The Girl Who Wasn't There

A Secrets of Redemption Novel

Books by Michele Pariza Wacek
MPWnovels.com/books

Secrets of Redemption series:
It Began With a Lie (Book 1)
This Happened to Jessica (Book 2)
The Evil That Was Done (Book 3)
The Summoning (Book 4)
The Reckoning (Book 5)
The Girl Who Wasn't There (Book 6)
The Room at the Top of the Stairs (Book 7)
The Search (Book 8)
*The Secret Diary of Helen Blackstone (*free novella)

Charlie Kingsley Mystery series:
A Grave Error (free prequel novella)
The Murder Before Christmas (Book 1)
Ice Cold Murder (Book 2)
Murder Next Door (Book 3)
Murder Among Friends (Book 4)
The Murder of Sleepy Hollow (Book 5)
Red Hot Murder (Book 6)
A Wedding to Murder For (novella)
Loch Ness Murder (novella)

Stand-a-lone books:
Today I'll See Her (novella)
The Taking
The Third Nanny
Mirror Image
The Stolen Twin

The Girl Who Wasn't There

A Secrets of Redemption Novel

by Michele Pariza Wacek

ISBN 978-1-945363-60-3

Library of Congress Control Number: 2023933584

For my family, for always believing in me.

Chapter 1

"I can't believe it." Mia dropped her phone on the butcher block kitchen table with a clatter, a stunned look on her face. "Penny Schroeder is dead."

"Oh, that's too bad," I said. Admittedly, I was only half-listening as I stood behind the counter, measuring dried lavender for the custom tea blends I was making. It had been a productive, relaxing day—I'd caught up on all my orders and was even getting ahead.

The afternoon sun slanted through the side window, and Oscar, my black cat, soaked it up as he slept on a chair beneath it. The kitchen smelled like potpourri and coffee, as Mia had just made a fresh pot. Ever since she'd decided to return to school to become a lawyer while continuing to work part-time as a waitress at Aunt May's Diner, her coffee consumption had gone way up. I was surprised she was able to sleep at all with all the caffeine coursing through her veins. Although now that I thought about it, she had been drinking a lot more wine in the evenings as well … probably to counteract the coffee. "Who is Penny Schroeder?"

Mia ran a hand through her straight, dark hair, which was cut in a chin-length bob. Half-Japanese from her father's side, she was petite with a narrow face and high cheekbones. Like me, she was in her early thirties, but since returning to school, she appeared significantly older. "I always forget you haven't lived here very long," she answered.

"Nope. Barely a year," I reminded her.

I had moved to Redemption, Wisconsin, from New York with my husband at the time and 16-year-old stepdaughter Chrissy. My Aunt Charlie had died, leaving me the big, rambling old farmhouse Chrissy and I currently resided in, along with Mia, who had moved in to save money while she went to school. She paid for the utilities in lieu of rent, and we split the grocery bill.

The house, along with being well over 100 years old, was also haunted. Not so much by Aunt Charlie, although I did suspect she was one of the ghosts, but by former occupants "Mad Martha" and Nellie. Back in the early 1900s, Martha's husband built the house for his blushing bride, but sometime after the birth of their second child, Martha lost her mind and ended up killing her maid, Nellie, and then herself. No one was sure why Martha did it, but supposedly, Nellie and Martha's husband were having an affair. Ever since, the townspeople were convinced that Mad Martha, and probably Nellie, were haunting my house.

My house wasn't the only haunted place in Redemption, either. In fact, the entire town had the same reputation, ever since all the adults disappeared in the winter of 1888, leaving only the children behind. The children all swore they knew nothing about it—when they went to bed, the adults were there, but when they woke up, they were gone. To this day, it's still a mystery.

I wasn't sure how much I believed the children's story. I had a sneaking suspicion the kids knew more than they'd let on. But alas, since none of them were still around to question, I suspected the truth was also dead and buried.

"Penny Schroeder is, I mean *was*, a fixture in Redemption," Mia said. "Her family has lived here since the 1800s, and her great-great-grandparents—maybe it was her great-grandparents … I can't remember how many greats—were two of the adults who disappeared."

I paused, a sprig of lavender in my hand. "Seriously? I didn't realize there were people here who could trace their lineage back that far. That's actually really cool."

Mia didn't respond, as she seemed to have stopped paying any attention to me. Instead, she pressed her hands to her cheeks and slumped over in her chair. "Man, I can't believe she's gone."

I put down the lavender and walked around the counter to sit next to her as she stared down at the table. "I'm so sorry. Were you two close?"

Mia didn't respond, and I put a hand on her knee. I expected to see tears, but her eyes were dry. "I can leave if you need some time alone."

She still didn't say anything, but just as I was about to get up to give her some space, she released her breath in a heavy whoosh and shook her head. "No. Stay. It would help to talk. I'm just … I'm in shock, I think."

"I can imagine," I said, rubbing her knee gently. "Getting a text like that would definitely be shocking."

She scrubbed at her face. "That's part of it, sure. But mostly … I guess I just thought I'd have more time with her."

"So her death wasn't … expected?" I wasn't sure how to phrase it delicately.

"Not exactly. It's just …" she sighed again and dropped her hands in her lap. Her skin was bright red where her fingers had dug into her face. "The last time I saw her, we had a terrible fight."

"Oh no," I sympathized. "That's really rough."

"Yeah," she said, her voice wooden. "It was really bad. I've known Penny nearly my entire life. She was like a second mother to me. But in the past couple of years, she … wasn't herself."

"That's so sad. Was she sick?"

"Well, yes. But there's more." Mia blew the air out of her cheeks. "She was always busy … always doing something. She constantly volunteered while working full time as a teacher AND maintaining a massive garden in the summer. So, several years back, when her health started to decline, she had no choice but to stop doing so much. She put a good face on, but it was clear it upset her to not be as involved as she was used to. She started getting worse, and I suspect it became a vicious cycle—as she stopped being active, she became depressed, which made her health decline even further, causing her to stop doing even more stuff. Regardless, it was clear she wasn't doing well physically, which would have been bad enough. But then she started to deteriorate mentally, and it was just ..." She paused and shook her head again.

"That's when you argued?"

"Yeah." Her head was bowed, and her voice was so quiet, I had to lean forward to hear her. "It was awful. She was saying all these crazy things. Just ... really nutty stuff. All sorts of conspiracy theories and other insanity. There was no talking sense into her or convincing her otherwise, and if you tried, she would accuse you of being a part of it."

"Oh, Mia," I said, feeling my heart break for her. "I'm so sorry. Was that why you had the fight?"

Mia dipped her head in acknowledgment. "In retrospect, I think she was having a particularly bad day when it happened. She was convinced someone was sneaking into her house at night and poisoning her food. She had reduced her meals to items that came out of a can. The only exception was coffee, which she carried around with her constantly. She even slept with it at night, so it couldn't be contaminated. Since she wasn't eating much, she was losing an incredible amount of weight. One day, I decided to bring her groceries—some canned food, yes, but I also brought things like meat and cheese and bread. She told me not to leave the perishables, as she wouldn't be able to keep it all with her all the time. I tried to convince her that she was safe ... that no one was trying to poison her. And she just blew up at me. Threw me out of the house and told me to never come back." Mia paused to blink rapidly, and I noticed her eyes glistening. "So, I didn't. That was the last time I saw her."

"It wasn't your fault," I tried to reassure her. "When someone is that paranoid, there's not much you can do."

"I get that. Logically, I know you're right, but emotionally?" She pressed her hand to her chest, over her heart. "I feel like I should have done more. I should have gone back sooner or tried to get her help. Something. But …" she raised her shoulders helplessly. "I didn't. I didn't want to upset her any more than I already had. Plus, I had heard through the grapevine that people were keeping an eye on her and making sure she was eating and whatnot, so I thought it best to give her space. She had a doctor who was working to get her stabilized on the right meds, too. I honestly figured it was just a matter of time before she would be better, and I could go see her. But then it was one thing after another. I met you and decided to go back to school. I've been trying so hard to balance everything, and … I guess I ran out of time."

She looked so miserable, I leaned forward to give her an awkward hug. "Do you want anything? More coffee? Tea, or wine? I think we might have ice cream, as well."

"Maybe a glass of wine," Mia said.

I immediately got up and fetched a bottle of white from the fridge along with two glasses. "Did Penny have any other family?"

"No. Her husband died years ago, and she never remarried." Mia mashed her lips together in a flat line and stared off into space. I sensed there was more to the story, but she wasn't ready to share. I turned all my attention to opening and pouring the wine. When I handed Mia her glass, she immediately gulped down half of it without looking at me. I left the bottle on the table and returned to the kitchen and my custom tea blends. I figured if she wanted to keep talking, she would, but I didn't want her to feel pressured.

The house was quiet as I worked and Mia sipped wine. The only sounds that broke the silence were the ticking of the grandfather clock and Midnight's quiet snores, so when we heard the front door opening and closing, it seemed louder than normal. Both of us jumped, and what was left of Mia's wine sloshed in her glass.

"Becca? You here?" Daniel's voice floated in from the living room.

"In the kitchen," I called out.

A moment later, Daniel appeared in the doorway, still wearing his Redemption Police Department uniform. His blonde hair was messy, like he had been running his hands through it, which he did a lot whenever he was stressed or preoccupied. His dark-blue eyes looked exhausted. He leaned forward to give me a quick kiss, his eyebrows raising when he saw the wine. "You two are starting early."

"There was a death," I explained.

His eyes went wide. "Oh no. Who?"

"Penny Schroeder," Mia said, taking another sip.

"What?" Daniel looked stricken. "Oh, I'm so sorry to hear that. She was one of my favorite teachers."

"Mine too," Mia replied. She was still staring off into space, her glass almost empty.

Daniel watched her for a moment, his expression torn. He obviously wanted to say something but didn't quite know what. I came to his rescue, lightly touching his hand. "Would you like something to eat or drink?"

He turned to me, raking his hand through his hair. "Absolutely … but unfortunately, I can't stay. I just stopped by to tell you I have to cancel our date tonight."

"Oh, bummer," I said, feeling deflated. We had plans to go to Mario's, my favorite restaurant in town.

"I know," he said. "I normally would have texted, but I was close by and was hoping to at least see you for a minute."

"What's going on?"

Daniel sighed. "Oh, it's that case I've been telling you about."

"The gangs?" I asked.

That got Mia's attention. She swiveled around in her seat to face us. "Gangs? What gangs?"

"That's what we're trying to figure out," Daniel said. "It seems at least one, maybe two, have moved into Redemption, but we haven't narrowed down which ones they are yet."

"But it's been years since we've had any gang activity," Mia said.

Daniel nodded. "Exactly. Well over 20, actually, but it appears to be starting up again."

"That's scary," Mia said. "Is it drugs?"

"Drugs and theft, mostly, along with a little graffiti and vandalism. Thankfully, there's been nothing violent, but we know how fast that can change."

"Do you have a lead? Is that why you have to work?" I asked.

Daniel's expression darkened. "I wish. There's been another break-in."

I raised my eyebrows. "Another one?"

"Fifth this week alone." Daniel shook his head.

"Wow," Mia breathed.

"Yeah, 'wow' is right. Anyway, it's all hands on deck, at least in the short-term, to try and get ahead of it." His phone buzzed then, and he pulled it out of his pocket to look at it. "Oh, I gotta deal with this. Call you?"

"Of course," I said as he leaned over to give me another kiss, this one a little longer than the first.

"I promise to make it up to you," he said. The look in his eyes sent a shudder up my spine.

"You better," I teased.

"Oh, please," Mia said, her voice sounding more like herself. "Get a room."

Daniel laughed as he headed out of the kitchen. "Bye, Mia."

Mia waved at him as she drained the rest of her wine.

I went back to making my tea as Mia swiveled around to refill her glass. She eyed me as she poured. "Have you guys talked about which one of you is going to sell your house?"

"Why would either of us sell our house?" I asked.

"Well, unless you're planning a pretty unorthodox marriage, one of you is going to have to," Mia answered.

"Two marriages are more than enough for me," I said lightly.

Mia gave me a look. "Uh huh."

"It's true," I said. "Besides, I have Chrissy to think about. And you. Is that why you're asking? Are you worried I'm going to kick you out?"

"Just don't want any surprises," Mia said, setting the bottle back down.

"Trust me, you have nothing to worry about," I reassured her.

Chapter 2

"Becca," Mia yelled from the living room. "Hurry up. We're going to be late."

I was in my bedroom getting ready for Penny's memorial service. Even though I had never met her, it was clear Mia wanted support, and I didn't mind giving her that.

However, staring at myself in my ensuite bathroom mirror, I was starting to regret my decision. I had forgotten how terrible I looked in black. It made my skin look pale and sickly. I added blush, but that just made me look clownish. In truth, I had spent the better part of an hour trying to remember what I did in New York to look acceptable when I had to wear black, but all that came to mind was hours and hours in front of the mirror with a lot of different products, 'potions,' brushes, and sponges.

I didn't even own that much makeup anymore.

I tried adding a touch of eyeliner and mascara to bring out the green in my hazel eyes, which sort of worked. It wasn't enough to detract from my sickly skin color, but it was an improvement.

One thing I couldn't do a thing about was my hair. The high humidity made it even wilder than normal, causing it to spill over my shoulders in a brownish-blondish-reddish frizzy, curly mess. I tried to capture it in a ponytail, but it kept springing free. I finally just let it be.

"Becca, come on!" Mia yelled again.

Sighing, I turned away from the mirror, smoothing the simple black sheath dress across my hips. At least the dress still fit.

I headed down the stairs to see Mia pacing the living room. On her, black looked far better. "What took you so long? We're going to be late."

"Aren't we still waiting for Daphne?"

Mia's face darkened. "If she's not here in two minutes, we're leaving without her."

I kept my mouth shut.

Daphne was the third in our little friendship trio, although Mia had still not completely forgiven her. They had been best friends since childhood, but Daphne had kept a pretty big secret from her, and Mia was still struggling to move past what she considered a betrayal. To her credit, she was trying, but it was one of the reasons she had asked me to accompany them to the memorial service.

"Maybe I should text her again," I said, heading into the kitchen to find my phone. At that moment, the doorbell rang.

"Finally," Mia muttered as she walked toward the front of the house. I collected my purse, breathing a sigh of relief.

"You're late," Mia declared as she swung the door open.

"Nice to see you, too," Daphne replied before craning her neck around Mia. "Hi, Becca. You're joining us?"

"I am," I said. I couldn't help but notice that Daphne didn't look any better in black than I did. At least I wouldn't be the only one appearing pale and sickly.

Unfortunately for Daphne, it wasn't just the color of her dress that was doing her an injustice. The cut wasn't right for her tall, broad-shouldered body, either. Plus, she had pulled her dark-red hair away from her long, rawboned face, which accented her plainness. Luckily, her smile made up for all of it, lighting up her face whenever it emerged.

"Are we ready?" Mia asked, glancing between the two of us, her expression strained. She looked like she was biting her tongue to keep from snapping at us.

"Let's go," I said as I grabbed my phone.

Mia nodded curtly, clearly annoyed. I felt a pang of guilt around all the time I'd spent fussing with my appearance. Even though we were waiting on Daphne anyhow, I knew how stressed Mia was. It had been a rough week for her. She hadn't said much, but it was obvious she was both grieving and beating herself up. I knew she wanted to get to the memorial service early to pay her respects.

We piled into my car, Mia next to me in the passenger seat and Daphne in the back. No one spoke on the way to the church.

When we arrived, I was amazed how packed the parking lot was. "Wow," I said. "I guess Penny was popular."

"Well, she did live here all her life," Mia said, her eyes misty with memories.

"Yeah, and she was always volunteering for something," Daphne added. "I don't know if she ever had a day off. At least … until recently." Her voice caught awkwardly at the end, as she belatedly remembered it was still a sore spot with Mia. She tried to catch Mia's eye in the mirror, but Mia was staring straight ahead, her expression stony.

No one spoke again as I maneuvered through the parking lot hunting for a space. Finally, I found one and quickly pulled in. I turned off the engine and watched Mia fumble for her sunglasses, feeling a little sad that I hadn't gotten the chance to meet the woman so clearly beloved by my new hometown. "She sure seems to have been a very special person."

"She really was," Mia said, swiping at her eyes. "We should get going."

We exited the car and headed toward the church, falling in line with several others there to pay their respects. I recognized a few of them, and we returned their silent waves and nods as we crossed the threshold into the church.

A somber man dressed in a black suit greeted us, directing the crowd to the dimly lit sanctuary where the casket was displayed for viewing. I trailed after Mia and Daphne, the three of us picking our way between the white candles and dozens upon dozens of flower arrangements to the line of people waiting to pay their respects to Penny. Amongst the sea of flowers, I couldn't even find the ones Mia, Daphne, and I had chipped in on and delivered earlier.

We slowly approached the oak casket. Though Penny had been carefully made up—her hair a helmet of neat, tight, gray curls—nothing could hide the gauntness of her face and body, both ravaged by her illness, as she lay upon the cream-colored satin lining.

Mia removed her sunglasses and stared down at her friend. She murmured something I couldn't hear, but I saw a couple of tears run down her cheek.

Daphne had already stepped away, and I moved to join her, wanting to give Mia as much privacy as I could in such a public setting. "Think she'll be okay?" Daphne asked, her voice low. She tilted her head toward our friend.

I studied Mia as she stood at the casket with head bowed. "Eventually. I hope. It's been a difficult week."

"I can imagine," Daphne said, her eyes never leaving Mia. "I'm wondering if all of this has brought up memories of her mother's death, as well. That would surely make it even more painful."

"Yeah, I think that's part of it. And all the stress she's been under the past year with her crazy schedule isn't helping, either." For months, I had been gently suggesting Mia dial things back, or even take a break from school or work, but she always insisted she was "fine." She would remind me that her schedule would only be this crazy for a few years and insisted she had already lost too much time. She'd spent her twenties working as a waitress instead of going to school, and now that she had made up her mind to change her future, she was going to pursue her dreams of becoming a lawyer at all costs. She didn't want to wait any longer.

While I could sympathize with that perspective, if she ended up making herself sick, the process would surely end up slowing—or halting—altogether.

Daphne gnawed on her bottom lip. "No, I'm sure it doesn't. She doesn't look well. I wish she'd let me help her." Her voice was full of regret.

I reached over to squeeze her arm. "Give her time. She'll get over it."

Daphne's smile was sad. "I hope you're right. But it's been almost a year. I would think that's enough time."

"Well, she's barely given herself time to sleep and eat, much less work through her emotions. I'm guessing she'll move past it, eventually. You guys have been friends for a really long time."

Daphne sighed. "I suppose you're right." She turned to face me, narrowing her eyes. "How are you doing?"

"Me?" I was a little surprised. "I'm fine. Why do you ask?"

She continued to study me. Daphne had this penetrating gaze that made you feel like she was seeing far more than you wanted her to, but there was always so much compassion behind it, you didn't really mind.

Though she worked in technology (which I still had trouble wrapping my mind around, as it seemed like the last thing she'd be good at), she did some consulting on the side as a healer. She even helped me with my clients who were looking for health benefits in the custom teas I blended for them.

"So, nothing strange has been going on?" Daphne pressed.

"*Should* something strange be going on?"

She hesitated a moment. "No, not necessarily …" Her voice trailed off as Mia appeared at my elbow, interrupting her.

"We can sit down," Mia said. Her face was pale, and the dark circles under her eyes looked even more pronounced.

I wanted to ask Daphne what she was talking about, but I knew it wasn't the time. "You okay?"

Mia nodded brusquely. "We're holding up the line." She moved forward, clearly not in the mood for conversation. Daphne and I followed.

The pews were crowded with mourners, many of whom had apparently decided to use way too much cheap perfume/aftershave and not enough deodorant. The air was overly warm and sluggish. Despite the open door at the back of the room, there was zero airflow, let alone air conditioning. I made a conscious effort to breathe through my mouth, fighting to restrain myself from pulling my sweaty dress away from my body as we squeezed into one of the pews near the back.

As soon as we were settled, Daphne began to fan herself with the program. Her face was blotchy and red, and drops of sweat beaded her upper lip. Mia, on the other hand, didn't appear to even notice the heat. She sat hunched over, her expression glum.

My mind wandered as I tried to ignore how uncomfortable I was. Then, I felt Mia suddenly stiffen beside me. "I can't believe it. The nerve."

"What?" I craned my neck to look around us, but noticed nothing out of the ordinary amongst the mourners who were finding their seats or standing in line.

"Wendy." Mia spat the word out of her mouth like it had a foul taste. She gestured toward the back of the church with her head.

I turned to see a middle-aged woman wearing an ill-fitting dress and looking extremely uncomfortable hovering near the back. "Wendy?"

Mia glanced at me, her eyes hard. "Penny's daughter."

I did a double take. "Wait. Penny has a daughter? I thought you said she didn't have any family left?"

"She didn't," Mia said. "At least for all practical purposes."

"I'm not following."

Mia flattened her mouth into a thin, straight line. "Wendy ran away from home when she was a teenager. She's never been back. Or I should say, before now."

"Really?" I took another look at Wendy. The sleeves of her dress, which had to be agonizing in the heat, weren't quite long enough, as her knobby wrists poked out. Her hair was a mud-brown color and frizzy, like it had simply given up its fight against the humidity. "How do you know it's her then?"

"She's the spitting image of Penny," Mia said. Even though her face was hard, there was a pensive look in her eyes as she stared at Wendy. "I can't believe she decided to show her face."

I peeked again at Wendy, who was still standing all alone in the back of the church. I wondered if anyone else recognized her. "It is her mother's funeral," I said gently.

Mia made a face as she turned back to the front. "Yes. Her *funeral*. Where was she when Penny was still alive? When Penny was sick and needed help? Oh no, she of course couldn't show up then. But now, when there's an inheritance to claim, here she is."

"If she ran away as a teenager and hasn't been back since, it's possible she won't inherit anything," I said. "Penny may not have put her in her will."

"It won't matter," Mia said, her voice dripping with disgust. "She's Penny's daughter. If she wants to challenge the will, she'll likely win. It won't matter that she ignored her mother while she was alive and really ought to have no claim to anything. Gold digger."

Based only on my first impression, Wendy didn't strike me as a gold digger … at least not like the ones I had known when I lived in New York. They always had carefully arranged expressions of grief on their faces. Occasionally, they'd even throw in a few fake tears. But Wendy seemed genuinely upset by her mother's death.

Speaking of which, I turned back to Mia. "If she ran away from home as a teenager and hasn't been back since, how do you think she found out about Penny's death?"

Mia paused, frowning as she thought. "That's a good question. I don't know. Unless …" She closed her mouth with a click as the priest made his way to the pulpit.

The service was much shorter than I'd expected, though I wasn't complaining. The longer I sat in that packed church, the more uncomfortable it became. The priest was the only one who gave a eulogy, and it was a brief. Wendy was never acknowledged. At the end, he invited everyone to Penny's house for refreshments, courtesy of the volunteers at Redemption's Historical Society. Apparently, Penny was quite involved with them, so as a thank you, they decided to organize the post-funeral reception.

And then, just like that, it was over. I quickly got to my feet, glancing over my shoulder to see if Wendy was in the receiving line, but she had disappeared.

Mia noticed her absence, as well. "Well, at least she had the decency not to stick around."

"Who?" Daphne asked as we shuffled closer together, heading for the exit. I was trying to breathe through my mouth, as the overwhelming scent of whoever had bathed in perfume ahead of us threatened to make me retch.

"Wendy."

Daphne's eyes went wide. "Penny's daughter?"

"The one and the same," Mia replied.

"Wow," Daphne said, her expression stunned. "That's … surprising."

Mia reached up with one hand to pull her dark hair up and away from the back of her neck. "Yeah, I know. I thought she'd at least have the decency to wait until Penny's body was cold before coming to collect whatever is left."

Daphne shook her head, a couple of tendrils of hair escaping and floating around her head. "No, that's not what I meant. I just assumed she *couldn't* come back."

Mia glanced at her. "What, like she was dead?"

"Dead or gone," Daphne said. "You know as well as I do that when people go missing in this town, they rarely turn up alive again. I assumed that would be the case with Wendy, too."

"This was never like the other missing people though," Mia said. "Penny always said she had sent Wendy away."

"Wait a minute," I interjected. "I thought you said Wendy ran away from home."

Mia flapped her hand impatiently. "She *did* run away from home."

I rubbed my temples, trying to clear my head. The longer I was stuck in this church, the worse I felt. Maybe that was why I was having such difficulty following Mia. "I don't understand. You just said that Penny claimed to have sent Wendy away. How does that translate into Wendy running away from home?"

"Because Penny was covering for her," Mia said in exasperation. "Wendy ran away from home, but rather than make Wendy look bad, Penny pretended that it was her choice ... that she had sent Wendy away."

I was still struggling to follow the logic. "But if Wendy ran away, something could have happened to her to keep her away. Bad things happen to runaways all the time."

Mia let out a frustrated sigh. "Let me try again. Wendy ran away from home, but Penny obviously knew she was still alive, or she wouldn't have covered for her by saying she had sent Wendy away. If Penny hadn't known that, then she would have said something else ... probably something along the lines of Wendy being taken."

Daphne gave Mia a curious look. "Is that the only reason you think Penny was lying about sending Wendy away?"

"Of course not," Mia said. "It's also illogical. Wendy was all Penny had left. Why would she ever send her away?"

"Maybe to save her," Daphne offered.

"Save her?" I dug my fingers into my temple, trying to offset the dizziness. I was sure I wasn't hearing the conversation correctly. I also hoped I wouldn't faint before getting out of the church. "What do you mean? Save her from what?"

"From the curse," Daphne said matter-of-factly.

I stared at Daphne. Was I dreaming? "Curse? What curse? What are you talking about?"

"Wendy ran away," Mia insisted. Her cheeks had turned bright red; however, I had a feeling it wasn't entirely from the heat. "But even if Penny *had* sent her away to save her from the curse, if Redemption didn't want Wendy to leave, she couldn't have."

"What curse?" I asked again.

"The 1888ers curse," Daphne said. "You know her ancestors were some of the ones who disappeared in 1888, right?"

"Yes," I said. "Mia mentioned that."

"Well, it's believed that all the descendants of the adults who disappeared are cursed," Daphne said.

"Why would they be cursed?" I asked. "Do they know why the adults disappeared?"

"According to them, no," Mia said. "They claim they don't know anything more than the rest of us."

"Then how do they know they're cursed?"

"Dreams, I think," Daphne said. "It's not really clear, though. As a group, they're pretty secretive."

"Bad luck, as well," Mia said sourly. "There's not a lot of them left. They seem to be dying out. The family lines, I mean."

"Yeah, it's sad," Daphne said. "Either they can't get pregnant, or if they do, their children end up dying young."

Despite the heat, a shiver ran up my spine. "If that's the case, no wonder Penny sent Wendy away."

"She *didn't* send her away," Mia insisted again. "Wendy ran away."

"How can you be so sure?"

"I just am," Mia said flatly.

Daphne and I exchanged a glance. "It doesn't make sense to me why it matters either way," I said. "Why should anyone care?"

Mia stared straight ahead. "Precisely because of this day. Penny knew Wendy would eventually return. By telling people she had sent her away, the rest of the town wouldn't see Wendy as the ungrateful daughter she is. She can't fool me, though. I know what she really is."

Her voice had grown so dark, I shivered again. This wasn't the Mia I knew and had lived with for nearly a year. That Mia was friends with nearly everyone in town.

Which made me wonder what exactly Wendy had done to her to turn her into an enemy.

Chapter 3

We inched our way out of the church so slowly, I figured there was some sort of receiving line after all. As it turned out, though, a few elderly people with walkers were causing the delay. In retrospect, it probably wasn't even taking that long, but between the heat, humidity, and various odors, I was still afraid I might be sick.

Finally, we spilled out of the church and into the parking lot. I gulped in a few deep breaths of humid air. It wasn't much cooler outside than it had been in the church, but at least the overwhelming stench was gone.

"I assume we're going to Penny's house?" I asked as we walked through the parking lot toward our car. Traffic was already starting to back up all around us, and much to my dismay, exhaust fumes were now assaulting my sense of smell.

"Of course," Mia said. "It's not far. Maybe five, seven minutes away. Although, with all this traffic, it will likely take longer."

"I'm glad you're here to give me directions," I said, walking fast to get out of the way of a dark sedan that seemed to be in quite a hurry.

Mia smiled slightly. "I don't think you'll need me for directions. Just follow the line of cars."

Mia was right; Penny's house wasn't that far away, and I didn't need any help finding it. It seemed everyone at the church was also headed there, and we ended up parking about a block away on one of the side roads.

Located on the outskirts of Redemption, near the woods, the large, ramshackle house was missing shutters, and the front porch appeared quite broken down. It stood alone, a little way off from any neighbors, and was surrounded by tall, majestic oak, maple, and elm trees.

Mia stared at it from the bottom of the cracked driveway. The front yard was overgrown with dandelions and other weeds, and the grass was in serious need of mowing. "This house was just too much for her toward the end," she said softly. "I know she had people stopping by to help, but obviously not often enough."

"It's a big yard for one person to maintain," Daphne said. "I'm guessing people were probably more concerned about bringing her groceries and making sure the house was clean, rather than worrying too much about yardwork."

"I suppose," Mia said, her voice rough with sadness. "Penny just loved this yard so much. Gardening was such a huge hobby of hers. It must have broken her heart to look outside and see this."

Two older women walked around us, both with dyed, permed hair, one dark and one blonde. One of them shot us a glare as she walked by. The message was clear: *you're blocking the walkway.*

Mia must have gotten it, as well, because she started moving forward, her steps heavy. I shifted closer to her to give her arm a gentle squeeze. She glanced up and gave me a small smile that didn't reach her eyes.

The front door was propped open, revealing a house that was clearly packed. Still, we managed to squeeze our way inside.

Unlike the yard, the house was spotless. Apparently, Daphne was right about people having been more concerned about a clean house than a maintained lawn. It even smelled clean, of lemon polish and floor cleaner.

The furniture itself was old and well-used. The couch was a faded plaid, the cushions flattened by hours of sitting. An old, console TV was across from the couch, and a vase of flowers sat on the yellowing doily on top of it. Mourners stood in small, tight groups, drinking coffee and punch and holding small plates of food.

"Mia! Daphne!" A plump, middle-aged woman came toward us. Her hair was secured in a tight bun, and her cheeks were bright red. "I haven't seen you two in ages."

"Ruth Anne," Mia greeted the woman as she embraced her and then Daphne. When Mia introduced us, Ruth Anne's face lit up.

"Oh, you're Charlie's niece, right?"

"I am," I said.

"I heard you're starting up her tea business. Are you following her recipes? I'm in desperate need of her Deep Sleep tea. I haven't had a good night of sleep since I ran out of my last batch." Her eyes suddenly widened, and she pressed a manicured hand against her mouth. "Oh! I shouldn't be talking business here."

"It's okay," Daphne said hastily. "I'm sure Penny wouldn't mind. I believe she was one of Charlie's clients, as well."

"Yes, I remember how she'd always make me a pot of Charlie's lavender-lemon tea," Mia said. "That was her favorite."

Ruth Anne bobbed her head. "Oh yes, she loved that tea. Charlie made her a few different blends. In fact, I think Charlie's teas helped her more than any of her medications. She seemed to get a lot worse when she ran out of tea." Ruth Anne started fumbling with her purse, her eyes glistening, before pulling a tissue out of it. "There I go again. I've just been a wreck," she said, dabbing her eyes. "I'm so sorry."

"There's nothing to be sorry about," I said. "It's a funeral. We're supposed to cry."

She smiled slightly. "I can see the resemblance," she said, looking at me closely. "You have her eyes. And her hair. It always gave her fits."

I automatically reached up to try to smooth my wild curls. Back when I lived in New York, I was forever trying to straighten my hair. It was the bane of my existence. I could never look like the cool, polished, elegant women I knew. But here, I had allowed it to revert to its natural crazy state, although I still found myself occasionally wishing it was a little more controlled. "Yeah, it gives me a lot of fits, as well."

She patted my arm. "Well, it's beautiful. Don't let anyone tell you otherwise."

"Thanks," I said, feeling a little self-conscious.

Mia cleared her throat. "Not that I'm trying to break up the love fest over Becca's hair ..." I rolled my eyes at that, and her face brightened with an almost smile. "But do you know who told Wendy about Penny?"

Ruth Anne looked confused. "Wendy? You mean Penny's daughter?"

"That's the one."

Ruth Anne's mouth dropped open. "Wait. She's here?" Her eyes darted back and forth as if she expected Wendy to materialize from the kitchen holding a platter of sandwiches.

"I don't know if she's here or not, but she was at the church," Mia said. "You didn't see her?"

Ruth Anne shook her head. "I had no idea. I thought ..." she pressed a hand against her chest. "Well, I guess I didn't realize she was still alive."

A choked noise escaped Daphne's mouth, which she then automatically covered with her hand. I got the distinct impression she would have nudged Mia if she had been standing next to her.

Mia put her hands on her hips. "Why wouldn't she be alive? Penny always said she had sent her away."

Ruth Anne swallowed. "Well, yes, but ... you know, it's Redemption. People disappear all the time."

Mia twisted her lips, like she had just bitten into something sour. "But that makes no sense. Why would Penny say she sent Wendy away if Wendy had disappeared due to unknown circumstances?"

"Well, you know Penny," Ruth Anne said, waving a hand. "She always had these ... ideas, in her head."

"But this is her daughter we're talking about," Mia said.

Ruth Anne looked a little uncomfortable. "That's true, I guess."

Mia was looking more and more irked. "All right, forget about what Penny said or didn't say. Wendy is clearly still alive, and *someone* knew where she was, because otherwise, she wouldn't be here now."

"Are you sure it was Wendy?" Daphne asked. "It's been a while since anyone has seen her. Maybe it was someone else."

Mia shook her head. "She is the spitting image of Penny. I'm sure it was her."

There was an uncomfortable pause as Daphne and Ruth Anne exchanged a glance. There was something odd going on, but I couldn't figure out if the problem pertained to Penny, Mia, or both of them.

"Well, I haven't seen anyone who looks like a younger Penny," Ruth Anne said. "At least not yet."

"Hopefully, that means she's doing the right thing and staying away," Mia said. "Funerals should only be for people who are truly mourning, not just coming for the inheritance."

"Can't argue with that," Ruth Anne said as she started edging away. "If you'll excuse me, I'm going to refill my punch. It's really hot in here."

"I'd love some punch, as well," I said, stepping forward. "I'll go with you. Would you like some?" I directed the question to Daphne and Mia.

"You read my mind," Daphne said.

"Sure," Mia added, but her eyes were scanning the crowd, and her attention was obviously elsewhere.

"Great, I'll be right back," I promised as I started to follow Ruth Anne. While it was true I wanted punch, I also wanted answers.

"So, you and Penny were good friends?" I asked.

"Penny is a fixture in this town. Or *was* a fixture. Everyone knew her," she said, which didn't exactly answer my question.

"Ah ... that explains why it seems like all of Redemption showed up today," I said, half-smiling.

"Yeah, she was something," Ruth Anne said, a wistfulness in her voice. "It's too bad about the last couple of years."

"Yes, Mia spoke about her health declining. It's so sad when that happens ... especially to someone as vibrant as Penny seemed to be."

Ruth Anne pressed her lips together firmly. "It's even sadder when it's not the person's fault."

Well, that was an odd thing to say. I glanced over at Ruth Anne, but her gaze was firmly fixed ahead. "Why *would* it be her fault?"

Ruth Anne's eyes shifted back and forth as she worked her bottom lip with her teeth. For a moment, I wasn't sure she was going to respond, but then she took a breath and forced a smile. "Don't mind me. I'm just ... I'm just still really upset about her death."

"Well, of course you are," I said. "She was your friend, after all."

Her lips turned up in another fake, forced smile as her eyes became glassy. "She was. There was a time ... well, it doesn't matter now. What's so upsetting is that we had a huge fight near the end. It was just ... awful. We said some terrible things to each other."

"Oh, I'm so sorry to hear that," I said. I almost added that Mia had the same experience, but swallowed the words before they escaped. Even though Mia never said that was private in-formation, I didn't think it was my place to share it.

Ruth Anne dipped her head in acknowledgement. "It was the last time I ever saw her. I meant to go back and make up with her, but ..." she shrugged her shoulders delicately. "I guess I ran out of time."

Automatically, I reached out to squeeze her arm in a gesture of comfort, but at the last moment, I drew back. I had just met this woman and had no idea if she would be okay with being touched or not. "I'm so sorry to hear that," I offered instead.

I wanted to ask her if she had been arguing with Penny about the same paranoid delusions as Mia had, but I didn't know how to phrase the question without betraying Mia's confidence.

Ruth Anne gave herself a quick shake. "Well, anyway, it's all water under the bridge now. Oh, I see someone I have to talk to. I have to go, but I'll be in touch about the tea, okay?"

"Sure," I said, watching Ruth Anne disappear through the crowd. It was only when she had been swallowed up by it that I realized she never did refill her punch.

I continued my way into the kitchen and found the punch bowl on the table near a stack of paper cups. I quickly filled three of them before attempting to arrange them in such a way that would allow me to carry them all back to Mia and Daphne.

"Hello there!"

Startled, I turned around (and just barely avoided spilling the punch) to see an older woman filling a plate with tiny sandwiches. She had black, curly hair cut very short and neat around her head, and bluish-purple cat-eyed glasses. She wore a simple-yet-stylish black pantsuit. She smiled widely at me.

"Hello," I said, after glancing around to check if she was actually talking to me or to someone else.

"Thank you for coming today," she said. "I know Penny would have loved seeing how many people showed up."

"She certainly seems to have made her mark on this community," I said, wondering if I should admit I had never met her.

The woman sighed as she added one last sandwich to the plate, spinning it around to check it. "She sure did. I'm Sharon Ollie, by the way."

"Becca Kingsley."

Sharon's eyes sharpened. "Becca Kingsley? Are you related to Charlie Kingsley?"

"She was my aunt."

Sharon clapped her hands together. "Oh, I'm so glad to meet you! I've been meaning to come by and introduce myself, but it's been a little crazy."

"I hear that a lot. Are you one of Charlie's tea customers?" I was trying to remember if I had seen a Sharon on my aunt's customer list.

"I have bought her teas in the past, yes. I loved them. Are you starting the business up again? I should order from you, if you are. But I actually wanted to come meet you because I'm president of the Redemption Historical Society."

"Oh, you're the ones who are hosting this, aren't you?" I asked, nodding my head carefully so as not to disturb the cups of punch I was holding.

Sharon finished with the plate and brushed her hands on her pantsuit. "Really, it was the least we could do. Penny did so much for this community, and I knew people would want to pay their respects. We were happy to do it."

"Well, you've done a great job," I said.

Sharon beamed. "Thank you. Now, back to the Historical Society … I'd love to schedule a time to sit down with you and tell you about what we do."

"Um … okay," I said. Was she looking for a donation? Or volunteers? I started to edge away. "I should probably tell you that I've never been involved with a historical society before, though, so I'm not sure I'm the right person for what you're looking for."

Sharon waved her hand. "Don't be silly. Of course you are. You own Helen Blackstone's house now, right?"

"Yes."

"Well, if there's any house that needs to be registered with the Historical Society, it's Helen's." She wagged her finger at me. "Charlie was the same way, you know. Just as hesitant to get it on the register."

Oh, so that's what this was about. I could feel myself relax slightly. At least I wasn't going to have to refuse to donate or volunteer. "Yes, well, Aunt Charlie always had a mind of her own," I said.

"That's true!" Sharon laughed. "So, I can call you and set up a time?"

I shifted my weight from one foot to the other. I couldn't think of a good reason to refuse. Would it hurt to hear what she had to say? "Sure," I answered, deciding it wouldn't.

She clapped her hands together. "Perfect! I'll call you to set something up."

"Great," I said, taking a step back. Her exuberance was a little much for me. I held up the cups of punch. "I better go. My friends are probably pretty thirsty by now."

"I'll talk to you soon," she said with a wink. I smiled back, which felt a little forced, and headed out of the kitchen and back to the living room, where I had left Daphne and Mia.

The trek was slow going, as I ducked and shifted around all the people while concentrating on not spilling. Sweat continued trickling down my neck, and I could feel the punch starting to warm up through the thin cups.

Unfortunately, when I finally made it back, there was no sign of either Daphne or Mia.

Chapter 4

I took a deep breath, trying to tamp down my irritation. Even though it wasn't surprising they had wandered off to talk to the other guests, it was still annoying. They knew I was getting them punch. Would it have killed them to wait a few moments?

I started weaving my way through the living room, trying to see if I had simply missed them somewhere along the way. That's when my elbow knocked into someone's shoulder, and punch sloshed out of one of the cups, barely missing my dress.

"Oh, I'm so sorry," I said reflexively, jumping back to keep the red liquid from hitting myself or anyone else. "Did I get any on you?"

"I don't think so," the woman said, looking down at her outfit. "Not that it matters. This dress is so old. It barely fits me anymore."

"I rarely wear this one, either," I said, trying to keep my wet, sticky hands away from my outfit. A couple of droplets ran down my arm, and as I was trying to figure out how to keep them from getting on anything else, the woman reached out and patted my arm dry with a crumpled-up napkin.

"Thank you," I said in relief.

"No problem," she replied. "I'm a total klutz, so I always try to have a bunch of these on hand. I'm usually the one spilling things."

"I know the feeling," I said, finally glancing at her. My smile froze on my face as I recognized the frizzy brown hair and exhausted, pale face.

Of course, I needed to keep my cool. After all, what if I, or more accurately, Mia, was wrong? I decided to introduce myself.

"I'm Wendy," the woman returned.

So, Mia was right, not that I was going to let Wendy know. I suspected that if I wanted to keep Wendy talking, that would be the worst thing to say. "Nice to meet you," I said instead, and instantly felt my cheeks begin to burn. Her mother just died. Couldn't I have thought of something more compassionate? "Sorry. It's not really nice meeting someone at a funeral, I guess."

Wendy smiled slightly, but it didn't reach her bloodshot eyes. "That's okay. I know what you meant."

"I'm new to Redemption. Well, I've lived here for a year," I corrected before forcing myself to take a breath. I was babbling like an idiot. "Anyway, I don't know a lot of people here. I didn't have the chance to meet Penny, either. I came to support my friends."

"I don't either," Wendy said, a faraway look on her face.

"Oh, so you're new to Redemption, too?"

Wendy didn't answer, just kept gazing off into the distance for another moment before giving herself a quick shake. "Not exactly. I grew up in Redemption, but I haven't lived here in many years."

"Oh, so you must have known Penny fairly well, then. Are you a relative?"

Wendy gave me a small, sad smile. "You could say that. I'm her daughter."

This time, I made a point of widening my eyes to feign surprise. "Oh, I'm so sorry for your loss. I didn't know ..."

Wendy was already shaking her head. "It's fine. You couldn't have. In fact, I prefer it that way. I'd like to keep a low profile."

"But why? I'm sure people here would like to express their condolences."

Wendy looked horrified. "Oh, no. Absolutely not. I mean," she quickly amended, as if realizing her reaction was out of proportion. "It's been so long. No one remembers me, and that's fine. I didn't come here for attention. I just wanted to say goodbye to my mom."

Her expression was so grief-stricken, my heart broke for her, and I wished I could comfort her. "I'm so sorry," I repeated, even though I knew how useless that was.

She nodded, dropping her gaze and blinking rapidly.

"Were you estranged, or something? Not that it's any of my business," I added hastily, realizing how the question sounded. "If you don't want to talk about it, I completely understand."

"No, it's fine," she said, lifting her head. Though I expected to see tears, her eyes were dry. "I don't mind talking about it. We stayed in touch, mostly by phone, especially throughout these final years as her health began to fail and she was housebound. I … well, I should have made an effort to come visit. I know that now, but you know … life." She lifted her hands helplessly. "You can have all the right intentions, but then things happen, and you think you have all the time in the world. *Oh, I'll do it next month or later this year,* you think. Then something else comes up, and the next thing you know, it's too late."

"It's tough," I said sympathetically. I wondered if there was more to the story that she wasn't sharing—like maybe she and Penny had fought near the end, too. Or maybe Penny's paranoid delusions had driven a wedge between them, and Wendy was beating herself up for letting that keep her from seeing her mother one last time.

Although that didn't explain why Wendy hadn't visited her mom before her mental decline. It was possible she hadn't been in touch with her then, but if that were the case, why would she make the effort now?

And if she *did* have a relationship with her mother all this time, did that mean she hadn't run away from home after all?

So many questions, none of which I had any business asking.

Just as I was trying to figure out a way to draw her out more, Wendy's spine suddenly stiffened, and her gaze darted around the room. "Oh, where did she go?"

"Who?" I asked, glancing around myself even though I had no idea who she was looking for.

"Jill. My daughter." She was becoming more agitated. "I told her to stay where I could see her."

"Oh! You have a child." I wondered how Mia would react to learning that. "How old is she?"

"She's ten."

I bit down on my lip, trying to keep the surprise from my face. Wendy looked a little too old to have a ten-year-old.

I must have done a poor job of it because Wendy shot me a knowing look. "She's my miracle child. I had her late in life. I didn't think I could get pregnant, so I was ecstatic when it happened."

"No wonder you've had a hard time juggling everything," I empathized.

Wendy nodded. "Yeah. I'm a single mother, as well. Her father didn't want anything to do with her, so it's been just me. I've definitely had my hands full over the years."

Well, at least her letting life get in the way of visiting her mother made more sense now. It was still sad and unfortunate, but maybe it wasn't as cold as it first seemed. After all, she was surely working full time while raising her daughter. That wouldn't leave much time for anything else.

"I'm going to have to go look for her," Wendy said. "I don't suppose you noticed a ten-year-old anywhere around here?"

"Sorry," I said, shrugging my shoulders.

Wendy pressed her lips together before excusing herself as I continued my search for Daphne and Mia. I still had punch to deliver, although at that point, it was warm and surely less refreshing. More importantly, though, I had to share what had just happened with Wendy.

I finally found Daphne and Mia in a corner of the family room, and immediately, my heart sank. They were in a small group that included Barry and Celia. While I got along with Barry alright, Celia, his wife, made no secret of her dislike of me.

"Oh, there you are," Mia said when I approached. "I thought you might have gotten lost."

"Actually, I almost had a punch catastrophe," I said lightly, handing her a cup before nodding at Barry and Celia. Barry grinned in return, while Celia shot me a tight, perfunctory smile.

Daphne was knee-deep in conversation with a woman who looked about our age. She had dark-brown hair cut in a cute pixie style, huge dark-brown eyes, and a faint dusting of freckles across the bridge of her nose. I nudged Daphne to get her to take her cup.

"Oh, thank you," Daphne said, a little flustered. "Becca, have you met Robin?"

I shook my head as Daphne introduced us. Apparently, Robin had gone to high school with them. Daphne still seemed a little out of sorts, which was unlike her. I instinctively wondered if she maybe had a crush on Robin.

I caught Mia's eye, and she shot me a knowing look, which seemed to confirm my suspicion.

The conversation continued, but I wasn't paying much attention. They were swapping stories about things that had happened years ago, so there wasn't much I could contribute. On top of that, the room was uncomfortably warm. The windows were open, along with a sliding glass door at the back, and a couple of ancient fans were doing their part to keep the air circulating. Still, it felt heavy and hard to breathe. My dress was sticking to me, and my hair was plastered against my neck. Adding to the discomfort was being immersed again in the same overwhelming stench of perfume, which was now also mixed with lemon furniture polish.

I'd finally had enough. "I'll be right back," I said to Mia, since Daphne was completely fixated on Robin. Mia nodded, and I edged away.

I wove my way through the crowd again, edging toward to the sliding glass door. Once I reached it, I could see some of the guests standing around the backyard, fanning themselves with the programs from the church.

I opened the door and stepped out. The yard was large, complete with a crabapple tree, an overgrown garden on one side, and woods on the other. I wandered over to the garden, curious as to whether I could get a sense of what Penny had planted when her health was better.

Between the copious weeds, I found a few perennials—mainly Russian Sage and Bleeding Hearts—along with a sad-looking rose bush. An empty bird feeder hung next to a dirty birdbath. A bench that was once painted white but was now chipped and graying was positioned under the shade of a large oak tree.

Looking at the yard, I could see the traces of the oasis Penny had once created—it would have been a lovely, colorful flower garden filled with the chirping of songbirds and flitting butterflies. I imagined her taking breaks from her gardening to sit on the little white bench and enjoy the beauty and peace.

For some reason, seeing the sad, wild mess that remained of what was clearly one of Penny's great loves made my chest ache with grief. Years and years of work were reduced to a bunch of weeds in no time at all.

Nature had reclaimed what was hers without skipping a beat.

As I turned to head back to the house, a movement from the woods caught the corner of my eye. A small figure appeared to duck behind one of the trees.

I shaded my eyes, trying to get a better look, but whoever it was had already disappeared from view. Who would be out by the edge of the woods? Was it possible it was one of the mourners? But what would he or she be doing all alone out there?

It was more likely some kid just messing around. In fact, maybe it was Wendy's daughter.

The more I thought about it, the more I thought it likely. A ten-year-old would have no interest in hanging around with adults she didn't know, mourning a woman she likely had no memory of meeting. Of course she would run off to play in the woods. *That's what I would have done at her age, too*, I thought.

I remembered how frantic Wendy had become when she didn't see her daughter in the house and wondered if she knew where she was now. I figured I should find her and tell her that I may have seen her daughter in the woods, just in case she didn't know.

I was about to turn to head back to the house again when I noticed more movement as whoever it was edged deeper into the trees. I paused, suddenly uncertain.

It would take me a few minutes to get back to the house, not to mention how long to find Wendy. By the time I returned, her daughter might be long gone. These particular woods were next to the state park, and the trails went on for miles. If Wendy's daughter took a wrong turn, it could be a disaster.

Maybe it would be better to find her myself before looking for Wendy. It appeared she hadn't gotten that far yet, and I could have a conversation with her … let her know how dangerous the woods were. Maybe I could even convince her to come back to the house and find her mother, who was obviously worried about her.

The more I thought about it, the more it seemed the right decision. I set off, hurrying over the grass, not wanting to lose sight of her. I tried to remember her name as I walked. Was it Jen? No, Jill. That was it.

The ground was softer near the woods, and my modest heels sunk into the earth, which made it difficult to keep my pace. I gritted my teeth, wishing I had worn flats. Unfortunately, my black ones were falling apart, and I hadn't had time to replace them yet.

Finally, I made it to the tree line, where I was fairly certain the figure had disappeared. I peered between the trees, but it was gloomier than I expected. Even though the sun was still shining brightly overhead, these were old-growth, thick trees that blocked out most of the rays.

"Hello?" I called out. "Is someone there?"

There was a rustling in the branches and a flash of blue. Was it a bird? I couldn't really tell. I took a step toward the sound, but I still didn't see anything—not a bird or any other sign of life.

I started to feel uneasy. Was my mind playing tricks on me again? Even though it had been a year since the hospitalization and everything else that had happened, and even though I knew there was nothing wrong with me—I had been a victim of gaslighting and manipulation by some truly evil people—I still found myself wondering if maybe there was a weakness in my brain. Maybe there was a reason why I had been so successfully targeted.

No. I wasn't going there. I firmly pushed the thought away. I hadn't experienced a single odd episode for an entire year. I was fine. I had always been fine. I had to learn to trust myself more. Of course there had been something in the woods. It was the woods, after all. Lots of things lived there, and just because I couldn't see whatever it was now didn't mean it hadn't been there a few minutes before.

Brushing my hands down my dress, I squared my shoulders and prepared to turn away and head back to the house when once again, I detected movement from the corner of my eye.

"Hello?" I asked again. "Are you okay? Do you need help?"

A dark figure detached itself from a shadow from the trees and stepped closer to me. It was a girl, about nine or ten, with long, tangled blonde hair and a face smudged with gray. Her dress was also streaked with gray, like she had been playing in the dirt.

"Oh, hello there," I said in relief. *See*, I scolded myself. *There is nothing wrong with me. I am completely fine.* "You must be Wendy's daughter."

She stared at me, blinking slowly.

"It's Jill, right?" I continued. I paused again, giving the girl a chance to respond, but she only watched me closely. "I met your mom in the house. She's a little worried about you. You might want to come find her."

Jill's whole body seemed to tremble, and she took a step back into the woods.

"Wait," I called out, moving toward her. "Don't worry; you're not in trouble or anything. She's just … concerned. She's got a lot going on, you know. Plus, that's what mothers do … they worry."

Jill still didn't say anything, but at least she hadn't moved any further away. I felt my heart go out to her. She must be painfully shy, which would, of course, make a funeral torturous.

I softened my voice. "Are you okay? Is there anything I can do to help you?"

There was a long pause. The girl blinked slowly, twice, before finally nodding.

I was relieved to get a response. I took a deep breath, not wanting to scare her away. "What do you need help with? Are you hurt? Do you need me to find your mother?"

She trembled again, and her lips parted slightly but released no sound. I noticed her dress then … so old-fashioned under the dirt. It wasn't just out of style, either. It looked to be from a completely different era. Was she playing dress up? At a funeral? I knew some parents allowed their kids to wear pretty much whatever they wanted. Was Wendy one of them? Maybe she was simply too exhausted and in too much grief to care what Jill wore, just as long as it wasn't anything totally outlandish.

"Becca!" I turned and saw Mia walking toward me, waving her arm wildly.

I waved back. "Hold on. Give me a minute." I turned back to Jill, wanting to finish the conversation before Mia scared her off. Maybe, if I was lucky, I could coax her out of the woods.

But when I turned back, she was gone.

Chapter 5

My stomach dropped to the ground. Crap … I had lost her. "Jill!" I called out, taking a couple of steps toward the woods. "Jill! Wait! It's just my friend, Mia. We just want to help you!"

Ignoring Mia's shouts, I ducked past the edge of the woods, peering around to try and catch sight of the child while hoping against hope that she hadn't gone too far. But there was no sign of her.

The woods were completely silent.

"Becca! What is going on with you?" Mia asked from behind me, obviously out of breath. "What are you doing out here?"

"Talking to Wendy's daughter," I said, still looking around me. "Did you see her?"

"Wendy's daughter? Wendy has a daughter?"

I turned around to see Mia's puzzled face. "Jill. Did you see her?"

"I didn't see anyone but you. What's going on? Are we talking about the same Wendy? Penny's daughter?"

"That's her."

"How could you possibly know she has a kid? Or what she even looks like?"

"Because I was talking to her, and she told me she has a daughter."

Mia's eyes went wide. "You better tell me everything," she said. "And start from the beginning."

I took a final glance behind me, hoping to see some sign of Jill, but there was still nothing. It was as if she had never existed at all.

That feeling of unease I'd had earlier began creeping up my spine again, but I pushed it away. Apparently, Jill was not a fan of being around people, which wasn't that unusual for kids her age. I was sure Wendy would be able to find her once I told her where she was.

"Becca?" Mia was looking at me, her expression guarded. "Are you sure everything is okay?"

"Yeah, everything is fine. I just wish Jill hadn't disappeared like that. People can get lost in these woods. Especially a child."

Mia glanced at the woods. "Do you think we should search for her?"

"I don't know. It's possible we would just make everything worse. She's so shy, she might decide to run from us and get really lost. We probably just need to find Wendy and let her handle it."

"I guess we better go look for her then," Mia said, gently steering me toward the house. "And you better fill me in on what you two talked about."

I gave her a quick summary as we walked to the house. The more I told her, the more disgusted she looked. "So, she *is* just back for the money after all."

"Is there a lot of money?" I asked as I eyed the house. While it was certainly nice, I couldn't imagine it was overly expensive.

"I'm sure there's some," Mia said. "Penny was always careful with money. Plus, the house will be worth something once Wendy sells it." Her voice was bitter.

"I don't think it's just about money," I said, picturing the grief on Wendy's face when she talked about not having made time to see her mother at the end. "She seemed pretty broken up about not seeing her."

"Then she should have made different choices." Mia's voice was flat.

"I don't think she would disagree with you, but it was probably tough for her as a single mom. Maybe she couldn't get the time off or pull her daughter out of school."

"This is her mother we're talking about," Mia said. "Yes, I have no doubt life is difficult for her as a single mom. But she should have found a way to see her before she died. There's really no excuse for it."

"Yeah, I suppose you're right," I said, mostly because I could see there was no arguing with her. While she wasn't wrong about Wendy's choices, I thought she was being a little harsh. Who knew what had transpired between Penny and Wendy over the past year? Especially since it seemed clear Penny was not in her right mind.

On the other hand, Mia was grieving, too, along with suffering from her own guilt around how her relationship with Penny had ended, so I could hardly fault her for sounding unreasonable when it came to Wendy.

"If you want, I can help you look for her," Mia said, as if she was suddenly realizing how unsympathetic she sounded. "I was coming to find you because we're going to have to get going here pretty quick. I'm working the evening shift."

"Okay, once I tell Wendy about Jill, we can leave," I said. "Does Daphne know?"

Mia rolled her eyes. "No, we have to find her, too."

"I guess we have our work cut out for us," I said, sliding open the same glass door I had exited from. "Maybe we should divide and conquer."

"Yeah, I think that's a good idea. I'll stay here, and you head back to the living room."

"Got it," I said, weaving my way through the crowd. I noticed it was already sparser than when we arrived. It appeared we weren't the only ones ready to call it a day.

I found Wendy huddled near the bottom of the staircase. She was hunched over and pressed into the corner, like she was hoping to fade into the wall so no one would recognize her.

"There you are, Wendy," I said. "I'm so glad I found you."

She stared at me, her eyes wide with fear, pressing her back even more tightly against the wall. She reminded me of a terrified rabbit, poised to dart away from a hungry wolf but with nowhere to go.

Her reaction was so peculiar, I hesitated, unsure if I should apologize or simply back away. But then, she blinked a couple of times. "Oh, Becca, is it? Sorry, I was … lost in thought."

"No, I'm sorry. I didn't mean to scare you," I said, reminding myself that grief did a lot of strange things to people. "I just wanted to tell you that I found your daughter."

She gave me a puzzled look. "You found my daughter?"

"Yes. She's playing in the woods out back."

"My daughter is in the woods?" She still seemed confused.

"Yeah. I tried to get her to come inside, since it's …" I paused, not wanting to upset her any more than she already was, but also feeling like I owed her the truth. "People do get lost in those woods, so you might want to go find her and bring her out. She wouldn't come with me."

"The woods," Wendy repeated, like she was still trying to wrap her head around what I was telling her. "I don't under-stand. Why would she be in the woods?"

"Well, you know kids," I said. "Especially if they're shy, like Jill. Has she always been that shy?"

"Shy? Yes," Wendy said faintly. "I better … I better go get her." She pushed herself up from the stairs and hurried away, melting into what was left of the crowd before I could tell her exactly where I'd seen Jill.

"Did you find Wendy yet?" Mia was suddenly at my elbow, along with Daphne.

"Yeah, just now," I said, swiveling my head back to where Wendy had disappeared.

"What is it?" Daphne asked.

"It was just … weird," I said. "The whole conversation."

"It's probably just stress," Daphne said. "It can do strange things to people."

"Yeah, I know. That's probably it," I said, even though I didn't think that was it.

"Well, is she going to find her daughter?" Mia asked.

"I would assume so."

"Then I would say your work here is done," Mia said. "Which is perfect timing, as we really need to go. Now."

"I guess we better be off," I said, although a part of me didn't want to. I couldn't shake the uncomfortable feeling that there was something not quite right going on. The more I thought about Wendy's strange reaction, the more I wondered if some of Wendy's issues were deeper than just being an overwhelmed single mother. At the very least, I wanted to make sure that Jill was safely out of those woods before I left.

But Mia was staring at me with an expectant look on her face, and as I was the one driving, I figured I didn't have much of a choice.

Chapter 6

"I don't know about you, but I could use a drink," I said over my shoulder to Daphne as I headed into the kitchen. Mia was already halfway up the stairs to change for work. "Want a glass of wine?"

"Might as well," Daphne answered, as I headed to the wine cabinet to pull out a bottle of red. "It's 5:00 somewhere."

"For sure. But even if it wasn't, it wouldn't matter today," I said, poking around in a drawer for the bottle opener. "Funerals don't count."

"Ah. Good to know the rules," Daphne said, taking two wine glasses out of the cupboard as I uncorked the bottle. As I poured, Oscar appeared as if by magic and positioned himself next to his empty food dish.

"It's not time for your dinner, though," I said to him. "You didn't go to a funeral."

Oscar fixed his emerald-green eyes on me, his tail flicking slightly.

"I don't think he's convinced," Daphne said.

"No, it doesn't seem so," I sighed and reached down for his dish.

Daphne smirked and picked up her glass as Mia strode into the kitchen wearing her Aunt May's waitress uniform, which was jeans and a white tee shirt. "I'll be needing one of those, as well."

"Don't you have to work?" I asked, as Daphne turned to fetch another glass. "Or is this a quick one-for-the-road before you leave?"

Mia's lips flickered up into a slight smile. "Not this time. As it turns out, I'm not going in today."

"Oh," I said as Daphne handed Mia her wine. "What changed?"

Mia paused to take a long swallow before answering. "Teri texted and told me she would cover for me if I wanted the night off. At first, I wasn't going to accept. I had convinced myself I needed to stay busy, but then I suddenly realized that I do need a night off. So, I took her up on her offer."

"I think that was probably a smart move," Daphne said as Mia all but collapsed into one of the chairs surrounding the table. "You've been burning the candle at both ends for months now. You could use a little break."

"Yeah, I know you're right," Mia said, staring into her glass. Daphne and I joined her at the table, where Daphne set the wine bottle down. "I just feel like I'm already so behind in life and what I want to do. I don't want to waste any more time. But I'm also feeling really tired."

"It's okay to slow down," Daphne said as Mia reached for the bottle to refill her glass. "In fact, it's probably better if you do. The last thing you want to do is make yourself sick. That would definitely derail your goals."

Mia shifted uncomfortably. "True. Maybe once this semester is over, I'll see about taking a week or so off work." Her voice was flat, and it was clear she was done with the conversation, even though Daphne wasn't. "I still can't get over how Wendy decided to show up now. And with a daughter! Didn't she think that Penny might want to see her only granddaughter before she died?"

Daphne pressed her lips together. I could tell she was disappointed with the change of subject, as she was probably thinking the same thing I was—that a week wasn't nearly enough time for a real break—but she took the hint. "It was surprising she was there. Especially since she seemed to do everything she could to avoid drawing attention to herself."

Everyone seemed to be judging Wendy for her choices, but personally, I was not surprised that she had kept a low profile. Especially since I was getting the feeling that no matter what Wendy did, it wouldn't be the right choice. "Well, whatever the reason for not seeing her mother earlier, Wendy seems to regret it now," I said.

"She probably should have thought of that sooner," Mia said.

"Maybe," I said, trying to choose my words carefully. "But it's also possible that there was something else going on we don't know about."

Mia threw me a sharp look. "What? What could possibly get in the way of seeing a dying parent?"

"Penny's delusions, for one," I said. Mia turned her face away quickly, but not before I saw the flash of guilt there. "Ruth Anne told me she had also fought with Penny before she died."

"Really?" Daphne asked as Mia winced and stared into her wine glass.

I nodded. "That fight was the last time Ruth Anne saw her alive, as well. I'm guessing there are more people with that same story. Including Wendy."

"Did she say that to you?" Daphne asked. Mia continued staring into her wine glass.

"No, but I am a complete stranger to her. Why would she? She was obviously miserable, though. How much of that was guilt and how much was grief ..." I shrugged.

Mia let out a long sigh. Her entire body seemed to collapse in on itself, like a deflated balloon. "You're right, I'm being unfair to Wendy."

"This isn't about Wendy ..." I began, but Mia held up a hand to stop me.

"I know that. And I also know how I sound right now." Her lips twisted into a sardonic smile. "It's just ... it's easier to focus on Wendy and what a terrible daughter she is than to admit what a terrible friend I am."

"Mia, you're not a terrible friend," Daphne said immediately. "Honey, Penny was very sick at the end. She didn't know what she was doing. You're not to blame for that at all."

"Besides, you don't know what would have happened if you had kept trying to see her after your fight," I said. "You might have just upset her more. It was probably better to just let her be."

"Maybe," Mia said, draining half her wine. "I know in my head there wasn't much I could do. And I know she wasn't in her right mind. I couldn't get her to listen to me. But my heart …" She flattened her hand against her chest, her eyes welling up with tears.

"Oh, Mia," I said, feeling heartbroken. "I'm so sorry you have to go through this."

"The whole thing is horrible," Daphne said. "Penny was such an amazing teacher. I think about her back then, and I can't even fathom that this is how it ended for her."

"I guess she really was cursed after all," I said.

"She was cursed, alright," Mia said, her voice unexpectedly bitter. "Cursed with trusting the wrong people."

I did a double take. "What?" Even Daphne looked startled.

Mia glanced up, her expression confused, as if she hadn't meant to say the words out loud. "Sorry," she said. "I'm just … it's nothing."

"It doesn't sound like nothing," I countered. "It sounds like you're saying someone might have done something to Penny."

Mia ran a hand through her hair. "It's not … it's not that. I just … well, Penny and I didn't always agree on some of her relationships. But it doesn't matter now. It's not like anything would have changed."

I caught Daphne's eye and saw the question in my mind reflected there. While it was true Mia wasn't acting like herself, it also felt like there was something more to the story that she wasn't sharing. "What happened with those relationships you didn't agree on?" I asked.

Mia rubbed her eyes. "Nothing. Honestly, it's not important." She stood up so suddenly, she nearly knocked the chair over. "I think I need some alone time. I probably should just go to my room."

"I'm so sorry," I said quickly, guilt blooming in my chest. I shouldn't have pushed her. Why didn't I just let it go? "I didn't mean to pry. Just forget I asked."

Mia shook her head as she reached for the wine bottle to top off her glass. "It's not that. Honest. I just think I need to be alone for a bit to process everything." Her hand shook as she poured, spilling a few drops on the table.

"Well, of course, if that's what you want," I said, feeling even worse as I watched her. "Or I can leave if you'd rather sit here, or …"

She put down the bottle with a clink and scooped up her glass. "I appreciate all you're doing, Becca, but I think this is for the best. I'm really tired, so I'll probably lie down for a bit. Maybe take a nap before dinner."

"A nap is probably exactly what you need," Daphne said. "Grief is exhausting."

Mia shoved her hair out of her face. A droplet of wine ran down her wrist and then her arm, looking almost like blood. "No question about that. I'll be back down for dinner."

"Okay," I said, watching her leave the kitchen. I didn't bother telling her I wasn't going to be there for dinner since Daniel was taking me out. I was fairly certain she had no real plan to eat later, anyhow.

As soon as I heard Mia's bedroom door closing, I let out a sigh and slumped over the table. "I shouldn't have said anything," I said to Daphne.

"It's not your fault," Daphne said. "Mia was looking pretty ragged. I suspect she was going to head up to her room no matter what we said or didn't say."

While it was true that Mia looked like something the cat dragged in, I didn't agree about her going to her room unless she'd felt pushed or cornered. Mia was an extrovert, which was another reason why her online classes were taking a toll on her. I suspected she would have been much happier attending class in person, but that wasn't feasible at this point in her life. And since Daphne knew as well as I did that Mia was an extrovert, I suspected she was just trying to be nice to me.

"Well, I still shouldn't have questioned her. It's not like knowing the answer would have changed anything. Penny is still dead."

Daphne cocked her head as she picked up her glass. "True. But it might have done Mia some good to talk about it."

I looked up at the ceiling as if I could see Mia in her bedroom, maybe sitting on the edge of her bed drinking her wine or lying down like she said she was going to. "It probably would, if she was willing to talk about it."

"She hasn't been?"

I shook my head. "Not really. She hasn't said much of anything this last week. I tried a couple of times to get her to talk about Penny, maybe share some stories, but she just isn't interested."

Daphne frowned. "Hmm. That doesn't sound like her."

I lifted my hand up helplessly. "No, it isn't like her at all. And I don't know how to help."

Daphne exhaled loudly from her nose. "Oh man. I don't, either. Maybe we just need to give her some space, and she'll eventually work her way out of her funk."

"That's what I'm hoping."

Daphne shot me a small, sad smile. I wondered if she was thinking about what I'd said earlier about giving Mia time to get over her issue with Daphne, too. "So am I." She tipped her glass, draining the rest of her wine. "I have to get going. I've got some things to do. Are you going to be okay, or do you need me to come back? Maybe in a few hours for dinner?"

"I'll be fine," I said. "Daniel is actually taking me to out tonight, and I doubt Mia is going to eat. I'll prepare something for her that she can heat up later just in case."

"Oh good. I'm glad you're going out with Daniel," Daphne said, getting to her feet. "Maybe that is for the best, to give Mia some space tonight."

"That's my hope," I said, also standing up.

Daphne stepped forward to give me a quick hug. I breathed in her scent, lavender and lemongrass, and almost immediately felt myself relax.

"Call me if you need anything," she said as she stepped away.

"I promise," I said.

Daphne flashed me one more smile before slipping out of the room.

I emptied the final dregs from the bottle into my glass and headed into the kitchen to see what I had that I could turn into a dinner for Mia. After perusing the fridge and pantry, I settled on a chicken and rice casserole and got to work. I wasn't nearly as talented as Chrissy, but she had shared a few tips with me, so I could hold my own.

I sipped my wine as I chopped and diced and mixed, feeling more peaceful than I had in a week. There was something so soothing about cooking. Plus, it brought back memories of Aunt Charlie and how she used to spend hours in the kitchen cooking and baking. She always said how it helped her unwind. I had never experienced it for myself until that very moment.

Thinking of my aunt and her home-baked goodies made me start craving her chocolate chip cookies, so once I finished the casserole, I set to work baking a batch. Mia would probably appreciate a cookie or two.

The sun was starting to slant through the windows as I pulled the final sheet of cookies out of the oven. I wiped off my hands on a dish towel, surprised I hadn't seen Daniel yet. He had told me he was getting off a little earlier than usual to make up for all his recent overtime.

At that moment, my phone buzzed. *Oh no.* I felt my stomach drop as I went to get it. Man, I hoped it wasn't another gang issue. Daniel deserved a night off.

I swiped the phone and read the text. Then read it again.

No, I couldn't be reading it right.

I rubbed my eyes and tried again. The words hadn't changed.

I can't tell you how sorry I am, but I have to cancel again. Penny's granddaughter has been kidnapped.

Chapter 7

I quickly changed out of my funeral clothes, dashed a note off to Mia letting her know about the casserole and cookies, and drove to the police station as the sun continued to sink in the sky, casting long shadows on the sidewalks. It was still humid, although with the dying sun, it was finally starting to cool down.

I still couldn't get my head around that text. Wendy's daughter kidnapped? How could that possibly happen? Was it partly my fault? In my head, I kept seeing Jill in the woods, staring at me, her expression pleading with me to help. Why didn't I do more? I knew there was something wrong, and I had felt it at the time, but still, I let Mia lead me away. I should have gone after her. I should have tried harder.

There weren't many cars in the parking lot, so I was able to park close to the front doors and race into the building.

Other than the one bored-looking officer tapping computer keys, the lobby was empty. I was about to go up to him when I spied Daniel at the back of the precinct. He was by the water cooler, filling two glasses.

"Daniel," I called out, leaning over the divider and waving one of my arms.

"Can I help you?" the officer sitting at the desk asked, his voice sounding put out, like I had offended him.

"I'm here to see him," I said, pointing to Daniel as I called his name again.

Daniel started and looked around before seeing me draped over the divider. His expression was something between puzzlement and alarm as he started to walk toward me, weaving his way through the desks and chairs.

"You still need to check in with me," the officer said. "You can't be bothering our officers. They're busy working."

"I know," I said. "I have important information that could help him with one of his cases."

"I'll decide if it's important or not," the officer replied. "Our officers are all very busy and don't need to be bothered by every little thing."

"It's okay, Ralph," Daniel said as he reached the divider. He held both glasses of water with one hand, and with the other, he unlocked the half-door to let me in. "I'll take care of it."

"But you shouldn't be bothered," Ralph insisted. "That's my job."

Daniel flashed him a smile. "I know. But it's fine. I was taking a break anyway." He held open the half-door so I could slip in. Ralph pressed his lips together, clearly disapproving, but thankfully, he kept his opinion to himself.

"What are you doing here?" Daniel asked, his voice low. "Didn't you get my text?"

"It's because of your text that I'm here," I said, also keeping my voice hushed. "I may have information. Also, I need to see Wendy."

Daniel looked surprised. "Wendy? How do you know her name?"

"Because I met her at the funeral. And I also met Jill."

Daniel's eyes widened. "You met her? Okay, yes, you're going to have to give a statement. I can take you to one of the rooms to wait until we finish up with Wendy …"

I furiously started shaking my head, interrupting Daniel. "No. Take me to see Wendy first. She's all alone here, and she's probably terrified. And grieving."

Daniel frowned. "I don't think that's such a good idea."

"Please, Daniel. I'll tell you everything I know, but I just really feel like someone has to be in Wendy's corner."

Daniel ran a hand through his dark-blonde hair, mussing it up even more. He let out a sigh. "I guess it won't hurt to ask her if she wants to see you," he said. "BUT," he pointed a finger at me, "if she refuses, that's it. I don't want you badgering her."

"Deal," I said quickly. I was sure Wendy would want to see me. She just needed to know I was there.

Daniel didn't look all that happy, but he turned to lead me to the back of the precinct, then down a long hallway lined with a row of closed doors on one side. He paused next to one, gesturing for me to stay back. He knocked once, opened it a crack, and stuck his head in. "There's someone here who would like to see you."

"Someone to see me?" Wendy's voice was surprised as it floated out of the room. "But no one knows I'm here. Is it Jill? Did you find her?"

"I'm sorry … it's not Jill," Daniel said. "It's Becca Kingsley."

"Becca Kingsley? I don't … wait … there was someone at the reception today. I think her name was Becca. Is that who is here?"

Daniel glanced back at me, and I nodded. "Yes, that's her."

"I don't understand. How does she know I'm here? Does she know where Jill is?"

Daniel shifted uncomfortably, probably not wanting to admit that he had been the one to tell me. "It's a small town. Word gets around. Do you want to see her?"

There was a long pause. It went on for so long, in fact, I started to doubt myself. I was sure Wendy would welcome a friendly face to help her through every parent's nightmare, but maybe I assumed too much. She had just met me, after all. Maybe she thought it was really bizarre for me to show up unexpectedly at the police station.

For that matter, maybe it would be better if Wendy did refuse to see me. Why *was* I there, getting myself involved in something that had nothing to do with me? I had never even heard of Penny until after her death. And here I was, involving myself in a kidnapping. It might be better for everyone if I simply turned around and walked out of the station.

In that moment, I pictured Jill again, alone in the woods, staring at me, begging me for help. And I knew no matter what, I was now involved. No matter how nonsensical it might appear to everyone else.

Daniel glanced at me, raising an eyebrow. I could tell he was about to send me away when Wendy finally responded. I couldn't hear her answer, but I saw Daniel's expression shift to his blank, unreadable cop face as he opened the door wider, gesturing for me to go inside. I quickly stepped through the doorway.

Wendy was huddled in a chair, still wearing her ill-fitting black dress along with a faintly skeptical expression. "Becca? How did you know where I was?"

"I'm friends with one of the cops," I said, dragging one of the metal folding chairs to sit next to her. "He told me you were here, and I knew I had to come down to see if there was anything I could do to help."

"Oh." Wendy's face fell. "I thought maybe you knew where Jill was."

"I'm sorry … I don't. Unless she's still in the woods at the back of Penny's house. Did you find her there earlier?"

Wendy blinked confusedly at me. "Why would I check there? Jill was kidnapped."

The sound of Daniel adjusting his metal chair before he sat down kept me from answering. He smoothed his shirt down, then clicked on a recording device that he had placed in the middle of the table. A second, much younger officer had brought in an additional chair and was perched in a corner, holding an open notebook and pen. He seemed familiar, with his head full of black hair and gray eyes, but I couldn't place him. "Wendy, is it okay if we continue?"

Wendy nodded, straightening her spine and smoothing her tangled hair. I noticed it had flecks of red in it. "Yes, of course. Whatever we can do to find Jill."

Daniel's eyes flickered toward me. "Is it okay if Becca stays, or would you rather she leave?"

Wendy shook her head. "No, no. It's fine. Maybe she can help."

Daniel nodded, removing his notebook and pen from his pocket. "Okay, so you were in the kitchen making dinner."

"I was making tea," Wendy corrected. "Everyone had already left. I'm staying at my mom's house," she explained to me. "The ladies from the Historical Society were so nice. They cleaned everything up after the reception and left all the leftovers. There's so much food, I don't know if Jill and I will be able to eat it all."

"So, you were in the kitchen making tea," Daniel redirected.

Wendy bobbed her head up and down. "Yes. Neither Jill nor I were hungry. I asked her if she wanted anything … a glass of milk or a soda. I don't normally buy soda, seeing as it's hard enough to make ends meet and that I try to provide Jill with healthy options as my budget allows. But again, the ladies were so nice to leave a bunch of soda for us, and I thought one wouldn't hurt. Jill lost her grandmother, after all." Wendy looked sad, and I reached over to squeeze her hand.

"One soda wouldn't hurt at all," I offered.

Wendy raised her red-rimmed eyes to mine and gave me a watery smile. "That's what I thought. But Jill didn't want anything. She went up to the room she's staying in, and I decided to make myself a cup of tea.

"Just as I filled the kettle and got it on the stove, I heard a noise by the front porch. It was like a thump, or something. Not necessarily a knock, but like something was dropped on the porch. I thought maybe someone had delivered a package. Or something fell over, but I didn't think there was anything on the porch that would make that noise. So, I went to go check it out. I opened the door, but there was nothing there. Nothing at all. I even went outside to look around. I was sure I had heard something. I knew it wasn't in my head. But there was nothing there.

"I thought maybe it hadn't come from the porch at all, but from inside the house. It's been many years since I've lived in that house, so I'm not used to all the creaks and groans. I went back in and took a quick walk through the downstairs, but nothing seemed out of place. I wondered if maybe it had come from upstairs ... maybe Jill had knocked something over. But as I didn't hear anything else, I figured it was probably not important.

"I decided to put it out of my mind and finish making my tea. I returned to the kitchen and started digging around for a mug. The next thing I know, I was waking up on the floor with a horrible headache. I heard a dreadful screaming, which was making my headache worse. I had no idea where I was at first, but I finally pieced together that I was still in my mother's kitchen, and the screaming was the teakettle boiling. I dragged myself to my feet, turned the stove off, and moved the water. I had no idea how much time had passed or how I ended up on the floor. I just knew my head hurt." She touched her head, right by the red spots.

"Is that why ... is that blood in your hair?" I didn't mean to interrupt. The words just fell out of my mouth.

Wendy looked at me in surprise. "Blood? I don't ... I don't know."

"Did you look at your hair?" I pointed.

She shook her head, her confusion evident on her face as she started rubbing the area.

"We'll get you checked out by a doctor," Daniel said. "Are you feeling up to finishing your story now?"

Wendy stopped fiddling with her hair and nodded. "So, there I was, standing in front of the stove trying to piece together what happened when I remembered the thump I had heard on the front porch. I went to go look again and saw that the front door was wide open."

Chills ran down my arms, and I folded them across my chest, rubbing the skin.

"Are you sure you closed the door when you came back in before?" Daniel asked.

"Yes. I'm sure," Wendy said.

"Did you just close it, or lock it too?"

"Ah …" Wendy paused, seeming uncertain. "I know I closed it. I remember closing it behind me. But I don't … I'm not sure if I locked it."

Daniel made a note. "Okay, so then what did you do?"

"I went to check on Jill, of course. I was terrified. I shouted her name and ran upstairs as fast as I could, but her bedroom was empty. I checked every room, but there was no sign of her. She was nowhere in the house." Wendy's voice was getting more and more agitated, and I could see tears welling up in her eyes again.

Daniel raised his hand as if to calm her. "Okay. So, you checked the house. Did you go outside?"

"Of course I went outside." Wendy's voice was anguished. "I looked all over the yard, in the garage, everywhere. But she's gone! Whoever broke in and attacked me took Jill. We have to find her!"

"We're going to do everything we can to bring her back to you," Daniel promised. "Just a few more questions."

"But we have to *do* something!"

"And we are," Daniel said. "Remember, I told you we already have officers securing your house, and we're setting up an Amber alert. We're getting your daughter's information into our system as we speak. I just need a little more information, and then we'll go back to your house to see what clues we can find. We just need to finish here first, okay?"

Wendy swallowed hard and nodded once.

Daniel clicked his pen. "Why didn't you call us right away, instead of coming into the station?"

Wendy raised her hands helplessly. "I couldn't find my phone. You don't understand. I was so confused. My phone was supposed to be in my purse, but it wasn't. The kidnapper must have taken it with him. I didn't want to waste time looking for it, so I just grabbed my keys and came down here."

Daniel made a note. "We'll see if we can find your phone. Hopefully, you just misplaced it. Is there anyone you suspect might have done this? Maybe an ex-boyfriend or your daughter's father?"

Wendy shook her head. "Jill's father isn't in the picture. At all. He never knew her, never wanted to. No boyfriend, ex or otherwise. It's just me and Jill. Just the two of us." She lifted her head, her eyes shining. "You have to find her. She's all I have." Her voice was the sound of heartbreak, full of desperation and pain.

"Trust me, we're going to do everything we can," Daniel said again before clearing his throat. "Is there anyone else in your life who might want to hurt you in some way? Any enemies? Did you have a fight with anyone?"

"No. I'm too busy working to have enemies. I work two jobs. And if I'm not working, I'm focused on raising my daughter."

"Have you noticed anyone hanging around who shouldn't have been there? Or anyone who seemed off?"

"It was my mother's funeral." Her voice cracked. "I didn't recognize most of the people there. I have no idea who should or shouldn't have been there."

"Fair enough," Daniel said, making another note. "Any strange texts or emails?"

"No. Nothing like that." Wendy was getting agitated again. "I have no idea who would want to take Jill. I don't know that many people, and I certainly don't have time for friends. I didn't tell anyone I was coming here other than my employers, but they just know I was attending my mother's funeral. I didn't tell them it was in Redemption." Her voice cracked with unshed tears. "I didn't want to draw any attention to myself. I'm not looking for sympathy. All I wanted was to say goodbye to my mom. That's it."

"I'm so sorry for your loss," Daniel said, clearing his throat again. "And that you are now having to deal with your daughter being missing."

She nodded slightly as she pressed her hands to her cheeks, as if trying to physically keep the tears from overflowing.

Daniel dropped his head and busied himself turning off and pocketing the recording device, shutting his notebook, and standing up. "Okay, I'm going to have Trevor here ..." he nodded at the officer sitting in the corner, "take you to your mom's house, and I'll meet you there in just a few minutes." Trevor immediately leapt to his feet, at which point, I recognized him. He was the way-too-young officer who had been flirting with Chrissy when the police had come to my house the year before. Not that I blamed him. Chrissy was drop-dead gorgeous. "He'll to take you to your mom's house, and I'll meet you there in just a few minutes."

Wendy stood up as well. "You're not coming with me?"

"I'll be right behind you. I just have a few things I need to do here first. Trevor will take good care of you."

"Come this way, ma'am," Trevor said, gesturing with his arm. Wendy hesitated, eyeing me and Daniel.

"I'll come by soon, too," I said. "I promise. Trevor can get the ball rolling."

Wendy nodded and looked a little more reassured. She obediently followed Trevor out of the room. Trevor glanced at Daniel, and they exchanged a look before Trevor turned and disappeared after Wendy. I could hear their footsteps as they moved down the hall.

Daniel sighed heavily. "I hate missing kids' cases. Just the worst."

"Yeah, I can imagine," I said, stepping closer to him so I could run my hand down his chest. His eyes were focused on something behind me, but when I touched him, he shifted his gaze back to me and forced a smile.

"I guess you better tell me what happened today. Where did you first meet Wendy? Was it at the church?"

"No, it was at Penny's house, although I first saw her at the church." I gave him a quick rundown of the events of the day. He flipped open his notebook to take notes as he listened.

"So, you knew who she was when you met her at the house," he said.

"Yeah, but she doesn't know that. It seemed a little weird to try to explain how I knew of her."

"Did Mia or Daphne talk to her?"

"I don't think so. Neither said that they did."

"And Jill wasn't around?"

"No. I didn't see her until the woods."

He frowned, his brow furrowing. "Jill didn't say *anything*? Like what she was doing in the woods?"

"No."

He paused to rub his forehead. "This is just so strange. All of it. Who would kidnap a girl after her grandmother's funeral? No one even knows her here."

"Do you think it has to do with Wendy?"

He flipped his notebook closed and put it in his pocket. "That makes the most sense. It seems Jill was specifically targeted, with someone breaking into the house and incapacitating Wendy. It sounds like they used some sort of drug, like chloroform, which means they came prepared. That's not the work of some random child predator who sees an opportunity to snatch a child off the street. No, Jill was chosen. I'm just not sure if it was because of her or Wendy."

"But who would have chosen them?" I asked. "Wendy doesn't even live here."

"I know. I was sure this was going to be some sort of domestic situation. The father, or an ex, taking advantage of the opportunity to grab Jill during Wendy's mom's funeral. But as you heard, she says there's no one. And it doesn't seem like money could be the motivation, either, unless Penny has a much bigger estate than she's letting on."

I still couldn't shake the image of Jill in the woods, nor could I understand how it fit into what had happened. "Is it possible Jill ran away?"

Daniel shot me a curious look. "Why would you ask that?"

I shrugged. "I'm not sure. It seems more likely than the kidnapping angle, though, doesn't it?"

"It would, except for Wendy's story of being attacked in the kitchen."

"But was she attacked? She collapsed, that seems clear, but maybe she just … fainted, or something. Jill heard her mother fall, came down the stairs, saw Wendy on the floor and maybe even some blood—head wounds do bleed a lot, after all—freaked out and ran off to get help. And since she's not familiar with Redemption at all, she ended up getting lost."

Daniel's expression was thoughtful. "I suppose it's possible. Definitely something to look into. Speaking of which, I better get out of here. Call you later?"

I nodded as he leaned over to give me a soft kiss. "And if you think of anything else, text me. Or if Mia or Daphne saw or heard something, tell them to text me."

"Will do," I said as he led me out of the room and down the hall.

As I followed him, I felt strangely unsettled … like there was something I was missing. I couldn't imagine what, but the feeling was strong.

I tried to comfort myself with the knowledge that I had told Daniel everything I had witnessed, and I knew he would be examining any and all angles.

Still, I felt like there was something right in front of my nose that I just wasn't seeing.

Chapter 8

I was in the woods. It was dark, and I could barely see in front of me. Branches were tearing at my clothes, and twigs were getting caught in my hair. My skin was raw and red with scratches as I pushed my way through the trees. All around me were the sounds of tiny animals scurrying in the brush. An owl hooted from somewhere close by, an eerie sound.

I could smell the scents of dampness and decay. Of death.

A branch suddenly slapped me in the face, stinging my cheek. I reached up to shove it away, but I couldn't move it. Another snaked around my waist, pinning me in place. I yanked at it, pieces of bark becoming lodged underneath my fingernails, but it didn't budge. If anything, its grip tightened. I attacked it, hacking at it with all my strength, desperate to get out from under it. Finally, I snapped a piece off. The branch shivered, almost like it was in pain. I kept going, trying to peel the wood off of me. The owl hooted again … or was it the tree moaning? The branch trembled a second time before it loosened its hold enough for me to slip free.

But my escape was short-lived as another branch seemed to appear from nowhere, this one wrapping around my left arm. Were the trees ganging up on me? It sure felt like it, and I desperately struggled to pry myself away.

From the corner of my eye, I saw something flash. Something pale, like a bit of fabric or maybe a small hand, gesturing to me out of the dark. I turned quickly, trying to get a better look, but it had already disappeared into the trees, swallowed up as if it had never been there at all.

But it didn't matter. I knew what I had seen.

It was her. She was there. I *knew* it.

I furiously yanked at my left arm, trying to free it. I had to find her. I had to help her.

The branch was sharp, digging into my flesh, tearing it, but I refused to stop. I could see my blood dripping, bright red in the darkness as it stained the bark.

Finally, I was free, and I lunged forward, breaking limbs in my desperation.

And then, just like that, she was in front of me.

She was wearing the same dirty, old-fashioned dress she had on earlier. Her face was still smudged, and her long blonde hair was greasy and matted with leaves. Her eyes were huge in her face as she stared at me.

"Jill, there you are!" I exclaimed, relieved. "What are you doing in here?"

She didn't answer, just continued to stare, her gaze never wavering. In the silence, the sounds of the tiny animals scurrying in the dried leaves seemed louder than they should be.

"Why won't you answer me?" I asked. "What's wrong?"

She blinked once, twice, but made no other movement. The scurrying noises continued, seeming to multiply in the stillness.

"Why are you running? Is there someone after you? Are you in danger?"

Something flickered in her eyes as if in recognition, and I felt a jolt inside me.

"That's it, isn't it? You're in danger? Who is it? You can trust me. Is it someone you know?"

Her expression didn't change, but there was a deep fear in her eyes. She knew whoever was after her. I was sure of it.

I opened my mouth to ask more questions, but the crackling sound of the little animals running through the leaves was getting so loud, I thought it might drown out my voice. There was a strange smell in the air, as well. A thick, heavy smell. Bitter. I wrinkled my nose.

"Do you smell that?"

With a puzzled look on her face, Jill cocked her head and delicately sniffed the air. Her expression turned to horror, and she took a step back.

"Wait! Don't go!" I tried to step toward her, but she seemed to be going backwards faster than I could move forward. The smell was getting stronger, even more acrid, and every part of me was screaming to get out of there. "Jill, you need to come with me. I'll keep you safe. Please!" I stretched out my hand to her.

She shook her head slightly and seemed to recede even further from me.

"No!" I screamed, fighting to get to her. "Jill, please let me help you. Please come here. Come to me. Please!"

She paused then, her eyes never leaving mine. I reached for her, straining my arm toward her. If I could just touch her, that's all I needed to do. She would know she could trust me.

Her lips gently parted.

Find me.

"Find you?" I asked, not sure if I heard her correctly. Actually, I wasn't sure if I heard her at all. It was like her words just appeared in my brain. "You're right here. Right in front of me."

She shook her head slightly. *Find me.*

"But that's what I did," I said, feeling frustrated. "I'm trying to help you. Can't you see that?"

She shook her head again and started to back away into the darkness. All around, the crackling noise was increasing, and the thick, bitter smell was becoming overwhelming. Was it smoke? Were the woods on fire?

Find me.

"Jill," I screamed, but she had disappeared, swallowed up by the darkness. All around me, I could see the faint orange-yellow glow of flames as the fire grew hungrier, licking at the edges of the trees as they began to burn.

I awoke with a gasp, grabbing at my neck. I was sure my lungs were full of smoke ... that there was a fire somewhere outside. I could hear the sounds of the eager flames as they devoured the wood, sizzling in excitement for the feast in front of them …

I gave myself a quick shake.

There was no fire. The only light coming in through the window was from the sun just starting to peek up over the horizon. I was safe in my bed with Oscar next to me.

It was just a terrible dream.

I rubbed my face. It had been months since I'd had a dream like that. When I had first moved in, it seemed like I had nightmares nearly every night, but eventually, once I had gotten my life more or less on track, they had stopped.

It had been so long, I even allowed myself to think they were gone for good.

Boy, was I wrong.

A sense of unease crept through my body again. It didn't seem like a good omen that the nightmares had returned, but I tried to push it down. It was possible it was nothing more than a manifestation of the stress of being involved, even peripherally, in a missing child case.

Of course I would dream about Jill. It was only natural.

Right?

I rubbed my face again and decided I might as well get up. Even though it was early, I was feeling way too wired to be able to relax and fall back asleep in a reasonable amount of time.

Next to me, Oscar yawned, revealing all his teeth and making it clear he thought I should get up, as well. It was never too early for breakfast.

* * *

I was on my third cup of coffee when Mia stumbled into the kitchen, her hair a tangled mess around her head. "Morning," I greeted her.

She grunted in response and immediately headed for the coffeepot. I stayed quiet, sipping mine as she doctored hers and started a new pot.

When I had arrived home the night before, she was still in her room, door firmly shut, casserole and cookies uneaten. Well, I couldn't be completely sure about the cookies, as I hadn't counted them, so she may have taken one or two. But the casserole was untouched. I was a little disappointed but not surprised.

"You're up early," she said once she had sucked down half her cup. "Not that I'm complaining. I thought I was going to be the one to start the coffee."

"I had some trouble sleeping," I said. I didn't want to talk about my nightmare. It was still haunting me—every time I looked outside and caught a glimpse of the woods near the back of my property, I would see myself trapped in the trees, my nostrils full of smoke as I begged Jill to come to me.

"Yeah, I did, too," Mia said. Her face was pinched, like maybe she had experienced some bad dreams of her own but didn't want to share. She sat down next to me at the table and took another long sip. "Were you out with Daniel last night?"

"Yes, but it's not what you think." I cupped my mug with both hands, hoping to squeeze the warmth out of it. "I was at the police station with him."

Mia gave me a puzzled look. "Police station? Am I going to need more coffee to process this?"

"You might," I said, taking another sip myself. "Wendy's daughter was kidnapped."

Mia put her coffee mug down with a thump. "*What*?"

"I know. Crazy, isn't it? On the day of her mother's funeral, someone decides to kidnap her daughter."

Mia stared at me in disbelief. "I'm definitely going to need more coffee. What happened?"

I gave her a quick rundown of the night before while she drained her cup and fetched the pot to refill both our mugs.

"That's unreal," Mia said. "Someone just walked into her house and took her ten-year-old daughter?"

"Apparently."

Mia shook her head, staring into her cup. "Man, talk about the worst day ever."

"I'll say."

"Do you think there's any news yet? I know the police try to move quickly when a child has been kidnapped."

I shook my head. "Not yet. I checked my phone, but I don't have any texts from Daniel. Although it's pretty early. He might assume I'm not up yet."

"True," Mia said, tucking a chunk of matted hair behind her ear. "Hopefully, they got a break in the case last night, and he's busy with that."

"That's my hope, too," I said.

There was a long moment of silence as we sipped our coffee. Oscar snoozed in the sun, and I did everything I could to avoid looking at the woods.

Find me.

"Do you have plans today?"

"Oh man, I'm so behind," Mia said. "I've got two papers to write and like ten chapters to read. Why?"

"But no work?"

"No, thank goodness. As soon as I get enough caffeine in me, I'm getting my computer out and buckling down. Again, why?"

"I was thinking about heading over to Wendy's," I said. "See if she needs anything and offer her a little support. That sort of thing."

Mia eyed me. "And find out the latest on the investigation?"

I grinned. "Well, yeah. Obviously. But I'm also genuinely worried about Wendy. She's all alone here. Someone should be in her corner."

Mia took another sip of coffee, her brow furrowing. "I shouldn't," she said finally. "I have plenty to do here."

"We don't have to stay long," I said. "And it will all be waiting for you when we get back."

Mia groaned. "Don't I know it."

Chapter 9

Mia and I found Wendy in the living room, an untouched cup of coffee in front of her beside a couple of stacks of paper and an open notebook with a few notes jotted on the page. An exhausted Trevor had answered the door, a cup of coffee in hand. It appeared he had pulled an all-nighter. There was no sign of Daniel.

"Becca," Wendy said in surprise, jumping to her feet. "You came!" Her hair was tangled and greasy, and I caught the distinct scent of body odor, but she had at least changed into a faded blue tracksuit.

"I told you I would," I said, reaching out to squeeze her arm. I had wanted to give her a hug, but wasn't sure how she would react. She didn't pull away from me, but her body did stiffen slightly, so I quickly let go.

"And you are …" Wendy said, looking at Mia. Her face was squished up, as if trying to place her.

"Mia Moto," Mia answered.

"Mia," Wendy said, her voice hesitant and quiet, as if the name was familiar, but she was unable to place it.

"We met, but it was a long time ago," Mia said. "I was just a child."

"I think I do remember a Mia," Wendy said. "Vaguely."

"That would be me," Mia said. Then, her expression grew more solemn. "I'm so sorry for your loss. Your mother was a wonderful woman. She will be greatly missed."

"Thank you," Wendy replied. There was an awkward moment of silence that was broken by one of the officers walking past.

"Can I get you anything?" Wendy asked. "Coffee? Water? I'm not sure what else is there." She frowned.

"I'm fine," I said.

"Yeah, we're coffeed out," Mia said.

Wendy nodded, still looking uncomfortable, but indicated we should both sit down.

"So, any news?" I asked.

Wendy's face flattened. "Nothing yet."

"I'm so sorry," I said.

Wendy folded her arms across her chest, seeming to sink into herself. "I'm beside myself with worry. I can't stop thinking about her. Is she okay? Is she warm? Does she have anything to eat or drink? Is she asking for me?" She buried her face in her hands, silently sobbing.

"I can't imagine how stressful this must be for you," I said.

Wendy's body trembled in response, but she didn't lift her face.

"Have you seen a doctor?"

That caused her to raise her head. "Doctor? Why would I? I'm not sick. My daughter has been kidnapped."

"I know that, but you did collapse yesterday. Don't you think someone should check you out?"

Wendy stared at me like I was an idiot. "I collapsed because someone attacked me. I don't need a doctor to know that."

"But you hit your head," I said, "hard enough to have blood in your hair. You might have a concussion."

She shook her head in disgust. "You sound like the cops. I'm fine. I don't need a doctor. The only thing I need is to find my daughter." Her tone made it clear she wasn't interested in discussing it further.

Well, at least the cops were trying to get her some medical attention. I hoped that meant Daniel was taking my concerns about Wendy collapsing at least somewhat seriously.

Mia cleared her throat, leaned forward slightly, and rested her forearms on her knees. "Do they have any idea why Jill was

… kidnapped?" Mia asked. "Like, has anyone found a ransom note or anything like that?"

Wendy frowned. "Why would anyone send me a ransom note? I don't have any money."

Mia and I glanced at each other. "Yes, but there's normally a reason behind a kidnapping," she said gently. "There must be a reason why they picked Jill. It doesn't make any sense for it to be random."

"Of course it makes sense," Wendy said, looking at us both like we were stupid. "It's because of the curse."

"Curse?" I repeated.

"Yes, the family curse. You must have heard about it. My whole family is cursed."

"Remember, I've only lived in Redemption for a year," I said, giving the side-eye to Mia so she would stay quiet. I wanted to hear the story from Wendy's point of view. "What curse?"

Wendy reached over and picked up her cup of coffee, but she didn't drink it. Holding it tightly, she continued. "You know the history of Redemption, right? How all the adults disappeared in 1888?"

"Yes."

"Well, my family line directly descends from those missing adults," Wendy explained.

"Wow," I said. "Does that mean you know what happened to the adults?"

"No one knows what happened to the adults," Wendy answered. I noticed how she hadn't addressed the actual question. "What we do know is that everyone who is a direct descendent of those adults carries a curse. At least the ones who are left."

"Left? What do you mean?" I asked.

"Some of the families aren't around anymore," Wendy said. "They weren't able to have kids. And those who were able to lost theirs. It's part of the curse. Bad things happen. It's different for everyone." She clutched her mug tighter, some of the coffee sloshing over the edge. "I never should have come back. Never.

I should have known better. I've had terrible luck my entire life. Nothing has ever worked out for me. Nothing other than Jill, and now she's been taken away, too."

"Oh, you mustn't think that," I urged, reaching over to touch her arm again. "The cops are doing everything they can to find Jill. You can't lose hope."

"It won't matter," Wendy said, her voice full of despair. "They can't fight the curse. No one can. And now, it has my daughter."

"No, I'm sure it's not like that," I started, but the sound of a commotion by the front door interrupted me.

"What the ..." Mia asked as Daniel came striding into the living room followed by Trevor and a man I had never met before. He was older, at least in his sixties, with a weathered face and bald head. His eyes were dark and intense, and for some reason, they were zeroed in on me. I almost immediately looked away, finding it too difficult to return his gaze, although I could still feel his eyes on me.

Daniel blanched when he saw us sitting with Wendy. "What are you two doing here?" he asked.

"We just came to support Wendy," I said.

"Well, you're going to have to leave," he said. His face was grim, and a terrible feeling unfurled in my stomach. I met Mia's eyes, and I could see she was feeling it, too. Something dreadful had happened. I was sure of it.

Find me.

In my mind, I saw Jill disappear into the shadows as the fire burned around her. At the time of my dream, I had no idea what the message was, but now, I had a horrible feeling that it meant we were too late to save her.

Wendy stood up, swaying slightly. Her face was chalky white. "What ... what's going on?" she whispered, her voice broken.

"In a minute," Daniel said, still staring at Mia and myself. "You two really need to go. Now."

I stood up, as well. "But what if Wendy needs us?" I asked. "We should be here for support."

Daniel was shaking his head. "Wendy will be fine," he said. "We'll take good care of her." He pointed to the door, clearly done with the conversation.

I looked at Wendy, sure if she wanted us to stay, Daniel would have to let us. But she wasn't paying any attention to us. Her hands were pressed to her mouth, and her eyes were fixed on Daniel. She was still swaying dangerously, and I was afraid she might faint.

"Now, Becca," Daniel said, his voice like ice.

"Come on," Mia said, plucking at my arm. I hated to leave Wendy, but I didn't think I had much choice. Wendy was not helping, and Daniel was glaring at both of us. Even Trevor had started hovering closer and closer, like he was going to physically escort us out if we didn't get a move on.

Not to mention the third man, the one with the intense eyes, continued to watch me. I could feel my skin crawl wherever he looked. I felt the distinct urge to take a shower the moment I got home.

"Fine," I said flatly, allowing Mia to guide me out. At least I would be away from Intense Eyes. "Take care of her," I hissed at Daniel as we passed him.

"Don't worry about Wendy," he said, his voice sharp.

I stared at him, unable to believe my ears. What was wrong with him? This was not like him at all. How could he be so cold to a mother who was likely about to receive the worst news a parent could ever hear?

"Come on, Becca," Mia said, dragging me out of the room. I was so angry with Daniel, I could barely see straight.

"What is Daniel's problem?" I fumed the moment we were outside. "Why is he being such a jerk? And why wouldn't he let us stay with Wendy?"

"I don't know," Mia said as she propelled me down the driveway and toward my car.

"Wendy might need a friendly face depending on whatever it is she's about to hear. And what's the big deal about us being there, anyway? It's not like the whole town won't know whatever it is by this evening," I continued. I was on a roll. It didn't help that it was easier railing about Daniel's actions than it was to think about what happened to poor little Jill. Or why Intense Eyes wouldn't stop staring at me. Was it because I reminded him of Charlie? And if it was, was that a good or bad thing? The town seemed to be divided in terms of hating Charlie or loving her, and it was almost always one or the other. There weren't a lot of neutral feelings toward my aunt. And if Intense Eyes hated her … I pushed that thought away firmly. Better to focus on what a jerk Daniel was being.

"I don't know," Mia repeated as we reached the car. She glanced over her shoulder. "But I think we ought to leave now."

I had been fumbling for my keys, but I paused to stare at her. "Why? What's going on?"

Her eyes darted back to the house. "Let's get in the car first." I couldn't completely read her expression, but there was something about her manner that made my chest tighten and the air catch in my throat. I went back to searching for my keys. It took a minute to locate them and unlock the door, and the whole time, I could practically feel Mia's agitation as she watched me.

Finally, we were both inside. I put the key in the ignition but didn't turn it. "What's going on?" I repeated.

Even though we were in the car, Mia still didn't seem comfortable. Although, to be fair, it might have been because the car was stuffy without the windows open or the air conditioner on. She shifted in her seat, making a point of putting her seatbelt on, almost like she was hoping it would move me to start the car. "Did you see that other person with him?"

My heart seemed to stutter in my chest. Oh no. This couldn't be good. "How could I miss him? Who is he?"

Mia chewed on her lip, her eyes still on the house. "His name is Zane Eisner. He's an 1888er, as well."

"You mean like Penny and Wendy? He's related to the adults who disappeared?"

"Exactly."

I paused, mulling the information. "Well, maybe he knows Wendy, and that's why Daniel brought him."

"I'm sure he knows Wendy. He and Penny go way back. But …" she hesitated again, eyes back on the house. "Remember how I said yesterday that Penny and I disagreed on some of her relationships?"

My mouth dropped open. "It was him?"

She nodded. "He was one. Probably the main one."

Goosebumps rose on my skin as I folded my arms across my chest, almost as if I was subconsciously protecting myself from his gaze. "Why don't you like him?"

Mia worried her bottom lip between her teeth. "There's something about him. Actually, something about that whole 1888er group, but Zane especially. He was a huge believer in the curse. In fact, around the time Penny and I argued, he was convinced something dreadful was about to happen, particularly to an 1888er. It didn't help that he's also very suspicious of anyone who isn't an 1888er, to the point where he rarely even talks to anyone he calls 'normies.' I could always tell when Penny was spending a lot of time with him, because all she would talk about was curses and doom and gloom and… ugh." She flapped her hands. "It was so difficult to be around her after one of his visits. If she wasn't completely paranoid, she was super depressed. I would spend hours either talking her off a ledge or trying to cheer her up."

Due to my own paranoia, I found myself eyeing the house, as well. What if Zane could somehow sense us talking about him and came barreling out of the house to chase us down? "So he was one of the people who made Penny so crazy at the end?"

Mia let out a short bark of laughter. "I absolutely think he was behind it. Actually, I'm sure he was. But do I have any proof? Unfortunately, no." Her hands tightened into fists. "And trust me, I really tried to get it."

Looking at the determined expression on Mia's face, I had no doubt about that. "Why in the world would Daniel bring him to Wendy's?"

"That is the million-dollar question," Mia answered. "It's not like Zane is someone who would volunteer to talk to the police. He doesn't trust them anymore than any other normie. So, why would they be talking now?"

I tilted my head as I studied the house, but it remained as calm and peaceful as it was before. "Do you think Zane had something to do with the kidnapping?"

"I doubt it," Mia said, but her voice sounded less convinced than her words. "I mean, there's no question Zane is a conspiracy nut. But I can't see him being involved in something illegal and so awful. Especially the kidnapping of a fellow 1888er. He's always the one screaming about how they're being targeted; I can't see him doing the targeting."

"Hmm," I said. "Now I really want to know what's going on in there."

"You and me both."

I glanced at Mia, shooting her a mischievous smile. "What do you think? Should we go back in?"

Mia smiled back, but it didn't meet her eyes. "Tempting, but we should probably wait to talk to Daniel when Zane isn't around." Her smile disappeared. "I don't trust him."

I couldn't say I blamed her. I reached for the ignition.

I did a U-turn in the street and was just starting to speed up when I saw something flicker from the corner of my eye. A flutter of fabric disappearing into the woods.

Find me.

I slammed on the brakes and fishtailed toward the side of the road.

"Becca," Mia gasped, bracing a hand against the dashboard. "What is it? Did you hit something?"

"It's Jill!" I yelled, slamming the car into park.

"Jill?" Mia sat straight up, looking around. "Where?"

"In the woods." I flung open the car door and ran out, trying to gauge where I had seen the figure disappear into the shadows.

Mia was shouting at me, but I ignored her and took off toward the woods, so afraid I wouldn't find Jill before she disappeared again. I started peering through the trees, running back and forth, straining to see something, anything ... but as far as I could tell, there was nothing but branches and dead leaves. The air smelled like typical woods, musky and damp. To my relief, there was no sign of smoke anywhere.

But of course there wouldn't be. This was Wisconsin, not the Wild West. Wildfires were rare.

"Becca, where did you see her?" Mia had run up behind me, panting.

"Somewhere here," I waved at the edge of the tree line. "She was disappearing into the woods. Did you see anything?"

Mia shielded her eyes, trying to focus as they adjusted to the shadows. "No. I didn't see anything. Are you sure what you saw was her?"

"Positive," I said, thinking back to the flash of fabric, the glimpse of movement. "Well, almost positive."

Mia narrowed her eyes. "Almost positive?"

"It was just a quick look," I said. "I was driving, so I was focused on the road. It was only out of the corner of my eye. It looked like she was ducking back into the woods again."

Mia looked around. "Well, if it was her, she's gone now."

"It had to be her," I said. "Who else would be way out here in the middle of nowhere?"

Mia squinted at me. "It's possible it was some other person. Or maybe you saw a bird or deer or something."

I put my hands on my hips. "You don't think I know the difference between a bird and a person?"

"Of course I do," Mia said. "But you see something from the corner of your eye, and we've been talking about a missing girl ... your mind could just be playing tricks on you."

"I'm sure I saw her," I said, but I was already starting to question myself. Did I actually see what I thought I did? Or was it just an animal darting into the trees, and my mind filled in the blanks?

Find me.

I shook my head sharply. "I guess you have a point. If she was here, she's not now."

"Maybe what we need to do is tell Daniel," Mia said. "He has the resources to set up an actual search in the woods. With dogs and lots of people. You and I poking around isn't likely to do much."

"You're right," I said, although I was still irritated with Daniel. I glanced behind me toward the house, wondering if I should go back and interrupt him. But what if I was wrong, and Daniel had already found Jill's body? Me barging in there would be the worst thing I could do, especially to Wendy. Texting would be better.

Mia started walking to the car. "Coming?" she called over her shoulder.

"Yeah," I said, but I didn't move. I took one last look around, but the woods were still and silent.

"Becca?" Mia called from behind me.

"Yeah, I'm coming," I said as I deliberately turned my back to the woods. Mia was right; the best thing I could do was let Daniel know what I thought I'd seen.

As soon as I got back into the car, I dug my phone out of my purse. *It happened again. I saw something in the woods. I think it might have been Jill.*

"Should we wait?" Mia asked. She was peering over my shoulder, staring at my phone screen.

"Maybe a few minutes," I said, glancing around again. "I could always leave some sort of marker here for Daniel, so he knows where to look."

But the answer didn't take long. *Not now. I'll talk to you later.*

My stomach dropped with a sickening thud.

"Oh no," Mia breathed, and we both looked at each other. "Does that mean …"

Find me.

I slammed the car into drive and hit the gas a little too hard, so the wheels squealed. "We'll find out later." My tone was brusque. I didn't want to talk about it.

That didn't stop me from brooding about it the rest of the day, though. I spent hours in the kitchen, listlessly putting tea blends together as I continually refreshed my phone, looking for a text while Mia half-heartedly worked on her computer at the table.

It wasn't until the afternoon was starting to wind down and it was time to figure out dinner, that there was a knock at the front door.

"Is that Daniel?" Mia asked.

"Doubt it," I said, heading to the front door. "I haven't heard from him all day."

But I was wrong. Daniel stood on the porch.

We stared at each other for a moment without speaking. He had a peculiar expression on his face that I couldn't read.

"Well," I said finally. "I thought you were going to text me."

His expression didn't change. "Can I come in?"

I stared at him, trying to sort out the whirlwind of emotions swirling around inside of me. A part of me wanted to insist that he apologize first for how he'd treated me earlier, but another part wanted to know what exactly was going on.

I decided the apology could wait.

I took a step backward, allowing him to enter the house before turning on my heel and heading into the kitchen. Behind me, I could hear him shut the door.

Mia glanced up from the computer. "Who was at the do … oh. Hi, Daniel."

"Mia," Daniel said.

She closed her laptop, glancing between us. "Maybe I should go upstairs …"

"No, stay," Daniel said, looking between us. "This concerns both of you."

"Just say it," I said. "Is Jill … did you find her?" I couldn't say it.

"No, we didn't."

"Did you find a lead in who kidnapped her or where she is?"

"She wasn't kidnapped."

I stared at him. "So she ran away then?"

"No."

Mia and I glanced at each other. I could see the same question in her eyes. "So what, was she kidnapped by aliens? What happened to her then?"

"Nothing happened to her. Because there is no Jill."

I stared at him, utterly perplexed. "What on Earth are you talking about?"

"Exactly what I said. There is no Jill. Jill doesn't exist."

Chapter 10

I stared at Daniel blankly. "What do you mean, Jill doesn't exist? I saw her in the woods."

"I don't know who or what you saw in the woods, but it wasn't Wendy's daughter."

I couldn't believe what I was hearing. "How can she not have a daughter? She told me she did. She said she was ten years old."

"Apparently, she made it all up," Daniel said.

"She made up having a daughter?" Mia asked. "How does that even work?"

"It's not as complicated as you might think," Daniel explained. "Not if you don't have any close friends or family or anyone who wants to meet the child, that is. All Wendy has to do is talk about her. She's been telling this story for ten years now, and every year, her made-up daughter turns a year older."

"But *why*?" Mia asked. "Why would she do that?"

Daniel sighed and ran a hand through his hair. "I'm not sure yet. It seems Wendy might have some mental issues. She claims she never meant to mislead people, and that she just gets 'confused.'"

Mia's mouth dropped open. "Confused? About having a child?"

Daniel shrugged. "Like I said, mental issues. I'm also not sure whether she's getting treatment for them."

"But what about the kidnapping?" I asked, raising my hands in disbelief. "She just made all that up, too?"

"Apparently," Daniel said.

My mouth worked as if I were going to speak, but I struggled to find the words. "I need a drink," I finally said, heading to the wine cabinet for a bottle of cabernet. "Does anyone else want a glass?"

"Absolutely," Mia answered.

"The best idea I've heard all day," Daniel said.

"So, how does Zane fit into all of this?" Mia asked as I hunted for a corkscrew.

Daniel sighed. "Evidently, Penny knew Wendy was pretending to have a daughter, and one night, she confessed the whole sorry mess to Zane. She asked him to keep it to himself, though, since Wendy wasn't hurting anyone with her story. I mean, it wasn't like she was doing anything illegal, like claiming her fictional daughter on her tax returns. It might be unethical, and maybe even immoral, but she wasn't breaking any laws. Until now."

"Now?" Mia asked as I handed her a glass of wine.

Daniel's face was grim. "It's against the law to lie to the cops and file a fraudulent police report."

"Oh," Mia said.

"So, *none* of it really happened?" I asked incredulously, taking my seat at the table. "She was never attacked at Penny's house either?"

"That's what she says now."

"But what about the blood in her hair? How did that happen?"

"She claims to have accidentally run into a doorway after everyone left. That led to her confusion, and when she gets confused, that's when she hallucinates that she has a daughter. But this time, when Wendy tried to find her, she assumed she had been kidnapped."

"But the blood was on the back of her head," I said. "How does someone run backwards into a door?"

Daniel shrugged. "As she's no longer claiming to be a victim of a crime, there's nothing for me to investigate."

"Don't you want to get to the bottom of what happened to her though?" I asked. "If she was attacked in her home, that would obviously be a crime."

"There's no evidence of that," Daniel said.

"Nothing?" I asked in disbelief. "No blood on the floor? The door?"

Daniel took a sip of wine, his expression pained. "There did appear to be a blood stain on the kitchen floor in front of the stove."

My eyes went wide. "Then her story might be true! She might have been attacked in front of the stove."

"Possibly," Daniel said. "It's also possible it's what you said yesterday. She was standing in front of the stove and collapsed, hitting her head on the floor. When she woke up, she was confused, and maybe didn't have any idea what happened to her."

"She probably needs to see a doctor," Mia said. "Maybe she has a brain tumor."

"A brain tumor that's been affecting her for ten years?" I asked.

"Well, maybe not for ten years. But as Daniel said, she may have been suffering from mental issues for a long time, but they're getting worse now," Mia said. "Maybe the grief of losing her mother is causing it. That could explain her collapsing in the kitchen. Either way, it sounds like she needs to see a doctor."

"That's not really something I can force her to do," Daniel said.

"I know. I wasn't saying it's your responsibility." Mia frowned as she drummed her fingers on the table. "Ideally, a close friend or family member could intervene, but it doesn't sound like she has many of those. That's unfortunate and sad, as she's probably not going to get the help she needs."

I couldn't believe what I was hearing. "I think you're both forgetting something important."

They turned to look at me. "What?" Mia asked.

I leaned forward. "What I saw. I *saw* Jill. In the woods."

"You couldn't have. She doesn't exist," Daniel insisted.

"Then who was it?"

"Not Jill."

"But that's absurd," I said. "It's just a big coincidence that some other little ten-year-old girl was in the woods that day?"

"There are plenty of ten-year-old girls in this town," Daniel said. "And it's not that unlikely for any of them to wander off into the woods."

"Is anyone reporting a ten-year-old girl missing?"

"No. But that doesn't mean anything. She could have been gone for only a few hours before returning home. It's possible her family didn't even realize she was wandering around in the woods."

I shook my head, frustrated. Even though Daniel made a certain amount of sense, I couldn't let it go. I talked to Wendy about Jill. I saw the worry in her eyes. Jill *had* to exist. I couldn't believe it was all a figment of Wendy's imagination.

"When you first interviewed Wendy, you surely asked her for a picture of Jill. Or at the very least, a description. What did Wendy say she looked like?" I asked.

Daniel's mouth flattened. "She said she didn't have a picture on her. She claimed to have some in her apartment, though, and said she would call her neighbor to bring one to Redemption."

"No pictures? Not even on her phone?"

"She doesn't have a smart phone, just a plain old flip phone. Says smart phones are out of her budget."

"You didn't ask her about Penny having one somewhere?" I asked. "She was her grandmother, after all."

"You saw Penny's house," Daniel said. "There were no personal photos at all."

"Not everyone displays family pictures," Mia said pointedly, giving me a meaningful look. She was right; my home had a serious lack of family photos, too.

"But yes," Daniel continued. "We did ask whether Penny might have a picture somewhere, but Wendy was vague. She said she didn't know where Penny put things. She also didn't think Penny had anything current."

"She had an answer for everything, didn't she?" Mia asked.

"It certainly seemed so," Daniel said. "But I guess if you've been living with a delusion for as long as she has, she would know how to sidestep the obvious holes in her story."

"I'm still having trouble buying it," I said. "There was nothing in her expression when she talked about her daughter that would indicate this was all fake."

"It might not have been fake," Mia said. "It's possible there are times Wendy truly believes she has a daughter. Especially if there is a mental illness."

"Okay, but what happened when you showed up there with Zane?" I asked.

"Not much," Daniel said. "Zane told her he knew it was all a lie. At first, she denied it, but Zane kept talking, and she eventually folded. Apologized for all the trouble she caused. Said between hitting her head and the grief, she lost her mind a bit."

"So, she didn't admit to having any mental issues," I said.

"No, but Zane had mentioned something about it. I didn't think it was my place to push."

"Are you going to charge her with anything?" Mia asked.

Daniel shook his head. "I don't think so. The police chief will ultimately decide, but no one has the heart or the stomach to charge a clearly sick and grieving woman."

"Totally get that," Mia said, shaking her head. "Poor Penny. Now it makes more sense why she protected Wendy so much."

"Yes, it's sad all around," Daniel said.

I still wasn't buying it. "But what about Zane?"

"What about him?" Daniel asked.

"Is he credible?" I looked pointedly at Mia. "You didn't think so earlier."

"And I still don't," Mia said. "I wouldn't trust him as far as I can throw him. But it's my understanding that Wendy admitted everything, right? So it's not like we have to take Zane's word for what happened. We have Wendy's."

"That's right," Daniel said.

In my mind's eye, I could still see Jill standing in the woods, staring at me with an almost desperate expression. *Find me.*

"I still want to know who was in the woods."

Daniel finished his wine and reached for the bottle in the middle of the table. "Yeah, we'd all like that. A nice, neat bow on all our cases. The real world doesn't work like that, though."

"Does that mean you aren't going to look into whoever that girl was?" I asked.

"You haven't explained why I should. Where's the crime?" Daniel asked. "You saw a girl in the woods. Simple as that. That's not a crime, other than potential trespassing. But a lot of that is state land."

"You really don't think there's something strange going on here?" I asked. "Wendy claims to have a daughter who was kidnapped and then suddenly says she doesn't have a daughter. Meanwhile, I meet a girl who appears in the woods right behind the house she's staying in? That doesn't strike you as odd?"

"It's definitely odd, but that's not the point. The point is, has a crime been committed or not? Right now, the answer is no," Daniel said. "And unfortunately, I have way too much on my plate with real, actual crimes to do anything about weird coincidences."

"Are you still seeing a lot of gang activity?" Mia interjected.

Daniel sighed and ran a hand through his hair. "Unfortunately, yes. And there's been no break in any of the cases. There's also something suspicious going on outside of town that may or may not be related."

"What would that be?" Mia asked.

"It appears to be some kind of cult," Daniel said.

Mia stared at him. "A cult? In Redemption?"

"Not exactly in Redemption proper," Daniel said. "It's outside city limits."

"Where?" Mia asked.

"The old Hoffmann property," Daniel said.

Mia looked surprised. "Someone finally bought that old place?"

"Apparently so."

"What's the Hoffmann property?" I asked.

Mia waved a hand. "It's this seriously run-down property right outside of town. Old Man Hoffmann died a few years back, and the whole thing has been tied up in court and red tape ever since. He had it in a trust, but the kids were fighting over who got what, and while all of this was going on, it just sat there. I know some developers were interested in buying it, but nothing ever came of it. I didn't realize it was finally for sale."

"I don't know if anyone did," Daniel said. "It's also possible it hasn't been sold, and the cult is renting it."

"Why do you think they're a cult?" I asked.

"Well, to start, they call themselves 'The Church of the Forgotten,'" Daniel said.

"That does sound like a cult," Mia agreed.

I felt an icy shiver run down my spine. "What does 'The Church of the Forgotten' even mean?" I asked.

"Your guess is as good as mine," Daniel said. "All I know is that they're out there creating a communal living situation and certainly acting like a cult."

"How does a cult act?" I asked.

Daniel took a sip of wine. "Strangely. Like, for instance, the first thing they did was repair and fortify the fence around the property and add a brand-new, state-of-the-art lock to the gate. They claim it's to keep themselves safe, but this is Redemption. It's not like we have a lot of crime going on, although I admit the gang activity is worrisome. Still, what are they trying to do with that fence? Keep people out … or in?"

I shivered again and hugged my arms across my chest.

"That is a little peculiar," Mia said. "If they are a cult, I wonder why they chose Redemption."

"Me too," Daniel said. "I personally don't like coincidences, so the fact that gang activity has ramped up at the same time this so-called cult moved in is not sitting right with me."

It wasn't sitting right with me, either. Especially with what was happening with Wendy.

"Do you know how big this cult is?" I asked.

"Not too big. Maybe a few dozen people? Fifty at most, I would estimate. They're easy to spot."

"How so?" Mia asked.

Daniel grimaced. "You'll see."

Mia and I exchanged a look. "What does that mean?" I asked.

"Just wait. You'll see," Daniel said again.

Chapter 11

Find me.

I couldn't stop thinking about Wendy and her supposed nonexistent daughter … or the girl I saw in the woods. Why would she lie about something like that? Not just about having a daughter, but about the kidnapping?

And who had I seen in the woods, if she really was lying?

The next morning, Mia had the breakfast shift at Aunt May's, so she was already gone by the time I stumbled down into the kitchen. Even though she could have all the coffee she wanted for free at Aunt May's, she had taken the time to make me a fresh pot before she left.

Feeling grateful for her thoughtfulness, I poured myself a cup and fed Oscar. Then, I stood at the window and stared out into the backyard while I stewed. Not about my garden, which was looking a little overgrown and weedy, but about Wendy.

What I ought to do was spend the day in my garden. Admittedly, it was woefully neglected ever since Penny died.

But the longer I stood there, the more I recognized that as much as the garden needed my attention, it was going to have to wait another day.

Today, I needed to have a chat with Wendy.

***

I wiped my sweaty hands on my jeans as I mounted the steps of Penny's front porch. There was no reason for me to be nervous, yet I couldn't seem to control the fluttering sensation in my chest.

The morning was cool and clear. A few puffy clouds dotted the dark-blue sky, and a robin hopped along the too-long grass searching for a snack. There was a stillness around the house that made me wonder if Wendy was even there, or if she had packed up and left after her confession to Daniel.

I knocked on the door and waited, listening to the birds chirping happily in the surrounding trees. It was a little after ten in the morning. I had carefully timed my arrival, hoping it was late enough for her to be up and dressed but early enough to catch her before she left the house … or Redemption altogether.

It appeared my careful scheming didn't matter. Despite straining to listen, I didn't hear a single sound from inside the house, and my stomach, under the weight of disappointment, slowly started to sink.

I was wondering if there was any way to somehow track her down when the door suddenly flung open. Wendy stood there, her hair matted and face puffy and creased, like she hadn't slept in days. She was still wearing the same faded blue tracksuit as the day before, except it was now stained and wrinkled. Her body odor was even worse than before, too.

Her expression immediately fell when she saw me. "Oh. It's you." Her face puckered like she had eaten something bitter as she started to close the door. I quickly stepped forward and put a hand on it before she could close it all the way.

"Yes, it's me," I said. "Can I come in?"

"It's not a good time," she answered, shoving at the door. I didn't budge.

"Why? What's going on? Is something happening with your *daughter*?" I asked?

Her pale cheeks flushed an ugly red. "It's none of your business."

"You lied to me," I said. "Why?"

"It's complicated," Wendy said through gritted teeth, still struggling with the door.

"Then uncomplicate it," I demanded. "Why would you tell people you have a daughter when you don't?"

She suddenly gave up on trying to shut the door in my face and sagged against the frame. "I didn't … I get confused sometimes." She hung her head, causing her greasy, matted hair to cover her face.

I felt my heart soften toward her again. "Are you sick?" I asked. "Is there something I can do to help?"

She shook her head, still keeping her eyes down, and I noticed a few red flakes still on the back of her head. I sucked in my breath.

"You *were* attacked, weren't you." It wasn't a question.

Her head snapped up. "No, no, no. I told you. I was confused."

"But I can see the blood on the back of your head!" I countered.

Her hand rose automatically to touch the exact area I was referring to. "I ran into a door."

"How could you possibly run into a door with the back of your head?"

She took a deep, shuddering breath. "I … I fell down after I hit my head."

"Then where's the bruise from running into the door?"

She touched her temple, her eyes darting around. "I don't know. I can't really remember exactly what happened."

I took a step closer to her. "Wendy," I said, keeping my voice soft. "Why are you lying?"

Her eyes shifted to mine briefly before looking away. "I didn't mean to lie. I told you, I get confused."

"I'm not talking about before. I'm talking about now."

Her eyes went wide as she took a step back. "I … I … "

"You *do* have a daughter, don't you? Why would you tell Daniel she doesn't exist?"

She shook her head violently. "No, no, no. I keep telling you, I just get confused."

"Wendy, I *saw* Jill."

Her face jerked back toward me. "*What*?" The fear was naked in her eyes.

"I saw her. In the woods. I told you right afterward. Remember?"

She stared at me. "No, you couldn't have."

"But I did. She was back there, in the woods." I pointed. "She wouldn't come out when I talked to her, so I told you so you could go get her."

"But ..." she was blinking rapidly at me. "That doesn't make any sense."

"Why doesn't it make any sense?"

"Because Jill was ..." she broke off suddenly, pressing her hand to her mouth as if to keep herself from saying anything else.

I took another step forward. "Jill was what?"

She pressed her lips together, a haunted look in her eyes. "What did she look like?"

"Who?"

"The girl you saw in the woods. What did she look like?"

"Like a blonde ten-year-old," I said, thinking back. "Her hair was long and kind of a mess, like she had been in woods for a while. Actually, everything about her was kind of a mess. Her face was all dirty and smudged ..."

Wendy's expression sharpened. "Smudged?"

"Yeah, like with dirt or something. It was on her dress, too, although maybe that was because the dress was so old. Was it one of your mother's? Or maybe your grandmother's?"

Wendy's face went pale. "Dress? What kind of dress?"

"The old-fashioned kind. Like something they would have worn a hundred years ago."

Wendy gasped, pressing a hand against her neck. She swayed slightly, and for a moment, I was sure she was going to faint.

"Wendy," I said, reaching for her elbow. "Are you okay? Maybe we should sit down."

Wendy immediately shook her arm free, not allowing me to touch her. "That wasn't my daughter," she whispered.

"What?" I wasn't sure if I'd heard her correctly. "Then who did I see?"

Wendy suddenly burst into action, shoving me in the chest. I stumbled backward, landing flat on my butt on the porch. Her movement was so sudden and violent, it took me by complete surprise.

She slammed the door shut. I could hear her turning the locks, and I knew there was no sense in trying to get her to open it again.

I stayed where I was, trying to get my bearings as the cool wind ruffled my hair. Even though it didn't look like it was going to storm, I thought I detected the promise of rain in the breeze.

Everything around me seemed so normal, I was having trouble wrapping my head around what had just happened. Did Wendy admit to having a daughter after all? That last statement sure sounded like it. So why in the world would she lie and say she made it all up?

And who was the girl in the woods?

Find me.

The breeze blowing against the back of my neck suddenly didn't feel so cool and refreshing anymore. Rather, it was like cold, icy fingers trailing down my spine.

The feeling that something was wrong grew stronger, twisting my gut into a knot.

What was going on?

Chapter 12

Once I made it back to my car, I decided to go to Aunt May's. The idea of being by myself in an empty house, or even alone in my garden, was just too much. I was still feeling on edge and out of sorts. I needed to be around people and the hustle and bustle of normal, everyday life … where children who didn't exist weren't kidnapped or appearing in the woods for no apparent reason.

Also, I was sort of hoping Mia would be able to take a break, so I could tell her what happened. I definitely needed to talk to someone. My head was spinning, and I wasn't sure if I could wait until Daniel was off of work.

I ended up parking on the street and walking to Aunt May's, as the breakfast and lunch crowds were always the busiest. Even though it was mid-morning—a little too late for breakfast and early for lunch—I suspected it would still be crowded and decided not to waste time messing with the parking lot.

Teri, one of the waitresses, saw me walk through the door and waved me toward an empty booth in the back. I waved back as I wove my way through the crowd.

She was right behind me with a menu in one hand and a coffee pot in the other. After handing me the menu, she flipped over the mug on the table and filled it.

"You know me too well," I said appreciatively.

She grinned. "Of course I do. You're one of our favorite customers. Do you need a minute, or do you know what you want?"

I glanced at the menu and thought, *screw it*. Considering the last few days, I deserved to treat myself. Plus, I was famished. I ordered the blueberry waffles with a side of bacon and two scrambled eggs.

"Coming right up," she said, scribbling on her pad.

"Oh, and is Mia around?" I asked, searching the restaurant.

Teri frowned. "I think she left already, but I can check and see. It's been a crazy morning."

"If it's not too much trouble," I said, feeling oddly deflated. I hadn't realized how much I wanted to talk to Mia until that very moment. If I had known she had already left, I would have gone straight home.

But then I would have missed the blueberry waffles. And they were definitely worth it.

I doctored my coffee with cream and sugar and sipped it slowly, waiting for the caffeine to work its magic. *I'll have a nice breakfast, and then go home to talk with Mia whenever she can take a break from her studies*, I thought. *It will be fine. Better than fine, really, because I won't have to worry about sitting alone in an empty house.*

"Blueberry waffles? I thought you're watching your weight."

I looked up to see Chrissy holding my food. She flashed me a crooked smile.

"I didn't realize you were working," I said as she placed the plates in front of me.

"I'm on break," she said and gestured to the seat across from me. "Want some company?"

"Sure."

I watched as she slid into the booth, a little surprised she was volunteering to spend her break with me. While there was no question our relationship had vastly improved since the first few months we were in Redemption, she was still a 17-year-old teenager, and I was still her stepmother.

She took a sip of ice water she had brought with her before grabbing a paper napkin from the metal holder to mop her sweaty cheeks. Even with her bright- red face and messy hair falling out of its ponytail, she was still absolutely beautiful.

Her huge brown eyes, so similar to her father's, were rimmed with thick black lashes, and her narrow face and impossibly high cheekbones were framed by long, thick, black hair dyed hot-pink at the ends.

"It is really hot in the kitchen today," she said. "The air conditioner is on the fritz, and the main fan stopped working yesterday. Apparently, no one has done anything to fix or replace either of them. We're going to have to do something soon, though. It's like a sauna back there."

"Other than the heat, how's it going?"

"Good." She shrugged, a delicate movement. "I mean, it's diner food. So …"

"What, you don't like diner food?"

"It has nothing to do with 'like.' What's not to like? It's more about the speed of service. But once you get the hang of that, it's not much of a challenge."

"So, what? You want something more gourmet?"

She flashed another smile. "Something like that. Maybe Mario's, or The Redemption Supper Club."

My eyes went wide. "Oh! Pretty fancy." The Supper Club was a legitimate five-star restaurant. Located near the lake, it not only offered a gorgeous view, but also a fine-dining experience with a Michelin Star chef. I had never eaten there, since along with being one of Redemption's priciest restaurants, it was also difficult to get a reservation. People came from all over southern Wisconsin to celebrate special occasions there.

Her cheeks turned a little more red. "Well, I figured I might as well shoot for the stars. Otherwise, what's the point? But before I pursue anything like that, I have to finish culinary school, and that won't happen until after I graduate next summer."

"So, you'll come back after culinary school?" I wasn't sure of her plans. Like me, she grew up in New York City. Unlike me, she hadn't spent her childhood summers in this small, midwestern town. Needless to say, there was a culture shock. But once we had gotten over the initial difficulties, she seemed to find her place and had come to really like it. Still, it was very different from where she grew up.

Her face turned redder yet, and she didn't meet my eyes. "That's the plan." Her voice was quiet.

I frowned. "You don't sound overly sure."

She didn't immediately answer, taking a long drink of water instead. "I guess that depends on Redemption," she finally said. "If I'm supposed to return, I will. But if not …" She shrugged again.

Oh. So that's what was going on. The locals were convinced that Redemption itself determined who stayed and who left. If the town didn't want you, it would somehow become impossible for you to stay. On the flip side, if it did, you'd inevitably be stuck.

I wasn't sure how much I believed it, but as I did have my own strange related experiences, I couldn't completely discount it, either.

But there was something about Chrissy's expression that made me dig deeper. "But what do YOU want to do? Do you want to come back, or not?"

She looked away, squirming a little in her seat. I opened my mouth to say something else, but decided to eat my waffle instead. *If she wants to confide in me, she will,* I reminded myself. *I don't need to push her.*

Finally, she turned back to me. "Redemption is a weird little town, isn't it?"

That wasn't precisely an answer, but I nodded, my mouth still full of waffle.

"It doesn't exactly feel like home," she continued, playing with a corner of a napkin. "But neither does New York. At least not anymore."

I finished swallowing. "Are you looking for a place that feels like home?"

She glanced at me, a tiny smile on her lips. "Aren't we all?"

"I suppose so," I said, nodding in acknowledgment.

"And home might be Redemption," she continued. "But ... well, I guess I'm hoping for the chance to find out when I go to culinary school."

I tilted my head. "Are you afraid that something will keep you from going to culinary school?"

She shrugged, not meeting my gaze. "I just want to make sure there aren't any issues. If I'm supposed to come back, I will. But if I'm not, then that's fine, too."

I abruptly stopped eating, my fork frozen halfway between the plate and my mouth. "Chrissy, I know what the townspeople think, but this is a TOWN, after all. Not a person. I'm sure there won't be any issues with you leaving to go to school."

"But you don't know that," she said quietly.

"I know that sometimes people get a little too carried away with all these superstitions," I said.

She stared at me. "How can you say that? You of all people?"

"What are you talking about?"

She gestured with her arm. "Look at all the people who tried to leave and couldn't. Or were killed. Or had something else bad happen to them. Like that woman who had no sooner showed up here before her child was kidnapped."

"If you're talking about Wendy, Penny's daughter, there's some ... dispute as to whether she even has a child."

Chrissy looked at me in confusion. "What are you talking about?"

"I'm surprised you haven't heard. Isn't Aunt May's the center of town gossip?"

She gave me a look. "I'm serious."

"I am, too," I said. "But to answer your question, Wendy apparently doesn't have a child. I guess she 'gets confused,' or something. Anyway, she's now claiming to have hit her head, which caused her to think her nonexistent daughter was kidnapped."

Chrissy's jaw dropped open. "You're kidding."

I sighed. "I wish I was."

"But then who did she come to Redemption with?"

What? I stared at Chrissy, wondering if I had heard her right. "What did you say?"

Chrissy shot me a familiar look of irritation … one I had gotten used when we struggled to get along. "I asked who she came to Redemption with, if not her daughter."

"Are you saying you saw Wendy with a child?" I tried to control the excitement surging through me, but I was cognizant of the fact that I was also failing miserably. Was it possible that I wasn't the only one to have seen this non-existent daughter? Although based on Wendy's reaction, the girl in the woods may not have been her daughter after all. I pushed that thought aside. If Wendy was lying about her daughter, she could also have been lying about who I saw in the woods. "Are you saying you saw Jill?"

"Who's Jill?"

"Her supposedly non-existent daughter."

"Her name is Jill?"

"Yes. Do you not approve of that name or something?"

"Well, no, it's just …" She shook her head. "Never mind. No, I didn't see Jill."

"Oh." The surge of excitement quickly morphed into disappointment. "Then why did you ask who she came to Redemption with?"

"Because she stopped by here once and got two meals to go."

"That doesn't mean she had someone with her," I said. "Maybe she intended to have the second meal later."

"She got a tuna melt and a grilled cheese, both with fries," Chrissy said. "Do either of those sound like meals you'd warm up later?"

Careful, I warned myself as the excitement began to flicker through me again. *There could be a million other explanations other than her having a daughter.* "Maybe she was meeting someone."

"Maybe. But then why did she take a menu back outside before she ordered?"

My eyes widened. "She took a menu to her car?"

"I'm assuming so. She came in, asked for a menu, said she'd be right back, and returned a few minutes later to order."

"How do you know this?"

"I was on break, so I was sitting at the counter watching the whole thing. She wanted coffee, too, I remember. Just one cup, to go, and she was drinking it while she waited. She seemed nervous … kept looking around the restaurant. Teri went over and tried to start a conversation with her, but Wendy just shook her head. It was obvious she didn't want to talk."

"So, that's how you knew it was Wendy? Because Teri recognized her?"

Chrissy nodded. "Yeah. I thought maybe she was one of the weird cult members …"

"Wait, you know about the cult?"

Chrissy rolled her eyes. "Seriously, Becca? Everyone knows about it. That's all the talk around here. People are saying we might end up with our very own Jim Jones Kool Aid situation out there."

"You know who Jim Jones is?"

"What, you think I don't watch documentaries on YouTube?"

I decided not to answer that. "So, you think the Church of the Forgotten is some sort of doomsday cult?"

She gave me a look, her expression full of teenager disdain. "I mean, with that name, is there any doubt? What does it sound like to you?"

I had to admit she had a point.

"Anyway, Teri was the one who recognized her. Said Wendy looked just like Penny when Penny was younger."

I pictured Wendy, haggard and exhausted-looking from her grief and long hours of driving, sitting in the middle of Aunt May's, clutching her cup of coffee while she waited for her food. "If there was someone in the car, why didn't she bring her into the restaurant?"

"I have no idea. Teri said that Wendy was always ... high-strung, I guess. She was surprised to see her. I guess she thought Wendy had disappeared for good."

"A lot of people thought that," I said, remembering Daphne's reaction. Mia, on the other hand ...

"Was Mia here when Wendy stopped by?"

Chrissy dropped her gaze to the crumpled-up napkins she had used to wipe the sweat off her face. "I don't think so. Why?"

"I'm just curious. Mia was shocked when she saw Wendy at the funeral. I would have thought Teri would have mentioned something to her."

Chrissy's fingers reached out and she started nervously tearing a corner of the used napkin. "I think this was the day before the funeral, so I don't know if Teri would have had time to say anything to Mia."

I frowned. That didn't seem right to me. Teri and Mia were good friends. I couldn't believe she wouldn't have texted Mia. Or, for that matter, one of the other waitresses. Mia knew everyone in town. How someone hadn't reached out to her seemed unimaginable to me.

"And you didn't think to say something to her at home?"

The little pile of napkin pieces continued to grow. "I don't know. It was a busy day. I had a lot on my mind. And I don't know if I even saw her at home that day, anyway. It's not like she's around a lot."

I stared at her. Mia not around? If she wasn't working, she was home on her computer, focusing on school. What was Chrissy talking about?

Before I could ask any more questions, Chrissy continued. "Anyway, this is yet another example of something weird happening when this town doesn't approve of what you're doing."

"I don't think we can assume what Redemption wanted Wendy to do or not do," I said.

"Well, from my standpoint, whenever people try to do something that Redemption doesn't want them to do, something bad happens to them." Her voice was flat.

"I agree that a lot of strange things happen here," I said. "And I also agree that Redemption has a higher-than-average disappearance rate, but that's probably just coincidence. Especially since I don't know if we can definitively say that anyone was truly trying to stay or go when something happened to them."

Chrissy leaned forward, her eyes glinting. "What about Jessica?"

My mouth went dry. "What happened to Jessica was horrible. But there's no proof that Redemption had anything to do with it. And but more than that, it's a completely separate situation from you going to culinary school."

"You don't know that," she said again. "I think it's better to be safe than sorry."

"Well, okay," I said, going back to my waffle. Clearly, pressing her about whether or not she wanted to return to Redemption wasn't going to give me any more answers. "You know I'll do whatever I can to help you. With culinary school, I mean."

Her gaze softened. "I know that. And thank you. I don't even know what would have happened to me if you hadn't stepped up to help. I don't think I'll ever be able to repay you."

"I'm not looking to be repaid. I only want you to have a happy life. And cooking seems to make you happy. So, let's both do whatever we can to get you to culinary school."

"Thanks," Chrissy said, glancing over at the clock. "Oh. Break's over. I better get back to work." She started to slide out of the booth.

"I'll see you at home," I said. She smiled and gave me a little wave before suddenly pausing. "Them again." Her voice was full of disgust.

My back was to the front door, so I had to turn around in my seat to see who Chrissy was referring to.

I froze in place.

Even though I could only see the back of the two women standing by the counter talking to Teri, I immediately recognized the dresses they wore.

They were the exact style as the one the girl in the woods was wearing: long and old-fashioned, the material some sort of muslin or cotton, loose and flowing with long sleeves and a decorative hem. They appeared identical, except one was decorated with tiny blue flowers, whereas the other had tiny pink flowers. Unlike the girl in the woods, the dresses appeared clean.

Both women wore their hair up in a tight bun. While their dresses were so similar to the girl's in the woods, they were obviously different people. One woman was way too tall to be her, and the other shorter one was much rounder.

Still, it had to be more than coincidence. Was the girl related to them somehow? And why did they wear these get-ups? Were they a part of some reenactment I didn't know about?

"Who are they?" I asked when the initial shock wore off and I was finally able to find my voice.

Chrissy snorted. "They're part of that cult we were talking about."

They're easy to spot, Daniel had said, and I could see exactly what he meant.

The taller woman held a basket that she kept trying to show Teri, who was shaking her head.

"Why are they here?" I asked.

"Oh, they're trying to sell their eggs and vegetables to us," Chrissy said, rolling her eyes. "All organic and free range, of course."

I gave her the side-eye. "What, you don't like organic stuff now?"

Chrissy made a face. "You know I do. I just don't trust them. The first time they came in, fine. It never hurts to ask. But this is like the third or fourth time I've seen them in here. For a group that's supposedly all about love and light and being 'all connected,' they're awfully pushy."

That made me chuckle, which brought a small smile to Chrissy's face.

"Anyway," she said, pushing herself out of the booth, "I better get back to work."

The women's backs were to us, and they were far enough away to ensure there was no way they could have seen or heard Chrissy. Yet right at that moment, one of them suddenly spun around to face us.

She was older than I had initially thought, as she appeared to be in her mid-forties. Her skin was tough and leather-like, and her eyes were a piercing blue. Her hair was brown, but I noticed some gray mixed in.

Her eyes lit up when she saw us. "Hello, Chrissy! It's so nice to see you again." She headed toward us, weaving her way across the restaurant.

Chrissy muttered a hello in return as her gaze shifted around the room, like she was looking for an escape that wasn't completely rude. I glanced curiously at her. She hadn't mentioned she had been the one to talk to the cult members before. Was it because she happened to be cooking that day? Even so, I was relatively sure she was not the one who would be making the decisions around the diner's food purchases.

The woman fixed her intense gaze on me. "And you must be Becca Kingsley."

My mouth dropped open, and even Chrissy looked startled. "How could you possibly know that?"

Her eyes were even more piercing now that she was closer, and I found myself wanting to slide further back into the booth and somehow shield myself from them. "It's hardly a secret that Chrissy lives in the most famous haunted house in Redemption with her stepmother, who is a gifted tea maker."

I shifted uncomfortably. "I would hardly call myself 'gifted,' but thank you."

Her pale lips stretched into a smile that didn't reach her eyes. "And modest, too! I've actually been meaning to get in touch with you about your teas."

I stared at her. I had no idea how to respond. In a million years, I never dreamed that the Church of the Forgotten would be the least bit interested in my teas. "Uh … I …"

"Oh, silly me," the woman said, keeping the same plastic smile plastered on her face. "I'm Eleanor, and this is Fanny." She gestured to the young woman standing next to her, who avoided my eyes and bowed her head. She looked to be a little older than Chrissy, with mousy brown hair and a round face.

"Nice to meet both of you," I said.

Eleanor's eyes were still fixed firmly on me, but she bobbed her head. Fanny kept her gaze firmly down. "So, tea," Eleanor said, her voice brisk. "We'd love to learn more about it. As you can imagine, we drink a lot of it." The fake smile was back. "Can we set up a time to chat more? We're happy to come to you."

"Uh …" I wasn't sure how to answer. There was something about Eleanor and her intense gaze that made me uneasy. Was this a client I actually wanted? The idea of regularly seeing her made me queasy. "Let me get back to you. I'm going to have to check my calendar and find a time. Things are really busy right now."

"Of course," Eleanor said. "I completely understand. If you want to give me your phone number, we can call you later today or tomorrow."

I was feeling trapped, but I didn't know how to say no. I was running a business, after all. Plus, they could easily find my number with a quick Internet search, since it was posted on my website. "Uh, sure. Do you want to put it in your phone?"

Eleanor gave me a puzzled look. "My phone? Why would I have my phone? That's back at our ranch."

"I meant a cell phone. Or I can give you my website, if that's easier."

Eleanor laughed. "Oh heavens. We don't have cell phones or the Internet. We live a very simple life."

"Okay," I said, thinking I probably should have guessed that based on their outfits. "Do you have something to write on? Or," I picked up my phone. "I can take your number and call you later?" That would be ideal. Then I would be the one deciding whether or not I wanted to see them again.

For the first time since the conversation started, Eleanor looked faintly uneasy. "Our phone is a communal phone," she said, her voice hesitant. "There's not always someone around to answer when it rings."

Even better. 'That's fine. I can always leave a message."

She shook her head. "We don't have an answering machine either, if that's what you're referring to."

I clicked on the notes section of my phone. "Not a problem. I can keep calling if that's the case. I'm not home a lot myself, so you'd probably end up leaving a message for me, anyway. So, what's the number?"

Eleanor paused again, but finally relented and rattled it off. I typed it in, wondering why she was so reluctant to give it to me. She was the one who wanted the tea, after all. So why not be happy to have me call her?

"Could I get yours, as well?" she asked after I set my phone down. My heart sank, but her voice was so firm, and I didn't see how I could refuse.

"Do you have any paper?"

Eleanor didn't, so I grabbed a napkin while Chrissy found me a pen. She had been standing there the entire time, watching the exchange.

Eleanor definitely perked up once I handed her the folded napkin, and after assuring me she would be in touch, she glided away, Fanny following dutifully behind her.

"That was weird," Chrissy said the moment they left.

"I'll say," I agreed. I noticed Teri giving us a curious look, as well, but as she was busy taking an order, she couldn't come over.

"Think you'll call them?"

I looked down at my phone. When I had first asked for their number, I assumed I would never use it. But after Eleanor's reaction, I was no longer so sure. "I don't know. Probably not."

"Yeah, that's kind of what I assumed, until Eleanor didn't want to give you her number. Now, I'm kind of wishing you *would* call it."

I laughed. "The thought crossed my mind. I am definitely curious."

Chrissy tilted her head, shooting me a crooked smile. "Makes you wonder what they're hiding out there, doesn't it?" Before I could answer, she glanced at the clock and did a double take. "Oh, I really have to get back into the kitchen. See you tonight."

"See you," I said, but she was already trotting off.

I went back to my breakfast, which was now cold, my mind running through everything that had happened that morning. Between Wendy's reaction to my questions, Chrissy's cryptic comments about Mia, and the sudden appearance of Eleanor, which was also my firsthand introduction to the cult, it had been a very odd day, to say the least. I wished I could unpack it all with Daniel or Daphne, since I couldn't talk with Mia right then. On second thought, though, maybe not Daniel. I wasn't sure how he would feel about me having the cult as a tea customer.

My thoughts returned again to the girl in the woods. She and the women were dressed so similarly. Was it possible it was a coincidence? It certainly seemed unlikely. Unless it was some sort of costume, I never saw anyone else wear dresses like that.

But if the girl was a member of the cult, what was she doing in Penny's backyard? I didn't think the Hoffman property was anywhere close to Penny's house.

So, what was she doing there?

Was she lost? Or maybe running away?

Find me.

The food in my stomach had turned into a hard lump, and I put my fork down, no longer hungry. What if that girl was asking me for help, and instead of helping her, I left her alone to fend for herself?

I tried to swallow, but my mouth was so dry and my throat so tight, I thought I might choke. I reached for my water glass. If anything happened to that girl because I didn't do more to help …

No. I had to stop. *I shouldn't assume the worse,* I reasoned with myself. Kids run away from home all the time, even ones as young as ten. It didn't mean anything bad had happened to her.

An image of Eleanor popped into my head again as well as her hesitation to give me her number. Was that why she didn't want to give it to me? Because there was something going on out there she didn't want anyone else to know about? Something that might cause a ten-year-old girl to flee?

And what about Wendy's reaction? *That's not my daughter.* The fear in her eyes before she slammed the door in my face. If the girl was a member of the cult, that would explain some of it, because she *wouldn't* be Wendy's daughter.

But it wouldn't explain the fear.

I put my head in my hands, massaging my forehead with my fingers. If anything happened to that girl …

No. I couldn't go there again. Especially since I had no idea how to even try to find her. Daniel said no one had reported any ten-year-olds missing, and I doubted he would be willing to organize a search party based on something only I had seen. So unless I wanted to try to search the woods myself, I was out of luck.

Although … my eyes fell on my phone. I could try calling Eleanor and see about selling her tea after all. Maybe she would even invite me out for a visit, though I doubted it. She was so secretive about the phone number, I couldn't imagine her opening her home to me. And didn't she say she would come to me?

Regardless, it was worth a shot. I decided then and there to call her later that day to see if I could talk my way over there.

As I reached for my wallet to pay, I promised myself I wouldn't let trying to find the girl in the woods interfere with getting to the bottom of Wendy's situation. Was it possible the two were related? It was difficult to see how. Again, I saw the fear in Wendy's eyes when I described the girl I had seen.

Man, was there a lot to process. And that wasn't even all of it. I still wished I had been able to bring the conversation with Chrissy back to Mia. Especially since the more I thought about it, the more I realized it had been some time since I had seen Chrissy and Mia interact with each other at home. Maybe it was just coincidence, or maybe I simply wasn't around when they talked, but it still felt a little peculiar.

It was also possible that it was nothing. Mia and Chrissy worked together. There could have been some work-related issue that came between them, or maybe they were so sick of each other from work that they avoided each other at home.

There could be a million reasons that had nothing to do with anything.

I picked up my bacon, determined not to make a big deal out of it. I had enough strange things on my plate. I didn't need to invent problems between my stepdaughter and roommate.

Chapter 13

I had every intention of going to the grocery store once I was done eating, but as I stepped outside, I realized there was still plenty of time to get caught up on my gardening. It was the perfect day for it—warm, but not too warm, with a nice gentle breeze. The idea of being outside with my fingers in the dirt felt like the ideal way to get myself grounded and out of my head. I needed a break from all the spinning thoughts in my brain.

As I strolled down the street, I noticed someone coming toward me, pushing a shopping cart filled with various items. It was Maude, the local homeless woman. As usual, she was bundled up in various coats and scarves, including a dirty red-and-white striped stocking cap with a hole in it and a pair of gloves that were obviously too large for her hands. It didn't seem to matter how warm or cold it was outside; she was always dressed the same.

Maude was hunched over, muttering to herself, which was also normal. The mutterings were loud enough to be heard over the clacking of the wheels on the cracks of the sidewalk and the one bad wheel that made a constant clunking noise.

As she came closer, I tried to gauge what kind of mood she was in. If I greeted her and she didn't want the attention, it would upset her, and I didn't want to cause her any unnecessary distress. But if she seemed relaxed, even cheerful, then she'd be hurt if I didn't say anything to her.

Unfortunately, I had no clue how she was feeling, as she kept her head firmly down, the tip of the stocking cap hanging in her face.

I assumed that meant she wasn't interested in being friendly. I was prepared to pass her in silence when suddenly, she slammed to a halt in the middle of the sidewalk. Her head snapped up, and she stared at me. I was so surprised, I stopped in my tracks, too.

Her eyes were wide as she met my gaze. I could see the fear lurking in them. Her face went pale, and her mouth worked for a moment, but no sound came out.

"Maude? Are you okay?" Was she having a heart attack or a stroke? She didn't look well at all. Genuinely concerned, I took a cautious step toward her, preparing to catch her if she toppled over despite knowing she didn't like to be touched. She also didn't like doctors or hospitals or being inside any building, which would be a problem if she was having a medical emergency. The townspeople did a lot for her to keep her healthy and feeling safe, from one of Aunt May's wait staff handing her a meal each day to making sure she had enough blankets and somewhere to stay that was out of the worst of the weather in the winter.

"You saw her." Her voice came out in a hiss.

"Saw who?"

"Her." Maude made a stabby pointing gesture in the air. "In the woods."

My mouth dropped open. "Who ... who are you talking about?" *It doesn't mean anything,* I told myself. *After all, there is no possible way Maude could know about the girl I saw in the woods. Surely, she's just talking nonsense. There are woods all around us ... not exactly a leap of faith to imagine I could have seen someone in them.*

Maude nodded, her expression knowing. "You know who."

Find me.

The sun disappeared behind the clouds, and that nice cool breeze turned icy as it trailed along my bare skin. I tried to swallow, but my throat seemed to have seized up. The waffle had turned into a huge lump in my stomach again, and I wondered if I might get sick.

"I don't ... I don't know what you're talking about," I finally managed, forcing the words through my numb lips.

Maude took a step closer to me. "Be careful. Now that you saw her, *she sees you.*"

Find me.

I gasped. Every cell in my body urged me to run away as fast as possible, but I couldn't move. I couldn't speak. I could only stand there gaping at Maude.

She nodded again, a satisfied expression coming over her face, as if she had successfully completed her goal for the day. She went back to pushing her cart again, the wheels clacking loudly on the sidewalk.

She was halfway down the block before I was able to move. My limbs were thick and heavy, and my chest was tight, like bands were wrapped around it. Woodenly, I made my way to my car, trying to tell myself it was just Maude's way ... she said a lot of things that didn't mean anything or make any sense. Just because she happened to say something that seemed to describe an event in my life didn't make it true. It was more likely that I was making the whole exchange out to be bigger than it was. Especially since I had just seen the women from the Church of the Forgotten and what they wore. Considering it was possible I had seen a little girl from the cult, it was also possible that Maude had seen her, too.

Except that explanation didn't feel right. Just like it didn't feel right to assume Wendy had been lying about the existence of Jill simply because it wasn't Jill that I had seen in the woods after all.

Something else was going on. I could feel it, brewing just below the surface. Something dark and ancient. Something that had been around for a very long time, and was maybe just starting to wake up ...

Okay, enough, I admonished myself. I had to get a grip. If Mia wasn't able to talk, then I was definitely spending the afternoon in the garden, surrounded by my peaceful and calming plants.

Finally, I arrived at my car. I unlocked it and headed home, keeping my eyes glued to the road in front of me. The last thing

I wanted was to catch a glimpse of a girl with long, dirty-blonde hair and an old-fashioned dress on the side of the road.

Especially if that girl was watching me.

I made it home without incident and hurried into the house. I didn't allow myself to look around, focusing only on what was directly in front of me. Even the short trip from the car to the front door made my skin crawl, like someone was there, hiding in the trees, studying my every movement …

I was so frantic to get inside, I dropped my keys before I was finally able to unlock the front door. "Hey," I called as soon as I stepped through the threshold. "Anyone home?"

I shut the door behind me, locking it for good measure as I listened for a response. But there was none.

I looked around and saw Oscar sitting on the steps of the stairs, his green eyes blinking at me.

"Mia?" I walked into the kitchen, expecting to see her set up at the table, a cup of coffee at her elbow and headset on as she listened to music while she studied. But the kitchen was empty.

Was she upstairs in her room? She sometimes worked up there, especially if she was attending a virtual lecture or on a call with her classmates. That way, she could shut the door and not worry about disturbing anyone else or being disturbed. I went up the stairs and knocked on her door. "Mia?"

No answer.

I knocked again. Still no answer.

I stood by the door, chewing on my bottom lip. It was possible Mia was in her room, but she had her headset on and couldn't hear me. It was also possible she wasn't home after all. Now that I thought about it, her car was still in the same place as when I left that morning, which meant she had ridden her bike to work.

I contemplated checking the garage for her bike before opening her bedroom door to see if she was there.

Alternatively, I could march right back downstairs and head out to the garden, which was precisely where I had intended to spend the afternoon rather than stand there stewing about where Mia was. It wasn't like I was her mother. She was perfectly capable of taking care of herself and coming and going as she pleased. I had absolutely zero reason to open her bedroom door and check her room. There was no good reason to invade her privacy. None.

But I still couldn't bring myself to move away from her door.

I tried to tell myself that I just really wanted to talk to her, but I knew it wasn't the whole truth.

Deep down, I could acknowledge that at least part of why I was so frantic to find her was because I didn't want to be alone in the house.

There was a soft sound behind me, making me jump as I turned around. "Oh, Mia, you startled me ..." I started to say, but found myself talking to Oscar. He flicked his tail in response, and just like that, I realized how ridiculous I was being.

"I guess it's just you and me," I said to my cat.

Oscar flicked his tail again, his emerald-green eyes watching me unwaveringly.

"I bet you'd like to help me with the gardening, wouldn't you?"

Oscar immediately stood and padded down the steps. When he reached the bottom, he looked up at me as if to ask what was taking so long.

"Alright, I guess I have my answer," I said as I started down the stairs myself. "No killing songbirds, though." I shook my finger at him. "Got it?"

Oscar gave me a hurt look, as if he wouldn't dream of doing such a thing.

"Moles are a different story," I continued. "Feel free to kill as many of them as you want."

He blinked at me.

"We understand each other, then," I said as I headed toward the back door. "I'm holding you to it."

I let him out and went to fetch my gardening tools, which were in the back shed. At least, that's where I thought they were. I was sure I had left them there.

But when I looked, all I found were my gloves, a shovel, and a couple of different hand forks. My pruning shears, hand trowel, and hand cultivator were missing.

For a few moments, I just stood there, unable to believe what I was seeing. The shed was dimly lit, especially compared to the bright sun of the backyard, but even when I removed my sunglasses and gave me eyes a moment to adjust, I didn't see them.

Although the day was comfortable and warm, but not hot, I could feel the sweat starting to gather at the base of my neck under my hair. I was sure I left everything in the shed. So where were they?

I closed the doors and took a quick walk around the backyard in case I was remembering wrong and had left them out. But they were nowhere to be found.

The sweat was beginning to trickle down my neck, leaving a trail that was somehow both hot and cold at the same time. My skin prickled as I again sensed someone watching me, but no matter where I looked, there was nothing.

Had the tools been stolen? I supposed it was possible. I didn't keep the shed locked at night. But why those and not something else ... something of value?

Could Mia or Chrissy had used them and put them back somewhere else? But where would that be? The only place I could think of was the garage, so I headed to the front of the house to check it.

The garage was still more of a storage room than anything else. It was filled with boxes I hadn't quite figured out what to do with yet. Some contained remnants of my life in New York; some were Chrissy's; some were my ex's (I had thrown a lot of his belongings out, but not everything—he was still Chrissy's father, after all), and some were Charlie's that I wasn't sure if

I should keep or get rid of. There was even stuff of Mia's that hadn't fit into her bedroom.

After stepping around the maze of old belongings (and checking to see if Mia's bike was there, which it was not), I finally spotted my gardening tools hanging from one of the shelves.

I had no idea how they ended up there, but at least they hadn't been stolen. I collected them and headed back out to the garden to get to work.

Except I couldn't focus. My skin was still prickling with the now-familiar sense of being watched, and no amount of telling myself that there was no one there made any difference.

After what felt like an eternity but was probably only an hour or two, Mia finally came home. I heard the garage door open and nearly sagged into the dirt with relief.

Finally, I wasn't alone.

I quickly put my tools back in the shed, closed the door firmly, and went into the house. Oscar stayed where he was, watching me from where he lay in the sun, tail flicking lazily. I reminded him of his promise to leave the songbirds alone. He blinked his eyes at me and laid back down.

I got the feeling he was humoring me.

I found Mia in the kitchen, opening a bottle of wine. She wagged her eyebrows when she saw me. "It's 5:00 somewhere."

"I'll get the glasses," I said, moving to the cupboard. It was a little earlier than I would normally start, but quite honestly, after all that had happened to me that day, I felt it was justified. "Rough day?"

"You could say that," she said, working the cork free with a gentle pop. "I think Daphne is right. I need a break. Starting with this." She held up the wine bottle and tipped it toward me. "How about you?"

"Definitely a rough day." I paused as I watched her pour the wine into the glasses, her forehead wrinkled in concentration. "Did you happen to use my gardening tools?"

She glanced up, her expression surprised. "No. Why? Would there be a problem if I did?"

"No, no, of course not," I said hastily. "I don't care what you use, you know that. No, I was asking because they weren't where they're supposed to be."

"Where are they supposed to be?"

"In the back shed."

Mia finished pouring and straightened up, still holding the bottle with one hand. "The back shed? You mean there's stuff in there?"

"Yes, my gardening tools." I felt like I was repeating myself.

"Oh, I guess I didn't realize that. I thought you were keeping all that stuff in the garage. Everything else seems to be stored in there." She put down the bottle and picked up the wine.

"That's actually where I found them."

Mia gave me a curious look over her wine glass. "I thought you couldn't find them."

"No, I said …" I took a deep breath. Why was this so difficult? I felt like I was in a Laurel and Hardy sketch. "My tools weren't in the shed, which is where I always keep them. I found them in the garage."

Mia's eyebrows went up. "Oh, now I get it. Yes, you probably found them in the garage because I put them there."

Now it was my turn to stare at her in surprise. "You did? But I thought you just said …" I paused, taking another deep breath. I didn't want her to get the wrong idea and think I didn't want her using the tools when it was really just about putting them back in the correct place. "It's fine that you used them. I just thought you said you didn't."

"I did say that … because I *didn't* use them." She cocked her head, watching me over the rim of her wine glass. "I found them and put them away."

"You found them?" Now I was even more puzzled. "Where?"

"On the side of the house." She gestured to the area. "I was coming up the driveway and saw something laying in the grass. I went over to check it out and found your tools. There was that little shovel and rake and pruning shears, right?"

"Yes, my hand trowel and hand cultivator," I said, feeling more perplexed.

"Right. Those things. Anyway, I figured you got called away or something and weren't able to put them away, so I put them in the garage for you." She paused to take a sip. "I didn't know they belong in the shed."

"But I don't understand," I said. "How did they end up there? I didn't leave them there. I always put them away when I'm finished with them."

"Maybe you were doing something on the side of the house and got called away."

I shook my head. "No, I would remember that."

"Well, maybe Chrissy used them." Her lips curled up in a half-smile. "Not that Chrissy is much for gardening, but you never know with teenagers."

"I guess I'll ask her," I said, even though I couldn't fathom what Chrissy would possibly be doing with my gardening tools. She was most definitely an indoor type of girl. But Mia was right—when it came to teenagers, you never know.

"So, I'm guessing you spent your day gardening. Once you found your tools, that is," Mia said.

"Actually, I spent very little time gardening as a bunch of other stuff happened."

"Oh." Mia put her wine down and leaned against the counter. "I'm ready. Let's hear it."

"Well, to start, I went to see Wendy today."

A strange expression drifted over her face, but before I could identify it, it disappeared. "You did? Why waste your time?"

I stared at her. "Because I wanted to know why she lied. Don't you?"

She shrugged. "I figured it was because of her mental issues. That's pretty much what Daniel said."

"Yes, but don't you think there's something more going on? Remember, I saw someone in the woods."

"That could have been anyone," Mia said, waving her hand. "The two incidents probably have nothing to do with each other."

"How can you say that? How many girls play in the woods behind Penny's house? She's kind of out in the middle of nowhere without a lot of close neighbors."

Mia picked up her wine. "Maybe she was the daughter of one of the other guests."

"I can't see any of the other guests bringing their daughter dressed in some hundred-year-old dress."

Mia gave me a funny look. "What do you mean, hundred-year-old dress?"

It was on the tip of my tongue to tell her about the cult members and how similar the dresses were, but at the last moment, I decided to keep it to myself. I had a feeling Mia would dismiss what I saw even more if I told her and likely be even less inclined to want to help Wendy. And regardless of how Mia felt about Wendy's situation, I knew she needed help.

Unfortunately, though, since I had brought up the style of dress, I had to describe it and hope Mia didn't make the connection to the cult members, if she had seen them. "The dress the girl was wearing was very old-fashioned. It was also dirty and not in the best shape. I was thinking maybe it was something of Penny's ... maybe something that had been in her family for years ... and Wendy or Jill found it in the house, and Jill decided to wear it. I can't see someone allowing their daughter out of their home wearing it."

"Kids get all sorts of funny ideas in their head," Mia said, but that strange expression was back. She lowered her eyes to stare into her wine glass. I braced myself for mention of the cult members. "And maybe the parents were just exhausted fighting with her and decided to let her wear what she wanted. Sometimes, you have to choose your battles."

I reached for my wine glass and took a sip, deliberately buying myself some time before I answered. This conversation was nothing like what I'd expected. I had assumed it would have been more like the ones we used to have, where we would be more supportive of each other's ideas, even if they were a little out there. Where did that Mia go? Was it as simple as grief, exhaustion, and overwhelm? Or was something deeper going on? "I don't understand why you don't think something strange is going on."

Mia's eyes flickered up. "What are you talking about? Of course I think something strange is going on. I just found out that Penny's daughter has serious mental issues, which is likely why the two were estranged. And I'm also wondering why no one got Wendy the help she so desperately needs. What is wrong with us, as a society, that we allow people to fall through the cracks the way they do?"

"That is a problem, I agree," I said. "But what if Wendy doesn't have mental issues?"

"You think she was purposefully lying about having a daughter?"

"No, I'm saying what if she DOES have a daughter, and her daughter was kidnapped, but now she's being pressured to lie and say she has no daughter?"

Mia rolled her eyes as she drank her wine. "Oh, for heaven's sake. You've been watching too many *Lifetime* movies. Who would pressure her? And why?"

"I have no idea, which is why someone needs to be looking into it."

Mia waved her free hand. "This is all absurd. Wendy admits she made the whole thing up, but you're going to try and prove she is lying *now* and not before? How would you even do that?"

"We could track down Wendy's address and see if anyone has seen her daughter," I said.

"How? Did she mention where she's from?"

"Well, no," I admitted. "But Daniel probably knows."

Mia gave me a look. "Assuming Daniel tells you. But, okay, let's say he does, and we track her down. Then what? How are we going to ask people if they saw Jill when we have no idea what she looks like? We don't have a picture or even a description."

"We could ask her neighbors if they've ever seen Wendy with a little girl," I said. "I don't think it would be that hard. We could even call the local schools and see if there was a Jill Schroeder registered."

"And how do we even explain why we're asking? Don't you think the neighbors would be just a little suspicious?"

I hadn't considered that. "Well, maybe we work it into a bigger conversation about being worried about Wendy now that her mother is gone."

Mia didn't look convinced. "This sounds like a wild goose chase. But putting that aside, what about Penny?"

"What about her?"

"How do you explain Penny telling people that Wendy made up having a daughter?"

"We don't actually know if Penny said that or not," I said. "We only have that one guy's word, who no one trusts. I can't remember his name ... Zed, or whatever." I shivered despite myself. I could still feel his dark, intense eyes raking over my skin.

Mia reached over to grab the bottle to refill her glass. "You mean Zane?"

"Yeah, him." I watched her pour the wine, her eyes carefully fixed on her glass. "It doesn't sound like he's credible, so why should we believe him now?"

"Well, again, Wendy confirmed his story."

I leaned forward. "Are we so sure Zane isn't the one behind all of this?"

Mia jerked her head up to look at me. "What are you talking about? You think Zane kidnapped Wendy's daughter?"

"Maybe."

Mia set the bottle down with a thud. "But then why would Wendy say he was right? Why wouldn't she tell Daniel the truth?"

"Probably because Zane is threatening her in some way," I said. "Maybe he told her if she didn't recant the kidnapping claim, she'd never see her daughter again."

"But that's crazy," Mia said. "Why would Zane kidnap Wendy's daughter to begin with?"

"I have no idea. We'd probably have to ask him."

Mia sat back in her chair and took a long drink of wine, her face screwed up as she thought about it. "No, I don't buy it," she said.

"Why not? You were the one who said you didn't trust him."

"And I don't. But this is a whole other level of corruption you're talking about. Kidnapping and blackmail and who knows what else. I don't like the guy, but I don't think he's that evil."

"Well, from my standpoint, it seems far more plausible that someone is blackmailing Wendy to keep her quiet than her making up a daughter for ten years," I said.

"Why?" Mia asked.

I blinked. "Why?"

"Yeah, why is that?"

"Because …" I raised my hand in the air, making a gesture like it was obvious. "Humans have been kidnapping and blackmailing each other for hundreds, thousands, of years. I've never heard of anyone who pretended to have a daughter for a decade."

"People lie all the time," Mia said. "In fact, I would say lying is more common than either blackmail or kidnapping. Sure, maybe that specific story isn't that common, but almost everyone lies, and some people have constructed their entire lives around a lie."

I shook my head. "I don't buy it."

"Again, I ask why?" Mia leaned forward slightly. "Why are you so sure Wendy is the victim and Zane is the perpetrator?"

I shot her a hard look. "Why are YOU so sure Wendy is the perpetrator and not Zane?"

"Because I don't know Wendy. At all. But I do know Zane." She returned the hard look. "You don't know either of them."

"But …"

Mia held up a hand. "This isn't to defend Zane. He is a crazy conspiracy theorist. BUT, and this is important, what he's fixated on is how the 1888ers are being attacked. There is no way he would hurt a fellow 1888er, and Wendy, as Penny's daughter, along with Wendy's daughter, is part of the 1888er club. He would never kidnap or blackmail one of his own. Someone else, like you or me, maybe. I wouldn't put it past him. But not a fellow 1888er. And especially not someone related to Penny. Now, let's talk about Wendy."

Mia paused and gave me the side-eye. "Neither of us knows anything about her. We have no idea what she's capable of. I'm giving her the benefit of the doubt that she has some psychological issues that led to her making up a daughter and a kidnapping, but it's just as possible that she's a serial liar who just happened to go too far. And this time, she got caught."

"Why would anyone lie about something like that?" I asked.

Mia shrugged. "Why does anyone do anything? I don't know. Maybe she likes manipulating people. Maybe she's a sociopath. Maybe it's all one big joke to her. Or maybe …" Mia paused and shot me another hard look as I opened my mouth to defend Wendy. "Maybe she's a sad and lonely person who made up this story because it made her feel less sad and lonely and, since she wasn't hurting anyone, thought it didn't matter."

I closed my mouth with a click. I felt deflated, like all the air had left my body, and I sagged against the counter. In my mind's eye, all I could see was Wendy hiding in a corner at her mother's funeral, wearing that ill-fitting black dress and looking awkward and uncomfortable. The way her face lit up when I started talking to her, like she hadn't expected anyone to be nice to her, was painful to see.

Was it possible for someone to be so sad and lonely, they would make up such a story?

I wanted the answer to be no, but every time I pictured Wendy, I felt more and more depressed.

I could tell by Mia's expression that she knew she had hit the mark. "Becca, it's not your fault. You want to believe the best about everyone. That's always been the case, and it's not a bad thing. The world is a better place with people like you in it. But …" her mouth worked, but no words came out, as if she was trying to decide what to say next. "It can also get you in trouble," she said at last.

She didn't have to say more. I knew exactly what she was referring to.

I had been taken advantage of in the past. By multiple people.

I thought I had put all of it behind me. I was sure I was a better judge of character now.

But maybe I wasn't. Maybe I did misjudge Wendy.

"Hey," Mia said, moving closer to put a hand on my arm. "Don't beat yourself up. You're a good person. I know your heart is in the right place. You're trying to help Wendy. But some people can't be helped."

I gave Mia a slanted smile. "Maybe you're right. Maybe I am a little too naïve."

"Not naïve," Mia corrected. "I would say optimistic."

I thought that was a little too generous, but I didn't want to argue or make her feel like she needed to keep trying to make me feel better. Instead, I drained my wine and picked up the bottle.

As I did, I glanced through the window and caught sight of the woods. There was a flash of movement, and for a moment, I was sure there was a figure standing there, wearing an old-fashioned white dress, watching me.

Find me.

My throat seemed to close up, and I was having trouble swallowing. I blinked, and just like that, there was nothing there. Nothing but the trees gently swaying in the wind.

"Becca? You okay?"

I picked up the bottle and turned around to face a concerned-looking Mia. "Yeah. I'm fine. I'm just ... still trying to get my head around things, I guess. But I'm fine."

"Okay, if you're sure," Mia said, but she didn't sound—or look—convinced. Her eyes narrowed, as if she were trying to read my mind.

"Absolutely." I plastered a fake smile on my face as I topped off my glass. I had no idea what was going on, but there was one thing I *was* sure of ...

I wasn't done with either Wendy or the girl in the woods.

Chapter 14

"Thanks for meeting me here," Daniel said as he slid into the booth across from me in The Tipsy Cow. "I know I still owe you that nice, romantic dinner, but I'd rather do it on an evening when I'm not trying to squeeze it in-between work. Maybe this weekend?"

"Of course," I said, playing with the glass of red wine in front of me. I was pacing myself, as I had already split the bottle with Mia earlier. She had opened a second, but knowing I was meeting Daniel, I declined. "I'd rather have you relaxed and able to enjoy your evening, as well."

Daniel grimaced as he reached for the menu. "I'm not sure that will happen until I've gotten to the bottom of this gang activity, but at least I'm off this weekend, so that should help."

I watched him read the menu, drinking him in. He was so solid, so safe. I could still feel the prickles of unknown eyes as they crawled all over me in my backyard, no matter how many times I told myself it was only in my head. And I still couldn't figure out how my garden tools ended up where Mia found them. I kept telling myself to stop thinking about it—that there was a perfectly reasonable explanation for it—but the whole experience still left me feeling deeply uneasy.

The waitress came by. She looked like she was visiting from college, with her light-pink hair and gold nose ring. Daniel ordered a beer and wings as an appetizer. "I missed lunch today, and I'm starving," he said as he perused the menu. I already knew what I wanted, so I stuck to playing with my wine glass. Across from us, another couple sat at a table. The woman had a stormy expression on her face, while the man looked like he would rather be anywhere but there. At another table, four women surrounded by colorful gift bags toasted one another.

By the time the waitress returned with his beer, Daniel had decided on the bacon cheeseburger. I ordered a grilled chicken sandwich, despite feeling like I should be ordering the Cobb salad after my blueberry waffle breakfast. But I wanted something more substantial to soak up the wine I'd already had.

"No leads yet on the gang activity?" I asked.

He shook his head as he took a long drink of his beer. "Not really, although it's seeming more and more likely that it's tied to The Jack Saloon."

"That's not surprising." The Jack Saloon was a dive bar located near the edge of town. A lot of colorful and rough-looking characters frequented it.

"Especially since it's the bar that replaced the Lone Man Standing."

There was something distinctly familiar, and unpleasant, about that name, but for the life of me, I couldn't place it. "What's the Lone Man Standing again?"

"Oh, sorry." He smiled self-consciously at me. "I keep forgetting you aren't as steeped in Redemption lore as the rest of us. The Lone Man Standing was the bar that burned down in 1987, a few months after your Aunt Charlie moved to town. It happened the same summer as a lot of other terrible things— Louise's brother Jesse disappeared, along with Jonathan Decker. Of course, we know what happened to them now."

"Yeah," I said, thinking about my basement and what we'd found there.

"It wasn't just them. One of the waitresses at the Lone Man Standing disappeared, as well. We still don't know what happened to her. And Red, the owner, is also missing, although the general consensus is that he was killed in the fire."

Daniel paused as the waitress arrived with our wings. She deposited them, took Daniel's order for another beer, and left.

"You don't sound convinced that Red died in the fire," I said as Daniel helped himself to a couple of wings and sauce.

Daniel frowned. "It makes sense that he did. He disappeared the night it burned, and no one ever saw him again."

"Makes sense to me," I said, choosing a wing. "So why don't you sound convinced?"

"Because of Charlie."

"Charlie? My aunt?"

He nodded, a small smile playing on his lips. "She was sure Red survived that night. It didn't matter what anyone said to her. She was adamant that he was still alive and well and would one day return to Redemption, if he wasn't already here."

I shifted uneasily in my seat just as a shadow seemed to cross over Daniel's face. Did he feel it, too? Almost like the energy had morphed around us, turning the bar into something dark and heavy. Even the four women celebrating a birthday seemed to pause their celebration, and the angry couple looked even more upset. The woman, especially. Her expression had turned practically murderous. I was starting to feel a little concerned for her partner.

After a moment, Daniel picked up a napkin to wipe his mouth, and the spell seemed to break.

"Charlie was always pretty persuasive," I said.

"She was," Daniel agreed. "But I still wasn't convinced. Not until this past year, when I saw what was in your basement." He shot me a meaningful look. "Now ... I'm not so sure."

There it was again, that energy shift. I dropped my wing and wiped my fingers on a napkin, no longer hungry. "You think Red might be alive?"

Daniel shrugged. "If you're asking if I have proof, I don't. No one does. Despite Charlie's insistence over the years, there was never any evidence that Red survived or was hanging around. His bank accounts were never touched, nor his car or any of his personal belongings. I suppose it's possible he used the fire to just walk away from his old life, but then why would he come back?"

"Maybe Redemption didn't want to let him go."

Daniel half-smiled. "Well, that's true. Redemption can be pretty stubborn about getting her way. But there was also never any evidence he was here, either. Now, though, with all this gang activity going on, and especially since it's starting to seem like The Jack Saloon is at the center of it all, it's making me wonder."

I stared at him. "You think Red is the one heading up the gang activity?"

"It makes a strange amount of sense. If you removed the whole likely-died-in-a-fire-30-some-years-ago detail out of the equation, that is. Back then, the Lone Man Standing was the hub of much of Redemption's criminal activity. All sorts of shady deals were happening there—drugs, prostitution, maybe worse. No one could prove anything, though. There was also some talk about Red having bribed a couple of police officers to make sure no one *could* prove anything. After the bar burned down, all that criminal activity basically vanished, too, which made it seem more likely it was tied to the bar. Of course, it's possible that it was all a coincidence."

"But it sounds like you think that since the gang activity is back, Red may be back, as well?"

Daniel started to answer, but the waitress appeared with our food and his second beer. He thanked her with a smile, and she simpered in return. I kept myself from rolling my eyes. Daniel wasn't above using his rugged good looks and charm to get what he wanted, whether that was a confession from a suspect or better service at a bar.

"Well, when you say it like that, it sounds ridiculous," Daniel said, picking up a French fry. "It's not like Red is the only criminal around. But something about this just doesn't feel right. I don't know how to explain it, because I can't put my finger on it."

"I get it. There are a lot of things going on right now that don't seem right."

Daniel's gaze sharpened. "What did you do?"

I widened my eyes, trying to make myself look as innocent as possible. I didn't think I was that obvious. "What do you mean?"

His mouth flattened. "You know exactly what I mean. So spill it. Did you go see Wendy or something?"

Man, he really knew me. Maybe better than I knew myself. "I just don't think it's as simple as her making up a daughter and a kidnapping."

"As Freud famously said, 'Sometimes a cigar is just a cigar.' Not only do we have a witness, but Wendy herself admitted to making it up. What more is there to say?"

"Something doesn't feel right," I said. "I think it's worth looking into more."

Daniel stared at me. "Becca, haven't you been listening to me? I have my hands full with this gang activity on top of everything else that happens in Redemption, not to mention this new cult that's popped up out of nowhere. And you want me to put all of that aside and look into this nothing burger?"

"If she's being forced to lie about her daughter being kidnapped, it's not a nothing burger," I said.

"We have no evidence that she's lying."

"Not yet," I said. "But if we ask her neighbors and maybe call around to local schools to see if a student by her daughter's name was enrolled …"

"Becca, are you listening to yourself? You want me to stop working on very real cases to pursue this fool's errand? Do you have any idea what my captain would say?"

"It doesn't have to be you," I said. "I could do it. I just need her address."

Daniel's eyes went wide. "You want me to give you Wendy's address?"

"Well, it doesn't have to be that obvious," I said. "Maybe you can just bring her file home and leave it on the kitchen table while you take a shower or something."

Daniel looked up at the ceiling. "Ah, yes. That would definitely work. 'Oh, no sir. I didn't give my girlfriend Wendy's address. I just left the file on the kitchen table, and she looked without my permission. Oh, why did I bring Wendy's file home in the first place? I was just catching up on a little paperwork, that's all.'"

"I don't think it's that big of a deal," I said. "How would anyone find out?"

"Well, Wendy filing a complaint that you're harassing her would give it away," Daniel said.

"I wouldn't tell anyone I got it from you," I said.

"You're missing the point," Daniel said. "This is just not a good idea."

"Why?"

"Because at best, it's a waste of time. At worst, Wendy could slap a harassment suit on you."

"She wouldn't do that," I said, even though I didn't know any such thing. "Especially if I'm right."

Daniel snorted. "You have no idea what Wendy would or wouldn't do."

Drat. I couldn't slip anything by Daniel.

But he wasn't done yet. "Especially if you're right."

"What do you mean? If I'm right, and she really does have a child who was kidnapped, I would think she would be happy if I pursued it."

"Becca, if she did lie about not having a daughter, you haven't a clue as to why," Daniel said in exasperation. "What if she's being blackmailed and believes you put her daughter in danger by uncovering the truth? Do you think she'd be pleased about that?"

I sunk down in my seat. I hadn't considered that angle. "Oh. I see what you mean."

"And that's just one scenario. You have no idea what you're getting yourself into. It's better if you just let it go."

I pictured Wendy all alone in Penny's house, no friends or neighbors stopping by to check on her. "I hear what you're saying, but I feel like someone needs to be on her side regardless of what's true. If she is lying about having a daughter, especially if it's due to some untreated mental issue, she needs help. And if she DOES have a daughter, then she's probably in a different sort of trouble. Either way, she needs someone in her corner, and it doesn't seem like anyone is volunteering."

Daniel studied me, his expression softening. "I know you want to help. You have a good heart. But Becca, you're not responsible for helping everyone. Especially someone you just met and barely know."

"I get that, but it still feels like someone needs to step up."

"Possibly." Daniel's eyes narrowed. "But is she asking for help?"

I looked down into my wine, the image of Wendy slamming the door in my face still fresh. "Not particularly."

Daniel sighed. "I know it's difficult to accept, but I think you have your answer."

Daniel had a point. Wendy sure didn't seem to want any help or support, regardless of what the truth really was.

The only problem was, I didn't know if I could let it go.

Chapter 15

I yawned as I poured myself a second cup of coffee. I was off to a late start and feeling a little grumpy. I hadn't slept well. Between all the events of the past few days and feeling more than a little discouraged that neither Mia nor Daniel was taking me seriously, it was hard to get my mind to stop spinning around enough to fall asleep.

The evening before, I mentally debated whether or not to tell Daniel about meeting Eleanor and her involvement in the cult. Part of me didn't want to, as I was sure once he knew that the girl in the woods looked like a cult member, he would insist I drop all things Wendy. Obviously, he'd contend, I hadn't seen Wendy's daughter after all, therefore, there was no reason to believe Wendy ever had a child.

I also wasn't sure how he would react if he knew Eleanor wanted to buy tea from me. I had a feeling he wouldn't like it and would probably tell me not to have anything to do with her. And while I didn't have any intention of having her as a long-term client, that didn't mean I wouldn't feel the need to follow up with her at some point in the future.

I didn't think lying to him was a hot idea either, so keeping that little tidbit of information to myself felt like the best course of action, at least for the time being.

Still, another part of me insisted I tell Daniel. What if the little girl in the woods was in trouble, and telling Daniel about the cult connection could save her? Could I live with myself if I blew it by keeping quiet?

Of course, there was still a slight chance that Jill existed. And if she did, disclosing all of this to Daniel might complicate getting her help. But again, I was now seriously doubting her existence. Unlike the girl in the woods.

Find me.

Despite my reluctance, I realized I had no choice. After he had gotten the bill from The Tipsy Cow, I decided it was time.

"I saw the cult members this morning," I said.

Daniel's eyebrows went up. "Really? Where?"

"At Aunt May's. I went there for a late breakfast," I explained as I absentmindedly pushed a piece of chicken that had fallen out of my sandwich around on my plate. "I see what you meant about instantly knowing who they are."

Daniel's lips quirked up in a smile. "Yeah, they certainly do stand out."

"They do." I drained the rest of my glass of wine. "Do you know if there are children living there?"

Daniel frowned. "Children? I'm not sure. Why?"

"Because that girl in the woods I saw at Penny's house was dressed the same way."

Daniel put down the bill, his eyes narrowing. "That girl you saw looked like she was from the cult?"

I nodded. "She was a lot dirtier than they were, and her hair was loose, but yeah, she looked like one of the cult members."

Daniel sat very still. "Do you think she's a runaway?"

I held up my hands, palms up. "I have no idea."

"What did she say to you?"

"Nothing."

Daniel frowned. "Nothing?"

"Yeah, nothing. Not a word. I was talking to her and asking her questions, but she didn't respond."

"Hmmm." Daniel dug into his pocket for his wallet. "Maybe I'll stop by there tomorrow … ask if they've had any recent runaways."

I shot him a skeptical look. "You think they'd tell you the truth?"

"What else do you want me to do?"

I huffed out a frustrated sigh. What I wanted him to do was search the premises, and if he found any children, remove them, so they could be questioned by a professional in a neutral location. But even as I thought it, I knew it wasn't possible. At least not at this point.

"They haven't broken any laws," Daniel said as if reading my mind. "And even if the girl you saw did live there and run away, in and of itself, it isn't a crime."

"But what if she's being abused, and that's why she ran away?"

Daniel leaned forward slightly. "Becca, if we find out that a girl ran away from the Church of the Forgotten, we will investigate. But the truth is, and you know it as well as I do, that kids run away from home for all sorts of reason. It doesn't mean they're being abused."

"I know that, but this is a cult we're talking about."

"We need to look into it, yes. But again, not all cults are abusive. They certainly seem to be weird, but that isn't against the law … nor is it even particularly harmful."

I sat back feeling defeated, but unsure as to why. Daniel said he would stop by and talk to the cult members. Isn't that what I wanted?

He eyed me as he selected a credit card. "So, does this also mean you're coming to terms with the fact that Wendy doesn't have a daughter?"

I gritted my teeth, resisting the urge to reach across the table and smack him. This was precisely what I was afraid of. "The two have nothing to do with each other," I said. "It's entirely possible that there is both a kidnapping and a runaway situation happening at the same time."

Daniel moved the bill and his card to the edge of the table so the waitress could see it. "If you say so." A small smile played on his lips.

Argh. I was so tired of not being taken seriously. I covered the remains of my chicken sandwich with a napkin, refusing to look at him.

At least he didn't start lecturing me again to drop it. But the annoyance lingered. I knew I needed to shift my mindset. Daniel was going to check out the cult, and that was a positive step forward.

So, what I really needed to do was quit obsessing over it. I sipped my coffee and took a deep breath, trying to relax in the peacefulness. Neither Mia nor Chrissy were home, and Oscar was busy making himself comfortable on his favorite chair. Maybe I'd make myself a nice breakfast and then do a little gardening to make up for my lack of focus the day before. Then, I could spend the afternoon working on the tea business, which I had been sorely neglecting. It definitely needed a little love, as well.

The landline rang, and I felt a little twist in my stomach as I went to answer it. I hoped it wasn't an unhappy customer. I really needed to get myself caught up. It wasn't until I had picked up the receiver that I realized it might also be Eleanor. Ugh. I was going to have to make a rule to not answer the phone until I had at least two cups of coffee.

"Can I speak to Becca Kingsley?" The voice was unfamiliar. Maybe it was a customer after all. I automatically reached for the pen and pad of paper I always kept next to the phone.

"Speaking."

"Oh, wonderful! This is Sharon from the Redemption Historical Society."

It took a minute to place her, but finally, the gears clicked into place. The fact that I was still waking up didn't help matters. "Oh, yes. How are you?" I pushed the notebook away and swallowed a sigh. It was way too early, and I hadn't had the amount of caffeine required to tell her I wasn't interested in my house being added to the historical society, whatever that meant. Especially if it meant there was some sort of donation involved for the "honor."

"I'm doing fabulous! And you?"

I winced slightly. I also wasn't ready to deal with that level of perkiness. "I'm good."

"That's great to hear. I was wondering if we could set up a time to meet, so I could tell you a little bit more about the historical society? I'm happy to come to you."

"Uh, well …" I hemmed and hawed, trying to figure out a polite way of saying "never."

"What about tomorrow afternoon? Any time after 1:00?"

"Uh, tomorrow isn't good …"

"That's no problem. How about Thursday? I'm open most of the day. Or we can schedule something for next week, if that would be better."

"You know, this isn't a great time for me. I was just heading out the door. Could we do this later?"

"Of course! When should I call you back?"

I closed my eyes. I should have known it wouldn't be easy. "Maybe this afternoon?"

"Perfect! I'll talk to you then."

"Great. Looking forward to it." I replaced the phone onto the receiver, thinking it might be a good idea to just let all my calls go to voicemail, at least for the short-term. Between Eleanor and Sharon, it felt too risky to answer it.

I picked up my coffee, and my phone buzzed. It was a text from Daphne.

Hey! Did you still want to chat? I'm free for lunch.

I would love to, I texted back, already feeling my mood lighten. Maybe Daphne would be more supportive than Mia and Daniel.

She certainly couldn't be any less.

***

Daphne had suggested Aunt May's, but I was uncomfortable with the idea of Mia seeing us together. Not that it should matter. I wouldn't be telling Daphne anything I either hadn't already shared with Mia or was planning to tell her, but it still made me feel uneasy. Would Mia be upset if she knew I was confiding in Daphne? Would she continually stop by to reiterate how naïve I was being about Wendy?

Instead, I proposed The Tipsy Cow, even though I had just been there the night before for dinner. I promised myself to order the Cobb salad this time around.

I was the first to arrive at the bar. I chose a booth in the back, as far away from the other diners as I could manage. I knew I was being a bit silly—no one was going to overhear us anyway, considering how loud the bar was. Still, I felt better being a little isolated.

A waitress came to ask if I'd like a drink while I was waiting. Thankfully, she was an older woman, instead of the young, perky one who waited on Daniel and me. I really wanted a glass of wine, but I decided to be "good" and ordered iced tea instead. The last thing I needed was to start a day-drinking habit.

Daphne came in a few minutes later, and I waved at her. Her face lit up, transforming it completely, and she wove her way through the crowded tables to reach me.

"It's been ages since I've been here for lunch," she said as she slid into the seat across from me. Her red hair was pulled back in a messy ponytail, and she was wearing a gray shirt that didn't do her pale skin and freckles any favors.

"I was craving a Cobb salad," I said, deciding I didn't need to share how I was having my second meal there in less than 24 hours.

"They do have a good one," Daphne mused as she perused the menu. The waitress appeared after a moment, and we both ordered one.

"So, what's up?" Daphne asked after getting her iced tea.

I moved my straw around, making circles in the liquid. "Actually, a lot has been going on."

Daphne raised an eyebrow as she reached across the table for a couple of blue artificial sweetener packets. "Do tell."

"Well, first off, did you hear about the kidnapping?"

Daphne stilled. "What kidnapping?"

"Wendy's daughter was kidnapped. Of course, as it turns out, she may not even have a daughter after all."

Daphne stared at me, her eyes wide. "Wait. What?"

"You haven't heard any of this?"

She shook her head. "I've been knee-deep in a project from hell, working 60-hour weeks the last few. Even prying myself away for the memorial service was something of a miracle. But as of last night, the worst is behind me, so I thought I'd take a little time off and join you for lunch. So, fill me in."

I launched into the Wendy saga, including her cryptic message about whoever I saw in the woods not being her daughter.

Despite attempting to be as succinct as possible, it still seemed to take a long time to fill her in. I didn't finish until after we had gotten our food and iced tea refilled, and the waitress had departed again.

"So, Wendy seriously said she doesn't have a daughter?" Daphne asked when I finally took a breath.

"According to Daniel, yes."

She sat back in the booth, a stunned expression on her face. "That's incredible."

"I know. And no one seems to be considering the possibility that Wendy might be in a lot of trouble."

Daphne cocked her head. "What do you mean?"

"If you had a daughter who actually had been kidnapped, the only reason you'd lie about it would be if something really bad was going on."

Daphne scrunched her face like she was trying to process what I was saying. "Okay, so let me get this straight. Wendy has been telling people for the last ten years she has a daughter when she really doesn't, and after her mother's funeral, she changed the story that her make-believe daughter was kidnapped. She has now admitted to making the whole thing up, but you think she's lying, and she really does have a daughter who has, in all actuality, been kidnapped."

"Yes. Exactly."

Daphne's expression was unreadable. "Why do you think Wendy is pretending she doesn't have a daughter if she really does?"

I felt a little pain in my chest. Not Daphne, too. How could everyone not see what was happening? "Because it's the only thing that makes sense. I can't believe Wendy spent the last ten years lying about being a mother. Why would anyone do something like that, barring having some real mental issues? Wendy doesn't strike me as having any. To me, it seems far more likely she's lying now."

"But if she actually had a daughter who was kidnapped, why would she lie about her not being kidnapped?"

"Probably because she's being threatened or blackmailed."

Daphne scooped up a tomato. "Hmm. If that's the case, then it makes more sense, and yeah, I can see where you're coming from."

Finally! Someone believed me! I wanted to jump out of my seat and kiss Daphne, but I restrained myself.

"So, if that is what's going on," Daphne continued, still in the same thoughtful tone, like she was puzzling out the pieces, "I'm not sure what the next step would be to help her find her daughter. The cops are no longer involved. And when you tried to talk to her, she slammed the door in your face."

"I know. I'm thinking I might have to earn her trust."

"How are you going to do that?"

"By investigating on my own. If I uncover something, I can bring it to her, and it might be enough to get her to open up to me."

Daphne's expression was skeptical. "How are you going to do *that?*"

I toyed with a piece of lettuce. "Well, I guess I was sort of thinking I would start by proving she has a daughter in the first place. Because if I can prove that Jill actually exists, I can bring that back to Daniel and get the police involved again."

"Let's assume you're right. You don't think that could turn into a bigger headache for Wendy? She would then have to explain to Daniel why she lied about not having a daughter."

I held my hands up. "What else can I do? I have no idea where to start looking for a kidnapped child, especially without Wendy's help. But if I can convince Daniel that there really is a missing ten-year-old, he'll utilize the resources available to him to look for her."

Daphne mulled that over. "Okay, that makes sense. So, how are you going to prove Wendy has a daughter?"

"I thought I'd start with Wendy's neighbors. Ask them if they ever saw Wendy with a little girl. Maybe stop by the local schools and see if her daughter was enrolled."

Daphne nodded. "That could work. Do know where Wendy lives?"

I sighed. "That part, I'd have to figure out. Daniel already told me, in no uncertain terms, mind you, that he isn't going to help."

Daphne half-smiled. "Can you blame him? It's his job on the line. So, what are you going to do instead?"

"Internet searches, I suppose. Although I'm guessing Wendy isn't one for social media, so I probably won't find any accounts. I might have to pay to get her personal records."

"If you do that, you might as well see if her daughter has a record, as well," Daphne said. "Might be easier than asking her neighbors or calling the local schools. They likely have some sort of policy around not sharing information with random people asking about students."

"That's true," I said. It would be easier to just try and locate the records online. That would at least give me something to bring to Daniel to get the process started.

Daphne eyed me as she forked up another bite of salad. "That's not your only problem, you know."

I let out a laugh. "When did I say I only had one problem? I feel like there are dozens to sort through. Which one are you referring to?"

She smiled sympathetically. "Well, I was thinking about Wendy not wanting any help."

"Now you sound like Daniel," I grumbled, focusing on my plate.

"Well, he has a point," Daphne said gently. "It's difficult to help someone who doesn't want to be helped. But even more than that, if she's being blackmailed, is she going to want you nosing around? You might make things worse for her."

"That's exactly what Daniel said. He thinks it could be dangerous."

"Have you considered he might be right?"

"Maybe," I said, stabbing harder at my food. "But I also feel like I have to do *something*. Let's say there really is a Jill, and she really has been kidnapped. If I don't do anything and something terrible happens to her, I don't think I could live with myself."

"I get it," Daphne said. "That would be really difficult. But again, you don't know what's going on. Wendy could very well be doing something right now to get her daughter back. But even if she's not, it's like we said … she doesn't seem to want any help."

"That's true, but she also might not be thinking straight," I said. "She might need someone to step in and help her make better decisions. I guess …" I paused and looked up to meet Daphne's eyes. "I guess I feel like I need to at least try. If it turns out I'm wrong or making things worse, I'll back off. But I have to at least do something. Does that make sense?"

Daphne gazed back at me. "Yeah, it does. I would probably feel the same way if I were the one who had talked to Wendy at the service." She took a bite of salad and chewed it, her movements methodical. "Although the whole thing seems a little … strange, when you think about it."

I gave her a look. "Well, yeah. Everything about this seems strange."

She shook her head. "That's not what I mean. It just seems like there would be far easier ways to blackmail someone than to kidnap her child."

"According to Wendy, she doesn't do anything other than work and raise her daughter. If that's true, there really wouldn't be anything they could use to blackmail her."

"I suppose that's true," Daphne agreed. "But doesn't that make you wonder why she would be targeted in the first place? What would she have that a blackmailer would want so badly, they would kidnap her daughter? The whole thing seems extreme. There are so many moving parts that could go wrong, and I mean really horribly wrong. You'd have to be desperate to think this is the answer. What could Wendy possibly possess that would justify the risk?"

I opened my mouth and closed it. Daphne had a good point that I hadn't even considered. What was it about Wendy that would set a kidnapping in motion? On the surface, she seemed just about the least likely candidate to get dragged into something like that. So, what else could it be?

"Maybe it's connected to the curse. You know, since she's an 1888er."

I was joking, so I wasn't prepared for Daphne's reaction. She put her fork down and stared at me. "You're right. That's probably exactly what it is. In which case, Penny sending her away didn't save her after all. Poor Wendy."

Chapter 16

I blinked at her. "Are you serious?"

"Of course I'm serious," Daphne said. "You don't mess with curses. Especially in this town."

I wasn't sure how to respond. While I did agree that staying away from curses was, in general, good advice, it seemed a stretch to think that a curse was behind Jill's kidnaping.

On the other hand, this was Redemption. Strange things happening constituted a normal day.

Daphne must have seen something in my face, because she pushed her salad plate a little away from her and folded her arms on the edge of the table. "Has anyone told you about the 1888ers?"

"Just what you initially explained … that they're descendants from the children who were left behind in 1888 after the adults disappeared."

"So, nothing else?"

"Not really. Other than some of its members, like Zane, seem to have a screw loose."

Daphne looked amused. "I agree about Zane being a bit of a crazy conspiracy theorist, but quite honestly, I think all the members have a screw or two loose. At least the ones who are left."

There was something about the way she said it that made me put my own fork down, my appetite suddenly vanishing just as the adults had back in 1888. "That sounds ominous."

"Hence why you shouldn't mess around with curses." Daphne paused to take a sip of her iced tea, which I suspected was more about gathering her thoughts than satisfying her thirst. "Maybe I better start from the beginning. As you know, no one knows why the adults disappeared in 1888, but there is an awful lot of speculation. Some people think it's similar to what happened in Roanoke, or to the lost city of Atlantis. And while it's true there are some similarities, there are also some significant differences ... namely, that the children didn't disappear, too. That's the part that never made much sense.

"Because of that, a lot of the theories center around the adults and what they must have done or didn't do to have been targeted. As you can imagine, these theories are all over the place, ranging from digging up a Native American burial site to engaging in some sort of occult practices or black magic to stealing treasure from pirates or bank robbers ..."

I held up a hand. "Wait. Did you say 'stealing treasure from *pirates*'? Where would these pirates have come from? Wisconsin is nowhere near an ocean."

"You forget about the Great Lakes."

I stared at her. "The Great Lakes? There were pirates sailing around the Great Lakes?"

"Absolutely."

"Pirates. On a lake," I repeated, unable to believe what I was hearing.

Daphne cocked her head. "They're called 'great' for a reason. Have you seen how big they are?"

"I'm aware of their size. I guess I didn't realize they were *that* big, though." I made a mental note to plan a trip to Lake Michigan in the near future. "Okay, so the Great Lakes had pirates, and somehow, their treasure ended up in Redemption and caused the adults to disappear. Do I have this right?"

Daphne shook her head. "Is it really so hard to believe? Especially with some of the other theories out there?"

"Well, kind of," I said. "Even if you take out the logistics of transporting the treasure from the Great Lakes to here, then what? The pirates come to Redemption to kill all the adults and leave the children? And how that does that even translate into a curse?"

"Well, first of all, you're asking two different questions," Daphne said. "Curses don't just happen on their own. Someone puts a curse on something. So, in this case, maybe the treasure was cursed, and when the Redemption adults took possession of it, they also took possession of the curse. Or maybe one of the pirates cursed them when they took the treasure. Or maybe it wasn't even a pirate, but someone related to the pirates who cursed them. There are a lot of different ways Redemption could have been cursed.

"As for what happened to the adults, the pirates could have killed them and left the children because they didn't see the children as a threat. Or maybe they didn't kill them. Maybe they took them away, and something went horribly wrong."

"I suppose," I said, although I still had my doubts. "Does this mean there is treasure buried somewhere in Redemption?"

"Some people do believe that," Daphne said. "Over the years, we've had treasure hunters come and go, but nothing has really come of it."

"If that supposed treasure was responsible for the adults disappearing, you'd think they'd leave well enough alone."

"You would think. I agree. But you'd also think people would leave Egyptian tombs alone, and that show, *The Curse of Oak Island*, wouldn't exist."

She had a point. "So, is this where the 1888ers got the idea of being cursed? Because of the cursed treasure?"

"Not exactly. It's more about being the result of the adults doing something dreadful back in 1888. It was so bad, it also affected their families, just in a different way. And that's why the curse has continued to haunt them throughout generations."

"That must have been some curse," I said.

"Yes. Hence the assumption that the adults must have done something terrible."

"Makes sense," I said. "I can't even imagine how bad it must have been to cause their entire family lines to die out."

"Curses can be nasty," Daphne said. "Which is why you shouldn't …"

"Mess around with them. I get it," I said. "What I *don't* get is the kidnapping piece. If I knew I was targeted by this curse, I would understand not being able to get pregnant. Or if I could have children, I guess I wouldn't be surprised if something happened to them. But kidnapping? If the point of the curse was to eliminate Wendy's child, wouldn't she just be … well, eliminated?"

"Well, I'm not a curse expert, so I can't pretend to know all the ins and outs of how it works," Daphne said. "However, I will say that based on what I've heard from the 1888ers, the curse also just causes plain old bad luck."

"I guess being victim to kidnapping would certainly qualify as bad luck," I said, continuing to swirl my straw in my iced tea while wishing it was wine. Normally, I wasn't tempted to day-drink, so this particular craving was a little surprising. Then again, it had been a brutal week. "So that explains the 1888ers, but it still doesn't explain why Wendy was targeted, or Zane's role in the whole thing."

"How do you know Zane has a role in it?"

"He has to be involved somehow. He was the one who told Daniel Wendy was making it up."

"Hmm." Daphne pursed her lips in consideration. "That makes me lean toward Wendy making up having a daughter again."

"Why do you say that?"

"Well, both Zane and Penny were 1888ers, as you know. My understanding is that they were good friends, too. Although …" she puckered her mouth again. "He wasn't at the funeral or the service afterward, which is odd. At least, I didn't see him. Now that I think about it, I didn't see any of the 1888ers there."

"Maybe that's because they were busy planning the kidnapping of Wendy's daughter," I said.

"Daphne frowned. "I doubt that. The 1888ers are all about protecting each other, especially against outside threats and the curse. I can't see any of them being the masterminds behind the supposed kidnapping."

"What if they considered Wendy's daughter a threat?"

"Why would they? She would be one of them … one of the 1888ers."

"But she's not from here, right?" I asked. "She was raised somewhere else. So maybe that somehow factors into things."

Daphne looked skeptical. "Again, I'm not completely clear on the parameters of the curse, but that seems like a stretch. As far as we know, Penny was the one who sent Wendy away. I can't believe she would do that, if she thought it might put her only daughter in a dangerous position with the 1888ers."

"Maybe, but it seems like just as big a stretch to believe that Zane has this secret knowledge about Wendy that no one else knew about," I said. "Do you really believe that Penny would tell no one else that her daughter was pretending to have a child? Especially considering how badly Penny's mental state deteriorated toward the end of her life?"

"Well, to be fair, if Penny had said anything like that near the end, I suspect no one would have believed it," Daphne said. Despite her words, though, she appeared less convinced than she did just moments before.

"Still. It seems to me that Zane isn't terribly credible. So why should we take his word on what Penny told him?"

Daphne didn't answer right away. She seemed far away as she picked at her salad. I eyed the restaurant, seeing if our waitress was anywhere close by, but she wasn't.

"So, what do you suggest?" Daphne finally asked. "It's not like we can ask Penny anymore, and Wendy doesn't seem to want to talk about it. So unless we're going to hire a private investigator or try and actually do our own deep dive into it to see if Wendy ever gave birth to a daughter—which, again, would be a slog, since we don't know where Wendy has been living or where her daughter would have been born or even her birthday—how can we figure out the truth?"

I reached for a napkin to wipe my hands as I grinned at her. "I think it's time to give Zane a visit, don't you?"

Chapter 17

"I don't know about this," Daphne said as I pulled up in front of Zane's ramshackle house. She sounded nervous, which was unlike her. In fact, I couldn't even remember a time when she seemed this nervous before, and it made me second-guess myself.

"We're just talking to the guy. There's no law against that." I tried to sound more confident than I felt. Even though I knew we were doing the right thing in my gut, the idea of having those intense eyes on me again was making me uneasy, too.

Daphne wiped her hands on her jeans. "I suppose." She didn't sound convinced.

I parked on the side of the road, not wanting anything to do with the pitted and uneven driveway, and turned to face her. "What's the problem?"

Daphne didn't look at me. Staring out the passenger-side window, she said, "It's just … it's stupid."

"What's stupid?"

She sighed. "You're going to laugh."

"I'm not going to laugh."

"Don't be so sure." She glanced at me nervously. "You know how when you're a kid, you do stupid things like dare each other to prank call people and ask them things like, 'Is your refrigerator running?'"

"And if it is, they'd better go catch it?" I finished.

Daphne grinned, but there wasn't any real humor behind it. It seemed like more of a façade to hide how she truly felt. "Exactly. Well, one Halloween, my friends and I—I think we were about seven or eight or something—were daring each other to do these pranks. Things like sneaking around to the back of a house to knock on a window and yell 'boo.' Stupid things like that. My dare was to ring Zane's doorbell and say, 'Trick or treat.'"

"Doesn't sound like much of a dare," I said. "Isn't that what you normally do on Halloween? Or are their different customs in Redemption?"

Daphne's smile returned, this one a little more natural. "No, we do the same thing here. But Zane was known for being cranky and never having candy. So, the dare was that, when he opened the door and said he didn't have any treats, I was to tell him that I was going to play a trick on him."

"Were you actually going to?"

She shrugged. "Maybe. I can't remember anymore. But if I was, I'm sure it was supposed to be something silly, like throw a couple of water balloons against his house or something. Anyway, I trotted up and rang the doorbell. I remember it took him a bit to answer, because I had to ring it a couple of times. When he finally opened the door, boy, was he mad."

She looked down at her lap, two red spots appearing on her cheeks. "He was just screaming and swearing at me, calling me all sorts of names. Telling me how stupid I was, and 'Can't you see my lights are off? Everyone knows that means I don't have any candy! I guess you think it's funny to be a part of a holiday that's all about witches and demons and curses and whatever else you're summoning!'" Daphne's tone changed as she mimicked Zane's voice.

My jaw dropped. "Seriously?"

She nodded. "Anyway, as you can imagine, I was terrified. I took off as fast as I could. I still remember him screaming at me as I ran, telling me I should keep going and run away, right out of Redemption. Needless to say, I haven't been all that keen to have anything to do with him since then."

"Well yeah, I can see why. Talk about a grumpy old man screaming at kids to stay off his lawn."

"Pretty much," she said quietly.

I stared out the window at the sad, broken-down house. "Yet this is the same guy everyone thinks is credible?"

"Everyone knows he has credibility issues, but this just seems like a pretty strange thing to lie about," Daphne answered. "If Wendy had told him he was full of crap, and she did have a daughter, I'm guessing a lot of people would have believed her over him. But remember, she backed his story. That went a long way ... even more so than what Zane said."

"Yeah, I guess I can see that," I said, still staring at the house. The porch steps sagged as if they were exhausted under the weight of it all. "Are you okay doing this? If you want, I can take you home and come back on my own. I don't mind." Even as I said it, I knew I was lying. I very much did *not* want to face Zane on my own. But Daphne was my friend, and if she really didn't want to be a part of it, I didn't want to force her.

Daphne glanced over at the house. I could see her swallow hard before straightening her shoulders. "No. I think it's about time I faced this demon. And besides," she looked back at me, a seriousness in her eyes I didn't recognize. "I don't think you should be alone with him."

Before I could protest, she was opening the passenger door and getting out. I joined her at the bottom of the driveway.

"Ready?" I asked.

She didn't answer as she stared intently at the house. Finally, she took a deep breath and gave me a quick nod. "Let's do it."

We picked our way up the broken driveway, trying not to trip on the unevenness. Weeds sprouted from the cracks and threatened to take over the overgrown lawn.

The closer we got to the house, the more grateful I was that Daphne was with me. Everything about the place screamed that I should run away and never come back, but I refused to give in to my trepidation. Jill, if there was a Jill, was counting on me. I couldn't let her down.

We carefully mounted the steps onto the crooked porch. Daphne was in front of me, but she paused in front of the door, seemingly unable—or unwilling—to knock or try the doorbell.

I gave her a moment, the only sound being the whistling of the wind through the broken gutter. She remained frozen in place, no doubt remembering that night so long ago.

"You okay?" I whispered.

She stirred and glanced my way. "Yeah. I was just ... I'm good."

I gestured toward the door. "Do you want to do the honors?"

She took another deep breath and rang the doorbell.

Neither one of us spoke as the chimes sounded, followed by a practically palpable silence. After a few moments, Daphne rang it again.

"Wouldn't it be something," I said, "if after all that buildup, he wasn't even home?" I couldn't decide if I was disappointed or relieved.

"Not home or not answering," Daphne said, her eyes never leaving the door.

"Either way, it's no help to us," I said. "I guess we'll probably need to come back ..."

My voice trailed off as we heard a distinct creaking from inside the house. It came closer before abruptly disappearing, as if whoever was on the other side of the door was looking through the peephole and debating whether or not to open it. The pause went on for so long, I was about to suggest that Daphne ring the bell one more time, but she seemed to have the same idea as she raised her hand and began moving toward it. Before she could, though, there came the unmistakable clicking of locks being disengaged, and the door finally opened, revealing Zane.

He was taller than I remembered, although that might have been because when I had seen him before, he was next to Daniel, who was well over six feet. He was wearing a pair of very old and ill-fitting blue jeans secured over his bony hips by a frayed leather belt and a gray tee shirt. He seemed older and frailer than the man I had met just a few days ago, though his dark eyes were exactly as intense as I had remembered.

At first, he simply stood there studying us. His mouth worked for a moment, like he was chewing on a wad of tobacco. Finally, he addressed us.

"What do you want?"

I swallowed hard before answering, my mouth and throat unnaturally dry. "Hi, I'm Becca Kingsley. We met at …"

His eyes bored into mine. "I remember." His voice was flat. Then, he turned to Daphne. "But not you. Although you do look familiar."

"Probably because I've lived here my whole life," Daphne said matter-of-factly. Her voice was clearer and steadier than mine.

He grunted. "Doesn't matter. I'll ask again … what do you want?"

"We were hoping we could talk to you for a moment. About Wendy."

"Why?"

I blinked. Coupled with the intensity of his eyes, his terse responses were throwing me off. "Well, because I have questions about your claim that Wendy made up having a child."

"She did." He leaned out the door slightly and spat to one side of us, barely missing the porch. "Not that it's any of your business."

"I'm trying to help her," I said.

He fixed those eyes on me. "Why?"

"Because she needs help."

"So what? Lots of people need help."

"She's my friend," I said, stung by his nonchalance.

He let out a rusty bark of laughter. "I highly doubt that. If that were true, you'd already know the truth."

"And what IS the truth?"

His expression shifted, almost like he was surprised I would have the audacity to ask. "None of your concern," he repeated.

"It *is* my concern. Like I said, I'm trying to help."

"You can't."

"Why not?"

He looked at me like I was an idiot. "Because you're not an 1888er."

I put one hand on my hip. "What does that have to do with anything?"

He folded his arms across his chest. "And that's exactly why you can't help. Because you don't understand."

"What, about the curse?"

His eyes widened slightly. "You wouldn't be so flippant, if you were one of us."

"Then why don't you tell us more about it?" Daphne broke in. "Maybe we can bring some perspective you haven't considered."

His head jerked toward her, like he was a puppet on a string. "We don't need any perspective. What we need is protection."

"How can we protect you from something we don't understand?" Daphne asked.

Zane barked out a sarcastic laugh. "We don't need *you* to protect us. We can do that ourselves."

"Fine. But Wendy clearly needs help," I said. "If she *is* making up having a child, that's not normal behavior."

"As I just said, we'll handle it."

"Why didn't you handle it before then?" The longer the conversation continued, the more exasperated I felt. "She's been doing this for ten years. Why didn't you step in before?"

That seemed to land. For the first time, I saw a crack in his stony expression. "You think I didn't want to? Wendy belonged here, with us. I wanted to reach out to her ... to bring her back here, so she could be with her family, but Penny wouldn't ..." He slammed his mouth shut, as if he had said too much.

"Why didn't Penny want that?" I asked.

He shook his head. "It doesn't matter now. Wendy is here, so now, we can help."

"She's going to stay?" This surprised me. I figured she would be packing her bags and leaving Redemption the moment she could.

"Of course. This is her home. It's where her … it's where she belongs."

I felt a frisson of excitement shoot through me. Where Wendy's what was? Her family? Her daughter? What had Zane stopped himself from saying? "Why does she belong here? There's nothing here for her. No job, no family. Her mother's dead, and according to you, she doesn't have a daughter, so why should she stay?"

Zane's expression turned steely. "*We're* her family. We take care of our own."

Something clicked inside me, and I felt myself grow cold despite the sweat gathering on my forehead. "Is that why you kidnapped her daughter? To force her to stay in Redemption?"

Zane's mouth dropped open, and his entire body went rigid with shock. He recovered quickly, blinking rapidly and returning to his default upset expression, but the mask had slipped enough to reveal the truth.

And he knew it, too.

"We're done here." His voice was clipped, and he took a step backward into the house. As he began shutting the door, I darted forward to wedge myself into the doorway. "Where's Wendy's daughter now?"

"You're trespassing." His eyes glinted with a mix of emotions—anger and frustration for sure, but was there fear there, as well? He tried to slam the door in my face, but my body prevented it. "If you don't leave, I'm calling the cops."

"Go ahead. I'd be happy to tell them how you're not only guilty of kidnapping, but blackmail, too."

His face turned bright red. "I already told you, Wendy doesn't have a daughter. How can there be a crime when the daughter doesn't exist?"

"Maybe we should let the cops decide what is and isn't a crime."

He glared at me, his eyes so full of rage, I was a little surprised I didn't instantly catch on fire. "You'd do that, wouldn't you? Destroy us, without a second thought. That's why we don't trust you. You have no idea what you're dealing with, or what we're dealing with. The enemies we face on a daily basis, and what we're forced to do to survive. You have no idea what it's like to be one of us."

"Then tell me," I said a little more gently. "I have no desire to destroy you. I want to help you, but I can't do that unless you talk to me."

"Don't you get it?" he hissed through gritted teeth. "You can't help us. No one can." With a sudden burst of superhuman strength, he shoved me, catching me by surprise. I stumbled backward, almost toppling into Daphne, who steadied me. But before I could recover, he slammed the door closed. We heard the distinct clicks of multiple locks falling into place.

"Wow, that was intense," Daphne breathed behind me. She squeezed my shoulders gently, as if to make sure I was steady before moving to my side.

"I'll say." I ran a hand through my hair, trying to calm my racing heart and slow my breathing.

She studied me. "Are you okay?"

"Yeah, I'm fine. Just had a little *déjà vu*. I've had just about enough of getting pushed out of doors this week." I looked back at the door, which of course remained closed. What did I expect? For Zane to have a sudden change of heart and invite us in to share the full story?

Daphne leaned closer to me, her breath tickling my ear. "Maybe we should go," she murmured. "I didn't hear any footsteps. Did you?"

I took another sharp look at the door and realized Daphne was right. I hadn't heard any sound once the locks were engaged.

Which meant Zane was likely still there, watching us through the peephole.

"Good idea," I said, turning around to make my way down the driveway and back to my car. Daphne followed close behind me.

Neither of us spoke until we reached the car. "What did you think?" I asked Daphne as I unlocked the doors.

She pursed her lips but didn't respond until we were both inside and I had started the engine. "I think I'm now much more open to the idea that Wendy does actually have a daughter, and she really was kidnapped."

Chapter 18

I felt my body sag in relief at Daphne's words. Finally, someone believed me! It felt like a huge weight had rolled off my shoulders as I shifted the car into drive and pulled away from Zane's house.

"Careful," Daphne said as I nearly hit the curb.

"Sorry," I murmured. "You just have no idea how it feels to finally have someone take me seriously."

"I can imagine," Daphne replied, a small smile on her lips.

"Especially considering Mia and Daniel's reactions," I continued. Now that I had started talking about it, I could feel the words that had been bubbling beneath the surface, getting ready to pour out. "They've both been so dismissive of me and what I saw. I was the one who was talking to Wendy at the reception. Of all of them, I was the only one who had spent time with her before the whole kidnapping fiasco. Not to mention also being the only one who saw the girl in the woods. She's probably from the cult, but still …"

"Wait a minute." Daphne raised her hand. "Cult? What cult?"

I shot her a sidelong glance. "Oh, you haven't heard?"

"No, remember what I told you? I've been lost in a tech hell over the past few weeks. I haven't heard anything."

"Well, Redemption is apparently now home to a cult called 'the Church of the Forgotten.'"

Daphne wrinkled her forehead. "The Church of the Forgotten. Forgotten what?"

"Daniel didn't say."

"Hmm." She chewed on her bottom lip as she contemplated.

I glanced over at her. "Does that mean something to you?"

She didn't immediately answer. "I'm not sure. It's just ..." she gave her head a quick shake. "It's probably nothing. But how do we know they're a cult? Is that what they're calling themselves?"

"I suspect they're calling themselves a 'commune,' or something like that. They live just outside of Redemption."

"Where?"

I frowned. "I think it's the Hoffman property?"

Daphne looked surprised. "I didn't think that was for sale."

"I didn't say they bought it, just that they're living on it. I'm not sure who owns it or anything."

"That's interesting. My understanding was that it was tied up in some trust and couldn't be sold," Daphne said. "Although I guess it could be rented. Honestly, it's a good property for a cult or a commune. It's on the outskirts of town, up against the forest. There aren't many neighbors around there, either, so there's a lot of privacy."

"Daniel said they apparently like privacy. The first thing they did was repair the fence and gate."

Daphne's smile quirked up again. "You have to have your priorities, I guess. So, is that why he thinks they're a cult? Because they want their privacy?"

"That's part of it. There's also the name, of course. But I think it's mostly because of how they dress and act."

"And how is that?"

I pulled into the parking lot of The Tipsy Cow as Daphne pointed to where she had parked. The lot was nearly empty, so it was easy to find her car. Normally, she would have walked over to my house, or one of us would have picked up the other. But since Daphne had other errands to run, she said it was just easier to meet me today.

"Like they're living in the early 20th century," I said, pulling in next to her.

"What do you mean?"

I turned the car off and sat back in my seat. "I haven't seen the men yet, but the women wear these long, old-fashioned dresses and always have their hair up in a bun. They also don't have cell phones, only a landline, and no computers, of course."

"So, like the Amish?"

"I guess. If the Amish were a part of some weird church called 'The Church of the Forgotten.'"

Daphne sat back in her seat, as well. "It does make you wonder about the church's denomination."

"No kidding."

"So, these … 'church' members. You see them around Redemption?"

I nodded. "Yeah. I saw two of them in Aunt May's."

Daphne raised an eyebrow. "In a restaurant? I wouldn't imagine that fitting their lifestyle."

"Well, they weren't actually eating there. They were trying to sell their eggs and vegetables."

"Everyone has to make a living, I guess. Is Aunt May's going to buy from them?"

"I don't think so. Chrissy didn't sound impressed, and apparently, she's been promoted to food purchasing."

Daphne straightened. "Wow. That's impressive. She's not even 18 yet, is she?"

"No. Still a few months away."

Daphne nodded. "So, any other reason why Daniel thinks they're a cult? I don't suppose you talked to them, did you?"

"Actually, I did."

Daphne stared at me and started to laugh. "Of course you did. I should have known."

"What does that mean?"

She shook her head. "Nothing. It's nice to know someone who has no issue walking up to strangers and having a conversation."

"Well, in this case, she came up to me."

"Really?" Daphne shifted in her seat so she was facing me. "This ought to be good."

I reiterated the conversation between Eleanor and myself as Daphne listened without interruption, although she couldn't hide the surprise that flashed across her face when I talked about how Eleanor wanted to buy tea from me.

"I had no idea your tea was so famous," she said.

"What do you mean? I keep hearing how everyone wanted to buy tea from Charlie."

"Charlie, not you. No offense," she quickly added. "But you've been doing this for what, a year?"

"Not even."

"And Charlie was making tea since the 1990s, so yeah, she built up quite a reputation. I figured you wouldn't have too much of a problem capitalizing on that, but I didn't think it would extend to people who recently moved here and don't know who you are."

"I was surprised as well," I admitted. "Especially since I know they're self-sustaining. You would think they could plant their own herbs and flowers for tea."

"Maybe they need the land for food more than tea," Daphne said. "Or maybe there's no one who wants to make teas. But I agree … it is kind of weird. Are you going to sell to them?"

"I haven't decided yet, although I'm leaning toward no," I said. "I have no desire to do business with a cult."

"Makes sense," Daphne said. "Although we don't know if they really are a cult yet."

"What are you talking about? Of course they are."

"It's possible they're just a community of weird people who choose not to live in the modern world," Daphne explained. "After my past few weeks of tech hell, I can't really blame them."

"But the name," I said. "The Church of the Forgotten? Why would they call themselves that?"

"It's a strange name, for sure. But it still doesn't mean they're a cult."

I shook my head. "I don't know. It all sounds pretty cultish to me."

"Are they programming people? Keeping them against their will?"

My mind flashed to the girl in the woods. *Help me.*

"Does abusing children count?"

Daphne's face went slack. "They're *abusing* children? You know this?"

"Well, I don't know it for certain," I said, a bit reluctantly. "But remember that girl in the woods I saw at Penny's house the day of the funeral? She was dressed in the same style as Eleanor. This long, old-fashioned-looking dress."

Daphne looked stricken. "You think she ... did she say she was being abused?"

I held up my hands. "She didn't say anything at all. But she had to be a member of the cult. Her matching outfit couldn't have been coincidence."

"You're probably right. But was she bruised, or cut, or something like that?"

"She was dirty and unkempt. Her clothes were all stained."

Daphne gave me a sharp look. "With what? Like, blood?"

I saw the girl again in my head. It looked more like dust than blood, if I were being honest, but I still found it suspicious. "I don't know. The woods were dark, but she was clearly filthy."

"Okay, but how do you know she was being abused?"

"She was just ..." I waved my hands in frustration.

Find me.

"She was just really upset. And scared. Her body language and expression seemed to be asking me for help, but she was too frightened to actually say anything."

Daphne didn't look convinced, so I kept talking.

"Daphne, think about it. There's a girl in the woods in the middle of nowhere who was obviously upset and frightened. What explanation could there be, other than her being a runaway? Is it really a stretch to think she was probably running from a really bad situation?"

Daphne stared at me, her brow furrowing. "You do know that kids run away from home all the time, and it's not necessarily because they're being abused?"

"Yes, but ..." I huffed a frustrated sigh. *Find me.* "All right. Fine. I have no proof of it. It's just how I feel ... a gut instinct, I guess. And you're right, I could be blowing it all out of proportion. But I still feel like I need to do something. If she is being abused, and I do nothing ... if she ended up back in that situation *because* I did nothing ... I would feel terrible."

"I understand. And I do think we need to at least look into it," Daphne said. "Did you tell Daniel?"

"Yes, and he said he'd stop by and see if there are any children there, and if there are, if any of them had run away recently."

"That's a good start."

"Yeah." Daphne was right; it was a good start. So why did I feel like I wasn't doing enough? I glanced in the rear-view and saw a couple of well-dressed people walking into the bar. I wondered if it was happy hour. I wouldn't mind a drink, if it was, especially considering how I had decided against one at lunch. I gestured toward the bar with my head. "Want to continue this inside over a quick drink?"

Daphne made a face. "I'd love to, but I've got errands I really have to get to today. In fact, I should probably get going."

"Oh, of course. I didn't mean to keep you so long. I appreciate you coming with me to see Zane."

"No problem," she said. She reached for the door handle before turning back to me again. "Is everything okay? You don't seem happy," she said gently.

Inwardly, I sighed. Daphne was always a little too good at reading people. I didn't want to admit my disappointment in not getting a drink, especially since I had plenty at home. "It's just … are you sure we're doing enough? For the girl in the woods, I mean. Daniel has so much going on investing the gang activity …"

"Wait a minute." Daphne held up her hand again. "Gang activity?"

I smiled despite myself. "Oh, that's right. You haven't heard anything in weeks."

"Pretend I'm new to Redemption," she said.

I shared with her what Daniel had told me about the gang activity. By the time I stopped, she was shaking her head. "All right. That settles it. I'm not going to take on any more projects that bury me for weeks at a time. I miss way too much."

"What can I say? Things come at you fast in Redemption."

She rolled her eyes. "That's for sure. So, to recap, we had an unconfirmed kidnapping, a possible new cult or commune, AND a new gang in town. Anything else? An alien abduction, perhaps?"

"No, I think that covers it," I laughed.

"Hmm." Daphne tapped on her lips with her finger. "It's really odd, don't you think?"

"What is?"

"That a new group of people who have some questionable behaviors moved into Redemption at the same time the criminal activity started up again."

"Daniel said the same thing when he first told us," I said.

"Makes sense to me. It seems very suspicious that both of these things showed up in Redemption at the same time. A bit much to be a coincidence."

I frowned. "While I agree in theory, does it fit into reality? Would cult members be interested in graffiti? Petty theft, sure. Maybe drugs and prostitution, as well, since they seem to be looking for an income source. But I can't see a cult telling its members to cover walls with gang graffiti."

"Why not?" Daphne seemed to be warming to her theory. "It might be a great way to deflect. The cops see gang graffiti and assume there's a gang, when really, it's the cult doing the criminal activity."

"That would be one heck of a distraction," I said, contemplating the idea. Really, was it more likely that a cult AND a gang both moved into Redemption at the same time, or that there was only one entity responsible for everything?

Daphne threw me a look. "Isn't that the point?"

I chuckled. "Agreed. Next time I see Daniel, I'll bring it up to him. I must say, it seems more probable than his current theory."

"Which is ..."

"That's it's related to that bar that burned down back in the 80s. The 1980s, I mean." I half-smiled again. "Nothing to do with the 1888ers."

Daphne didn't smile back. If anything, her face grew more serious. "Are you talking about the Lone Man Standing?"

"Yeah, that's the one. I guess the owner was involved in a lot of shady deals."

"Yes, there was a lot of criminal activity attributed to Red." She paused, her brow furrowed. "But he was killed when the bar burned down, so how does Daniel think the two are related?"

"It seems Aunt Charlie didn't believe that Red died in the fire, and she wasn't shy about expressing it."

"Well, that's true," Daphne said. "I remember her talking about how she was sure Red was still alive somewhere. But still ... he would have to be in his 70s or 80s by now. And why would he return to Redemption? There's not been any sign of him for years."

"Daniel agrees it's a long shot. But I guess the crimes are really similar."

Daphne didn't look convinced. "I guess it's good to investigate a few different angles." She glanced at her phone and her eyes bugged out. "Oh man, it's getting really late. I better go."

She opened the car door and slid out. "I expect you to keep me posted from now on."

"I promise," I said. She waved at me as she shut the door and got into her car.

Chapter 19

I drove home wondering what I was going to do about dinner. Daniel was coming over after work, which meant I would either have to figure out something to cook or get takeout. If Mia was home, I would lean toward the former. Left to her own devices, she would be living on cold cereal and frozen pizza, if she even remembered to eat.

The late-afternoon sun was slanting across the neighborhood as I pulled into my regular parking spot in front of the house. I got out and was almost to the porch when I noticed a small, gray lump on the stoop.

I squinted at it as I walked toward it, trying to figure out what it was. Was it a package of some sort? Or maybe a rock? But why would a rock be on my porch?

As I got closer, I suddenly realized it was a dead mouse.

I immediately stopped in my tracks. Ugh. It had to be Oscar's work, although it had been a while since he'd left me a "gift." Yuck.

Although … where *was* Oscar? I glanced around the yard. Usually, if he was outside, he would be waiting for me to come home. Especially around dinner time.

Come to think of it, I didn't think I'd let him out that morning when I left. Had Mia or Chrissy, maybe? Thinking back, they were both already gone when I got up. Unless they had come home at some point and let him out, for some reason.

Well, regardless of how Oscar got out, the mouse was going to have to go in the garbage. I set my purse down and went to get a shovel.

As I walked toward the garage, the uncomfortable sensation of being watched washed over me.

I paused to glance around the neighborhood, but I saw nothing. It was a lovely summer day. The sun was just about to set, and a gentle breeze blew against my skin.

Other than the dead mouse, it was a quiet, normal afternoon. There was nothing to justify the alarm bells sounding in my head.

Nonetheless, I suddenly felt the urge to run into the house, slam the door behind me, and lock it.

I had taken two steps toward the front door when I caught sight of the dead mouse again. No. This was ridiculous. I wasn't about to leave it on my porch all night. I would clean it up first and then go inside.

Besides, it was all probably a figment of my imagination, no doubt brought on by the stress I'd been under and all the weird things that had been happening around me. No wonder I thought someone was watching me.

I squared my shoulders and strode toward the garage, determined to get the unpleasant task taken care of as quickly as possible. I opened the side door, fetched the shovel, and marched back to the mouse. The entire time, I could feel the skin crawling at the back of my neck, and suddenly, I recalled being in my garden just a few days before and feeling the exact same way.

I also remembered that I hadn't yet asked Chrissy if she moved my gardening tools.

I quickly scooped up the mouse, trying not to look too closely at it or analyze if it really had been killed by a cat. (Really, Becca. How could you possibly know by looking at the thing?) I dumped it in the garbage, returned the shovel to the garage, and hurried back to grab my purse, unlock the door, and get safely inside.

I locked the door behind me, leaning against it for a minute. I was breathing hard, harder than I should have been for the little work required to throw a mouse away. Sweat was trickling down my cheek, but I was shivering.

Okay. Pull yourself together, I scolded.

A glass of wine would help.

I pushed myself off the door, smoothed out my clothes, and went into the kitchen.

Mia was sitting at the kitchen table, laptop open in front of her, and Oscar was asleep in his normal spot on the chair below the window.

Mia turned to me. "Hey. Everything okay?"

For a moment, I couldn't respond. The scene in front of me was so normal, it somehow didn't feel real. Or maybe it was what had happened outside that wasn't real. Was I dreaming? Had I gotten stuck in a nightmare? Suddenly, I couldn't tell anymore.

Mia was still staring at me. "Becca? What's going on?"

I blinked, trying to get my bearings. "Sorry. I was … it's been a day. Want a glass of wine?"

"Sure." I could feel her eyes watching me as I moved to get the bottle. I could feel her concern. "Is everything okay?" she repeated.

"Why wouldn't it be?" I grabbed a bottle of white from the fridge and started digging around in the drawer for a corkscrew.

"Because you didn't say anything when you came in."

I opened the cupboard and grabbed two glasses. "I didn't realize you were here."

"I called out to you. Didn't you hear me?"

"Sorry. I guess I didn't." I uncorked the bottle with a soft pop and started pouring. "Hey, did you let Oscar out today?"

Mia stared at me. "Oscar is right over there."

I glanced at my cat, who flicked his tail as if to wave at me. "I know where he is now. I meant earlier."

"Why would I have let Oscar out earlier?"

"I don't know, but someone must have." I handed Mia her glass and gulped down a healthy swallow of mine.

She took the glass but didn't drink it. Staring at me over the rim, she asked, "Why do you think someone let Oscar out?"

"Because there was a dead mouse on the porch."

"Oh." Mia thought for a moment and took a drink. "It might have been Chrissy. She was home for a while."

I took another drink, feeling the warmth of the alcohol trail down my throat and into my stomach. I was already breathing easier. "Oh, then it was probably her."

Mia turned her attention back to her computer. "Or it was kids playing a prank. Or maybe the mouse died there."

I leaned against the counter. "You think a mouse happened to die right on the porch?"

"Stranger things have happened. It also could have died somewhere close by, and another animal dragged it there and left it." She gave me a closer look. "Becca, it's not that big of a deal."

But it felt like a big deal.

"Mia, have you been feeling like you're being watched lately?" I asked hesitantly.

Mia did a noticeable double take. "What?"

"Just what I said. Have you gotten the sensation that someone has been watching you?"

Mia's expression was bewildered. "Where?"

I waved my hand. "Here. The house. Or maybe you've seen something?"

"Becca, are you okay?"

"I'm fine," I said, gulping down another swallow of wine and reaching for the bottle.

Mia eyed my wine glass. "You're not fine. You're scaring me. And maybe you want to ease off the wine."

I took a breath. Maybe I did need to slow down a bit. "For the past few days, I've gotten the distinct feeling of being watched when I'm outside. And then my garden tools weren't where they were supposed to be, and now, the dead mouse. I'm just wondering if you've had the same feeling at all."

Mia shook her head. "No, but I've been so busy with work and school, I'm not sure I would have picked up on anything."

She paused to take a sip. "Have you talked to Chrissy yet about moving the tools?"

"No, I haven't had a chance. I haven't seen her."

Mia made a face. "Yeah, she's been working even more hours than me. Good luck trying to track her down. But like I said, if it wasn't her, it was probably just kids."

"Why would kids move my garden tools? Or leave a dead mouse?"

"Why do kids do anything? Besides, you're still living in the infamous Blackstone haunted house. You're always going to be a target for this sort of crap."

Mia had a point. Living in a haunted house did come with its own peculiar set of challenges, and not limited to the ghostly variety.

But still, something didn't sit right with me. It didn't feel like a prank at all. It felt like something else … something darker. Like something in Redemption had been awakened and was moving in unexpected ways …

I gave my head a quick shake as I took another drink of my wine. I was aware that I needed to stop this train of thought. Mia kept shooting me furtive glances, so I knew couldn't confide in her about everything going on. I had to try and pretend to be as normal as possible.

"I'm sure you're right," I said, forcing a smile. "All this talk about fake kidnappings and fake children and cults and gang members has left me more on edge than normal. I probably just need a break from it all."

Mia gave me a curious look. "Why do you need a break from it? Did you go see Wendy again?"

I turned away and started busying myself in the kitchen. I didn't want Mia to see my face. "No, I didn't go see Wendy. She made it pretty clear she wasn't interested in talking to me. I just meant I need to stop thinking about it so much. You know how I like to overthink things." I threw her a weak smile.

What I said was true, but it wasn't the whole truth. At the moment, though, I had no interest in sharing anything more than I already had. Mia had made her feelings clear about all of it, and I had no interest in listening to her disregard my thoughts anymore.

She smiled back, but it didn't quite reach her eyes. "Oh, if you're trying to figure out what to make for dinner, there's a casserole in the fridge."

"You made a casserole?" I opened the fridge door to see.

She snorted. "Are you kidding? Who do you think made it? There's a salad in there too, I think. And a note on the counter with the directions."

I shut the fridge and craned my neck forward until I saw the note, written in Chrissy's elegant, looping handwriting. She apologized for not being around to make dinner as much as normal, even though I had told her it wasn't necessary. If she was home, great, but she was also supposed to be living her life as a teenager. She had actually made two meals; one was in the freezer, and she left baking instructions for both. I returned to the fridge and pulled out what looked like a beef and pasta casserole and a salad.

"Well, this makes my life a lot easier," I said.

Mia was back to typing on her computer. "Daniel coming over?"

I inspected the casserole, making sure there was enough for all of us. "Yep, but we can eat in a different room if you're busy."

"No, that's fine. I probably need a break anyhow." As if to illustrate, she stretched her arms in front of her.

I checked the time. Daniel would arrive in an hour, maybe a little longer. "Think I should put it in the oven now, or should I wait? How hungry are you?" Knowing Mia, she probably skipped lunch and would want an early dinner. Actually, now that I thought about it, Daniel likely missed lunch, as well.

"Probably wouldn't be a bad idea to bake it now," Mia said with a pointed look at my half-empty glass. I decided to ignore her and focus on the food.

"Anything else going on?" Mia asked once I had the casserole in the oven. On the surface, her voice sounded casual ... too casual, like she was trying to hide her real motivation behind the question.

I busied myself with looking to see what I could make for an appetizer. We had some cheese and sausage, and I was fairly certain I had crackers, as well. The problem was, if I got to work cutting everything up, there was an excellent chance Mia would spend most of that time grilling me.

"Other than having a bunch of to-dos that really need my attention, nothing much." I picked up my wine. "How about you?"

She sighed and looked at her screen. "Busy. But that's nothing new. I am tired, though. More than I've been in a long time."

"Well, that's not a surprise, either. Grief does that to you, never mind how much you've been pushing yourself."

She nodded as she took a sip. "I'm realizing that more and more. When this semester ends next month, I'm absolutely taking a little time off. Not only to rest and recuperate, but to decide how I can keep moving forward without burning myself out."

"I think that's smart." I shifted uncomfortably from one foot to the other and pushed away from the counter. "I think I'm going to take a quick shower before Daniel gets here."

"Sounds good," Mia said. Her voice was light, but her eyes continued watching me. I got the impression she knew I was hiding something from her, and if she did, I also knew she wouldn't stop until she pried it out of me.

"I'll be back down in a minute," I said, fleeing from the kitchen with my wine glass in hand. I hurried upstairs and down the hall to my bedroom. It wasn't until I had closed the door that I felt like I could breathe again. No one was watching me in the safety of my room walls, nor judging me for some other nefarious purposes. I could finally relax.

Despite what I told Mia, I took my time in the shower, shampooing and conditioning my hair. I then spent quite a while blowing it dry with my diffuser. I decided to get a little dressed up, too, and put on my green sundress before applying a little makeup. When I was done, I stood back to examine the final result. I was a little pale, and there were lines around my eyes that I swore were getting deeper by the day, but for the most part, I looked pretty good.

"You're fine," I said to myself in the mirror. "Everything is fine. There is nothing to worry about."

My reflection nodded back in agreement. Good. I was ready.

It was getting close to when Daniel would likely arrive, so I figured it was safe to return to the kitchen. Mia was still on her laptop, but she glanced up when I came in. "Wow, you look nice."

"Well, I thought it might be nice to dress up a bit." I checked the casserole before pulling the cheese and sausage from the fridge to slice.

Mia shot me a look. "I hope you remember you still have a roommate living here. Actually, two roommates. Both within earshot," she teased.

"Don't worry, I didn't forget." I smiled as I grabbed a knife and cutting board and started slicing the sausage. "I just thought it would be nice to dress up a little and have a nice, restful evening."

"Hear hear." Mia held up her wine in a toast.

I picked up my wine glass to toast her back when I heard the front door open. "Hello," Daniel called out.

"We're in here," I said, continued my slicing.

Daniel appeared in the kitchen doorway. He was wearing a pair of faded jeans and a blue tee shirt that brought out the matching color of his eyes. His face was tired, but his eyes lit up when he saw me. "You look incredible."

I blushed. "Thank you."

His expression became uncertain as he patted his shirt. "Are we going out tonight? I'm not really dressed for it. I thought we were having a quiet dinner here."

"Relax, we are," I said, pouring him a glass of wine. "I just thought it would be nice to get a little dressed up. That's all."

He looked relieved as he leaned over to give me a kiss.

"Hey," Mia said. "Roommates. Remember?"

We broke apart. "Trust me, I'm always aware of you," Daniel joked as he sat down next to Mia. I opened a second bottle of wine for the table while I finished the appetizer.

"It smells wonderful. What did you make?" Daniel asked.

"I didn't make anything. Chrissy made us a casserole," I said as I started arranging the platter. "I'll need to take it out of the oven in a few minutes, but it should sit for a bit, so we still have time."

"Great," Daniel said as I brought the appetizer to the table. He was topping off Mia's wine as she typed furiously away.

"Just a few more minutes, and then I can relax the rest of the night," she announced.

"How was your day?" Daniel asked me.

"Becca found a dead mouse on our porch," Mia interjected before I could respond.

I closed my mouth. Slightly annoyed, I tried to catch Mia's eye, but she was still staring at her screen.

"Oh, that was nice of Oscar to leave you a gift," Daniel said lightly.

"We're not sure if it was Oscar or not," Mia said. She still didn't look up.

Daniel was glancing between us, his expression confused. "What do you mean?"

"It was probably Oscar," I said. "Chrissy was here, and she likely let him out."

Oscar, for his part, decided at that moment to sit up. His tail flicked as he stared at me with his green eyes.

"That's not what you said earlier," Mia said.

I glared at her, even though her face was buried in her computer. "I was wrong earlier," I said between my teeth, getting to my feet to feed Oscar.

"I don't understand," Daniel said. "What's going on?"

"Nothing," I said shortly.

"Becca thinks someone is watching the house," Mia said.

Daniel's eyes went wide. "What?"

I closed my eyes, resisting the urge to strangle my room-mate. "I told you, I overreacted." I picked up Oscar's food dish and tried hard not to slam it down on the counter.

"Why do you think someone is watching the house?" Daniel asked.

"Oh, and it's more than just today," Mia directed it at Daniel. "The garden tools were mysteriously moved, as well." She final-ly looked at me, an innocent expression on her face. "You told him about the tools, right?"

"What garden tools?" Daniel's expression was quickly turn-ing from confusion to anger.

I filled Oscar's dish with food and took a deep breath. "Look, it's not a big deal. When I was gardening the other day, my tools weren't where they were supposed to be."

"Where are they supposed to be?"

"In the back shed."

"And where were they?"

I went over to the stove to pull the casserole out of the oven, although I had completely lost my appetite. "In the garage."

"How did they get there?"

"Mia said she found them on the side of the house, and not realizing they belonged in the shed, she put them in the garage."

"I probably should have said something," Mia said.

Daniel looked between us. "When was this?"

"A few days ago," I answered, getting the salad out of the fridge. Now I was wishing Chrissy hadn't done so much. I would have liked an excuse to keep a little distance between me and Daniel and Mia, in that moment.

"That was when you put the tools in the garage?" Daniel asked Mia.

Mia shook her head. "No, that was ... I can't remember now. It wasn't that long ago. Maybe a week ago?"

Daniel looked back at me. "Why didn't you tell me?"

"Because I didn't think it was anything worth reporting," I said. As much as I didn't want to sit at the table with them, I also knew I didn't have much of a choice. I started gathering plates and silverware to bring to the table. "As Mia pointed out to me, Chrissy was probably the one who left the tools out."

"Did you ask her?"

"I haven't had a chance," I said. I moved to the table and nudged Mia's laptop, none too gently, with one of the plates. She got the hint and moved to put it away. "It's really not that big of a deal."

Daniel ran a hand through his hair. "Becca, you really need to tell me these things. Is this why you think you're being watched? Because of the garden tools and a dead mouse?"

I shot another murderous look to Mia, who was carefully avoiding my eyes. "I've probably been letting my imagination run away from me. With everything that's been happening in this town, I guess I just let it go to my head." I raised my hands helplessly.

Daniel didn't look reassured. "I hope that means you're done with the amateur sleuthing."

Mia looked at me then, but I ignored her, instead turning around to head back to the kitchen. "Of course," I said when Daniel couldn't see my face.

"Becca? Look at me."

I picked up the salad and gritted my teeth again. He knew me too well.

"What amateur sleuthing?" Mia asked.

"Where do I even begin?" Daniel asked. "With the cult, or tracking down Wendy's made-up daughter?"

Mia put her wine glass down with a thud. "Cult?" Her voice was sharp.

Oh no. I felt a sinking in my stomach. It suddenly occurred to me that I had made a very bad mistake not telling Mia what was going on. In my mind's eye, I saw the image of the longing in Daphne's expression as she watched Mia at the wake, and I realized I was making the exact same mistake Daphne had.

"You know. How she now thinks the girl in the woods is a member of the Church of the Forgotten," Daniel was saying as I approached the table holding the bowl of salad. I was desperately wondering if there was any way to stop him from talking.

"But I thought you said the girl in the woods was Jill?" Mia asked, turning to me.

"I did," I said quickly, placing the salad bowl in the middle of the table. Even though the damage was done, I had to do what I could to mitigate it. "But then when I saw what the cult members wore, I realized the girl was probably from the cult, since she was dressed exactly the same."

Mia's eyes widened. "Wait a minute. You saw one of the cult members?"

"You didn't tell her?" Daniel asked.

"I was going to," I said. "It just wasn't the right time."

"The right time?" Mia repeated, her voice getting louder. "What do you mean, the right time?"

"Both of us have been so busy," I said. "Not to mention stressed. I wanted to wait and tell you when we both had time to really talk about it."

"And we couldn't do that earlier?" Mia asked. "You were that desperate for a shower?"

"You were still working," I said, waving at her computer on the counter. "I didn't think it was time to get into a big discussion about the cult. I thought we could do it later when you were done." That wasn't exactly true, but I didn't think it was the right moment for the whole truth.

"That's not fair," Mia said. "I asked you if there was anything wrong. I would have been happy to talk to you."

"But nothing *was* wrong," I said. "It was fine to wait until you were done with your work."

Mia stared at me, her face contorted as if she couldn't figure out how to react ... whether she should be upset with me or admit I had a point. Finally, she crossed her arms over her chest and sat back in her chair.

"Anyway," Daniel said after a moment, glancing between us, his expression nonplussed. "I did go to the Church of the Forgotten today and asked if they had a missing child."

"And?" I found myself leaning forward slightly, balancing on the balls of my feet while barely breathing. Maybe this was it—the break I was so desperate for.

Daniel shook his head, and my heart seemed to crash to the floor. "According to Eleanor, they have no children at the Church of the Forgotten."

I stared at him, bewildered. "But they must have. Who else dresses their kids in those clothes?"

"What clothes?" Mia asked. "What do these cult members wear?"

"These long, old-fashioned-looking dresses," I said. "At least that's what the women wear. I don't know about the men."

"It's a similar style," Daniel said. "Cloth pants, suspenders, a loose shirt. Straight from about the 1800s. Or maybe early 1900s."

"Do you know why?" Mia asked.

"I wasn't there to talk about their sense of fashion," Daniel said. "I was there to ask if they had a missing child."

"But they must," I insisted. "The girl I saw in the woods was wearing that exact outfit. It can't be a coincidence."

"She did say there were a few teenagers," Daniel said.

"How old?"

"She said the youngest was 17."

I shook my head. "That's too old. It's possible the girl I saw was a young 13-year-old, but definitely not 17."

"She also said that some of their church members were quite young-looking, so it was possible one of them was mistaken for a much younger age."

I shook my head firmly. "No. The girl I saw was around ten years old. It just isn't possible."

"But she was in the woods," Daniel said. "Are you sure you got a good look at her? Maybe she was older than you thought."

I pictured the girl again, standing in the shadow of the trees, her expression pleading for me to help her. Was it possible she was older than she appeared? "She was just so small," I said.

"There are small women," Mia countered.

"Yes, but it was more than that. She was small like a child, not just short." I turned back to Daniel. "Are you absolutely sure there weren't any children there?"

"I didn't see any."

"Did you do a thorough search?"

Daniel picked up his wine glass. "I didn't do any kind of search. There was no cause to search."

"But what I saw -"

"You seeing a girl in the woods dressed like them is not cause," he interrupted.

I put my hand on my hip defiantly. "Are you saying you don't believe me?"

Daniel sighed and sipped his wine. "Not at all. I'm saying that you seeing a girl in the woods isn't proof of anything. You have no idea who she is or where she's from. Yes," he held up his hand as I started to speak, "I know the outfit is a very strange coincidence, and you know I don't believe in coincidences. But again, it's not proof. You also have no idea why she was there in the first place. She could have been out for a walk, for all you know."

"She was out in the woods by Penny's house, and Penny's house is in the middle of nowhere," I said.

"So maybe she was lost," Daniel said. "Or maybe she's a tourist, and she's camping with her family somewhere. There are a lot of explanations other than being abused by the Church of the Forgotten and running away."

I looked between Mia and Daniel, sure the disbelief was written clearly on my face. "So, that's it? We're just going to forget about this girl?"

"I'm not really sure what else to do," Daniel said. "If you see her again, or if we get another lead, then we'll have something more to work with, but for right now, there's nothing more I can do."

Nothing more he could do. I saw a child in need of help in the woods, and he was telling me there was nothing he could do.

Find me.

I opened my mouth and shut it, suddenly aware there was nothing I could say to convince either Daniel or Mia that something was truly wrong. Instead, I turned and marched into the kitchen to get the casserole.

"Did you at least ask them why they call themselves the Church of the Forgotten?" Mia asked Daniel.

"It didn't come up," Daniel answered.

I went to pick up the casserole, but I had been clenching my hands into such tight fists that it took me a second to relax them enough to carry the dish back to the table. Daniel and Mia continued talking about the cult, and how Daniel didn't see much other than a bunch of people gardening and tending some chickens. I could feel the loneliness rise up inside me, nearly smothering me. The emotion was so intense and my chest so tight, I was having trouble breathing. I stood there forcing air in and out of my lungs until I could trust myself to place the casserole carefully on the table.

I was all alone here. And if I was going to help Wendy or the girl in the woods, I was going to have to do it by myself.

Chapter 20

I sipped my coffee as I glared at the pile of work on my desk. It was way too early, and I hadn't had nearly enough coffee to deal with the multitude of administrative tasks.

To be honest, though, I didn't actually *have* to do any of it. I was really just hiding out, because I didn't want to be in the kitchen with Mia.

The night before had been exhausting. I had to sit at the table with a forced, pleasant expression on my face and listen to small talk all evening, when all I wanted to do was scream at both Mia and Daniel. I was so frustrated that they weren't taking me seriously, I couldn't even have a real conversation with them about what was really going on in Redemption. Couldn't they see how girls were being targeted? Jill and the girl in the woods were likely just the tip of the iceberg. Yet both of them wanted to pretend it wasn't happening.

I knew Mia was dying for me to tell her everything—she loved being in the center of things. It was one of the reasons she was such a popular waitress. She was always in the know, before everyone else. And she could sense there was more to the story than what I had shared. I knew it was driving her crazy that I wasn't giving her the full scoop like I normally would. And a part of me hated that I wasn't talking to her the way I used to. But I also was tired of being dismissed.

Mia had the day off from Aunt May's. It was a class day for her, and she was set up at the kitchen table bright and early with her laptop and coffee. After feeding Oscar, I poured myself a cup and escaped to my upstairs office after explaining how swamped I was.

Which wasn't a complete lie. I definitely had a very long to-do list for the tea business that needed to get done. But I also needed to figure out my next steps for both Wendy and the girl in the woods. For Wendy, I had to decide if I was going to try and do my own online research to see if Jill actually existed or if it made more sense (and I could afford) to hire someone. For the girl in the woods, it was trickier. The fact that Daniel wasn't going to help with the cult angle was a major blow, and I had no idea what to do next.

So, there was no question I had a busy day in front of me. But normally, I wouldn't start it until I had a pot (or two) of coffee and fully woke up. Typically, I remained in the kitchen and in close proximity to the coffeepot, and I would just sit there gazing out the window until I was awake enough to tackle my day.

Instead, I was still on my first cup. I hadn't even turned my computer on yet.

Well, I could at least do that. And maybe while I was doing some initial searches for Wendy, I could also open up my email program, so it could download the hundreds of unread emails that were likely waiting for me to sort through for the business. And then, I could multitask.

I turned on my computer and picked up my mug, intending to go down to the kitchen for a quick refill. But as much as I wanted coffee, I was even more reluctant to see Mia. If she wasn't buried in classwork, she might ask me how it was going, and I didn't want to have to admit I hadn't even started yet. Nor did I want to keep lying to her.

Instead, I opened my email program and watched the messages load. I recognized a couple from clients who looked like they were reordering, and it occurred to me that along with not checking my emails for the past few days, I also hadn't listened to my voicemail.

The realization hit me like a sledgehammer.

I had spent the last year slowly rebuilding my Aunt Charlie's tea business, and here I was ignoring paying customers in favor of chasing mysteries I wasn't even sure were mysteries. Everyone seemed to be convinced that Wendy had made up a daughter and a kidnapping. Wendy herself didn't want any help; she had literally slammed the door in my face. Sure, the encounter with Zane had been … troubling. But everyone also thought he was a nut. So, was it more likely that Zane was lacking in social skills, and that was why he came across as guilty, or that he was part of some elaborate kidnapping and blackmail scheme?

And then there was the girl in the woods. Again, I seemed to be the only one who thought anything of it. No one else had seen her. No one had reported a girl missing. And no one had seen any children with the cult.

Was I really about to throw an entire year of hard work away over two cases that no one else (well, no one else other than maybe Daphne) thought were real cases?

Especially since I knew for a fact that I wasn't the best judge of things. After all, I was the only one who had spent time in a mental hospital. And not just once, but twice.

Could I even trust my own thoughts and feelings? I thought about the last few days … how I was also becoming more and more paranoid that I was being watched, when no one else seemed to sense it.

Was that a sign that all of this was in my head?

But what about the dead mouse? And the garden tools? a little voice in my head said, but I pushed it away. Chrissy probably left the garden tools out. Yes, for the most part, she was pretty responsible, but she was still a teenager, and sometimes, she got distracted. As for the mouse, that was most likely Oscar. Chrissy was also likely the one who let him out and back in again. And even if she had seen the dead mouse on the porch, she probably stepped over it and kept going about her day. Again, she was a teenager.

No, I had to stop all of this nonsense and focus on what was real and important. Like my business. And there was no better time to start than right away.

On second thought, there was a better time—right after a coffee refill. I stood up and marched out of the room and down the stairs to the kitchen. Thankfully, Mia had her headset on and wasn't paying any attention to me, so I decided to make myself some toast along with the coffee. That way, I wouldn't have any excuse to not focus on my business for the next few hours.

Armed with my breakfast and extra coffee (I poured some in one of Aunt Charlie's teapots to take up with me) I headed back up to my office, determined to make some decent inroads with my business.

I decided to start with my voicemail, so I could listen while eating my toast.

I hit the speaker button on my landline and dialed the number to play my messages. There were a few from current and prospective customers, and two from Sharon from the historical society (I deleted both of those while trying not to roll my eyes too hard). The last one was from Eleanor.

I had my finger on the delete button, ready to permanently erase it. I was turning over a new leaf, after all. But something made me pause.

Hi, Becca. It's Eleanor from the Church of the Forgotten following up with you. I'm going to be in town again on Friday this week, and I was hoping I could stop by your house so we could chat about your teas. If Friday doesn't work, I'm sure I'll be in town next week, as well, so hopefully, you could meet on one of those days. We would really love to have a tea supplier, as we drink a lot of tea here. Give me a call, and we'll set up a time to meet.

I listened to it a second time.

I knew I should delete it. Yes, I was focusing on the tea business, and this Church of the Forgotten cult or whatever they were would probably be a good customer. But I also didn't get a good feeling about them. The fact that the girl in the woods was dressed like them continued to niggle at me. Even if it turned out that she had nothing to do with the Church of the Forgotten, it still felt like too big of a coincidence to ignore.

No, the smart thing to do would be to delete the message and move on. I had plenty to do already, after all. I didn't need to spend another second thinking about them.

My finger hovered over the delete key. I needed to push it and move on with my day.

Help me.

Instead of deleting the message, I found myself locating their number and punching in the digits before I could think too deeply about it.

Just once, I said to myself. *It's rude to simply not call them back. This is a small town. I should at least give them the respect to have the meeting and then decide if I want to do business with them or not. And, if I'm also able to look around the compound, or commune, or whatever it is, I could see for myself once and for all if there are any children there or not. And if there aren't, maybe I could finally put this behind me once and for all.*

The phone began to ring. I listened to it, wondering how long I should wait, considering they didn't have voicemail.

Luckily, I didn't have to wonder for too long. After five rings, someone answered. The voice was young and female, but it didn't sound like a child.

When I asked for Eleanor, she asked me who I was and then told me to wait. I heard the clatter as she put the receiver down, and a few minutes later, Eleanor was there. "Hello, Becca. I'm so glad you called me back."

"Of course," I said. "And I'd be happy to meet with you. I'm going to be out today anyway, and I thought I could swing by your place. It's the old Hoffman property, right?"

There was a pause. "Oh, you don't have to do that. I'm happy to come to you."

"Oh, nonsense. I often go to my clients. In fact, if you end up becoming a client, I'll probably be delivering your teas to you, so it makes sense for me to come out there now and get a lay of the land, so to speak."

There was another long pause. "I really don't mind coming to you. Like I said, I'm going to be in town on Friday, anyway. And we could always arrange tea deliveries for when someone is in town. We don't want to put you out."

"You aren't," I said brightly, but I was already wondering why she didn't want me to come to her. Was there a reason for not wanting me to see their property? Was she hiding something after all? "I do it for all my customers, and you would be no different. Is there a good time for you today?"

She didn't answer, and for a moment, I thought she was going to refuse and insist on coming to me, but then she surprised me. "How about 1:00?"

"Perfect! I'll see you then." I replaced the receiver and tried to push down the surge of excitement in my gut.

I was meeting with a prospective customer—that was all it was. And if I was able to also get a look around, that was a bonus, but it wasn't the point. I was there to focus on them as a client.

That was all.

Chapter 21

One thing I hadn't anticipated was how difficult it would be to figure out exactly where the Church of the Forgotten was.

I didn't have an address, so using my phone's map app was out. (And no, nothing came up when I tried typing in "Hoffman property" either.) I couldn't ask Eleanor, as she would probably use it as an excuse to come to me. Mia, who was in the kitchen, knew where the property was. But if I asked her for directions, she'd want to know why, and it would be impossible to avoid telling her what I was doing. Plus, if she didn't think I should go, that would open another can of worms. Ditto in terms of asking Daniel. Actually, Daniel would be worse, as he had already told me not to take them on as a customer. He would definitely not be pleased with what I was doing.

So, I texted Daphne. She responded right away, asking why I wanted to know, and upon receiving my answer, she called.

"Are you sure about this?" her voice was doubtful.

"No, but I also have no desire to have Eleanor in my home," I said. "This way, I can take a look around myself."

"You do know if they *are* abusing kids, this could be dangerous for you."

"I know. Which is why I'll check in with you after I leave. If you don't hear from me, you'll know there's a problem."

"I should go with you. 1:00, you said? I could rearrange my day …"

I was already shaking my head. "We're supposed to be talking about tea. How on Earth would I explain you being there?"

There was a long silence. "I don't like this."

"I'm not wild about it either," I said. "But I can't shake this feeling that we're missing something. And as Daniel has made it clear, he's not going to investigate unless something changes, it's up to me."

"And that's what worries me. If something goes wrong, you'll be out there all alone."

"I'm not completely alone. I have you."

Another long pause followed by a sigh. "What if you don't find anything? Then what?"

I shrugged, even though Daphne couldn't see me. "Then that's it. I'll admit Daniel and Mia were right … that there's nothing going on out there."

"Unless something changes, of course." I could hear the laughter in her voice.

"Of course. But at this point, I don't think I'm going to be able to let this go unless I personally take a look around."

Another sigh. "All right. I'm still not happy about it, but I get it. Text me when you get there and again when you leave."

"Will do."

After a little more grumbling about how she really ought to come with me, Daphne finally rattled off the directions and hung up. I was starting to get the feeling that it was more about her missing out on seeing the Church of the Forgotten in person than concern for my safety.

I still had several hours before I could leave, which meant I had plenty of time to make a dent in my to-do list. Not that I was looking forward to it, but it had to be done.

But first, coffee. Coffee made everything better, including plowing through to-do lists.

As it turned out, I ended up surprising myself. Not only did I get more done than I'd anticipated, but I became so immersed in it that I lost track of time. When I finally glanced up at the clock, I realized I was going to have to hurry if I was going to arrive on time, which meant I wasn't going to be able to take a shower like I had planned. Instead, I washed my face, pulled my hair back in a messy ponytail, and threw on a pair of jean shorts and a sleeveless, bright-yellow top.

I quickly packed up two different tea blends in case Eleanor wanted a taste test. I had to make it look good, even though I was fairly certain they were not going to become a customer.

On my way out, I noticed Mia typing furiously away, so I didn't disturb her. I simply collected my keys and purse and quietly left.

Luckily, and thanks to Daphne's clear instructions, the property wasn't difficult to find. And that was a blessing, as I was prone to getting lost. The large, imposing, gated fence was a dead giveaway.

I slowed down and carefully pulled onto the gravel road surrounded by a tangle of weeds. It led to a rusted, old gate, which was wrapped in a shiny, new chain and secured with a large padlock that glinted in the sun. Staring at it, an uneasy feeling began to uncoil in my belly. Daniel said securing the gate was the first task they completed when they moved in, and I found myself wondering exactly who they were worried about getting in … or out.

Eleanor had said someone would be there to let me in, but as far as I could see, no one was around. On the other side of the gate was a guard house much larger than I'd expect. It was in rough shape, with boarded-up windows and a partially caved-in roof. Everywhere I looked were weeds, tall grass, and trees. Nothing that said a working farm, as I was made to believe it was.

I was about to get out of the car to see if I could find anyone, but just then, a man suddenly appeared as if out of nowhere. He wore a round, black hat with a broad brim, a loose, brown tunic, and dark-brown pants. He hiked his way toward the gate and reached through the bars to unlock the padlock. After unwinding the chain, he pushed the gate open and gestured for me to drive through.

I sat there, my hands frozen on the steering wheel. Was I really going to do this? Drive into this padlocked property? What if they decided they didn't want to let me go? Then what would I do?

In that moment, I desperately wished I had brought Daphne with me after all.

I almost left. I was so close to putting the car in reverse, mashing the gas pedal, and peeling out of there. I could almost see the clouds of dust and gravel flying up behind me as I took off, never to return.

But then, in my mind's eye, I saw her again. The girl in the woods. *Find me.*

I was her last hope. Her only hope. No one else was even looking for her, much less coming to save her.

I had to do it.

The man was gesturing to me again, clearly impatient. Swallowing hard, I took my foot off the brake and eased my way onto the property. I could feel my tires sinking into the soft dirt, and I prayed I wouldn't find myself stuck when I was ready to leave.

He continued to wave at me until I was far enough in that he could close the gate. I could hear the click through my open window as he locked the padlock.

It was all I could do not to scream.

He sauntered over to my car.

"Go ahead and park your car here."

I stared at him, uncomprehending. "Park? Where's Eleanor?"

"At the main house. It's not a far walk, but she wants me to drive you." He waved behind him, and I saw an old pickup truck waiting behind the trees. *That's why he appeared so suddenly,* I figured.

I tightened my hands on the steering wheel, suddenly loathe to leave the relative safety of my car. "I don't mind driving myself. Just point me in the direction of where I should go."

He stared at me. His eyes were a very light blue and as piercing as Eleanor's. I found myself wanting to turn away, just as I had with her. "I will drive you," he said flatly. It was clear it wasn't up for discussion. I would either let him drive me, or I wouldn't see Eleanor.

Reluctantly, I put the car in park and turned off the engine. I gathered my keys and bag and opened the door, only to realize I had left the window open.

"Oh, give me a moment. I need to close the window." I started to shut the door again, but he fixed me with those piercing ice-blue eyes.

"We need to go. Eleanor doesn't have all day."

"But I have to lock up ..."

"You don't need to lock anything. Your car will be safe. Let's go."

I looked around and had to admit he had a point. I was inside a locked gate surrounded by nothing but trees and grass. Further in the distance, I could see more buildings and small, black dots moving around, which I assumed were people. But tucked away in this corner, there was nothing.

Still, I didn't like the idea of leaving my car unlocked. It made me feel exposed and vulnerable, even though I knew it wasn't rational. I could feel my sense of unease ratchet. But under the increasingly impatient and frustrated glare of my guide, I knew there wasn't much I could do.

I slid out of the car, closed the car door, and trudged over to the man who was still watching me intently. He didn't say anything more, but based on the frown on his face, I had the feeling he wasn't pleased. He turned and strode over to the truck, and I found myself having to hurry to keep up with him.

He was already in the driver's seat and turning the engine on by the time I got myself settled on the passenger side. The engine coughed and sputtered before finally catching. There was a long crack through the windshield, and I wondered how reliable the vehicle could be. But then I remembered he had said it wasn't far. I figured if he couldn't drive me back, I could always walk.

"I'm Becca, by the way."

He continued staring straight ahead, his eyes never wavering. "I know."

Well, I guessed he would know, as Eleanor sent him. Still, I waited a beat to see if he would introduce himself. "And what should I call you?"

He paused for a moment, long enough to make me wonder if he was going to tell me his name. "Edward."

"Hi, Edward. Nice to meet you."

He didn't respond. Instead, he focused on maneuvering around a particularly large hole next to a wooden shed that appeared like it might topple over with one strong gust of wind. Nearby was an equally decrepit barn. Both buildings were being choked by out-of-control weeds and had a sad, neglected air about them.

My escort was not exactly chatty, but I doggedly kept going. "So, how long have you been a part of the Church of the Forgotten?"

"Since the beginning."

I took a second look at him. This could be a lucky break, if I could get him to loosen up and talk to me. "Does that mean you are one of the founding members?"

For some reason, this made him smile. His black beard was thick and full, and his smile was like a crack in a thick piece of granite. "There is only one founding member, and she isn't here. Yet."

"You mean Eleanor?"

He eyed me again. "Not Eleanor."

Eleanor wasn't a founding member? That was interesting. "Who, then?"

"That's not important."

The truck jerked, and I instinctively reached out to brace myself against the glove box. He yanked on the steering wheel, causing the truck to jostle again.

"Sorry. Got to watch out for these holes," he muttered, but his expression looked more smug than apologetic, and I got the distinct feeling he had done it on purpose. Did that mean he wasn't interested in any conversation at all, or just not one about the origins of the church?

I was about to ask him another question to see if I could get a sense of which one it was when he pulled over to the side of a large, rambling farmhouse. "We're here," he announced and immediately opened the door and unfolded himself from the seat.

I exited a little slower, giving myself time to look around. We were in the center of a cluster of buildings made up of a strange mix of old and new. The farmhouse looked like it had been there for a while, and several hundred feet away from it stood a very old-looking barn with a matching and equally ancient chicken coup next to it. Dozens and dozens of chickens were strutting around a fenced-in enclosure, although I noticed that the fence itself wasn't in nearly as good of shape as the one around the full property. On the side opposite of the farmhouse were several manufactured homes that looked brand new.

Unlike what I had seen so far, this section of land was being maintained. The grass was neatly cut, and the weeds had been trimmed back on the edges of the house. Kitty-corner to the barn was an actual crop with rows and rows of small, growing plants. Members of the church were there, as well, weeding, hoeing, and pruning. The women wore their customary, uncomfortable-looking long dresses, especially considering the humidity, and the men were dressed similar to Edward. One of them briefly paused to wave at Edward, who waved back.

"I'll take you to Eleanor," he said, gesturing for me to follow him. He led me up a set of cracked wooden steps and onto a big wraparound porch. Finally, we approached the front door.

Once inside, I glanced around the very large and open front room filled with mismatched couches, chairs, and a few tables. It was clean, but not neat; everything was haphazardly placed, as though the church members had recently gathered for an informal meeting. The carpet was old and threadbare in places, and the furniture was faded and stained. On the other side of me was a steep, wooden staircase. From down the hall, I could hear quiet voices, though I was unable to make out any specific words.

"Wait here," Edward said before disappearing down a hallway. I stood motionless, feeling awkward and out of place. About a minute later, he reappeared with Eleanor, who was wiping her hands on a dishcloth. She was dressed in a similar outfit as the last time I'd seen her, except this time, she also wore a yellowing apron. "Becca, I'm so glad you were able to find us. Your timing is perfect … we were just finishing cleaning up after lunch. Here, sit." She waved toward the furniture, but I was unclear where exactly she was referring to, so I picked my way over to a mustard-colored chair and perched uncomfortably on the edge.

"If you don't need me, I've got things to do," Edward said. He was hovering by the front door, clearly ready to bolt.

Eleanor didn't look at him. "Of course, but don't go too far. Becca will likely need a ride back to her car, unless she plans on joining us."

Oh no. I could feel my face freeze. Was I going to be trapped there after all? I should have listened to Daphne and not come alone.

But then Eleanor smiled, and I realized she was joking. I forced myself to smile back. "I guess it depends on if you still want tea or not."

She laughed at that, the sound low and throaty. "Oh, I had a feeling about you. I think we're going to do a lot of good things together."

I kept the smile plastered on my face as I nodded, wondering what she was talking about. She just wanted me to sell her tea, right? Not go into business with her.

"So." She ran a hand down her apron, straightening out the wrinkles, and placed her dish towel on her lap. "Tell me about your teas."

Chapter 22

"I can do you one better," I said. "I brought samples." I leaned over and pulled two packages out of my bag to show her.

Eleanor clapped her hands together. "Oh, that's wonderful. I was hoping to try them. So, what are they?" She leaned forward, squinting as she tried to read the labels.

"They're my two most popular blends. This one is lavender-lemon, and this one is called 'Deep Sleep.'"

"Deep Sleep … I can imagine why it would be popular. Especially *Out There*," her nose wrinkled, like she smelled something bad. "With all the stress and noise and technology and … unhealthiness. Society has twisted people up so badly. We aren't meant to spend so much time in front of the television and computer. We need nature and community … to be a part of something bigger than ourselves." She held her hands out wide. "That's what being a human is all about."

"That's true," I said, still holding both bags of tea and feeling a little uncomfortable. Was this going to turn into a sales pitch about joining the Church of the Forgotten after all? "I'm guessing you aren't interested in the Deep Sleep tea then?"

She laughed again. "Well, yes, while it's true we don't have the insomnia problems they do *Out There*, we all experience nights when we have trouble getting our mind to quiet down. And I'm guessing it wouldn't hurt to drink even if you don't have sleep issues."

"No, it's quite relaxing," I said. "It's a good evening tea to help unwind from the day."

"That sounds perfect. Besides, you brought it, so we ought to try it." She stood up and reached for the bags, but I held onto them and got to my feet, as well.

"Oh, it's better if I show you," I said. "These aren't like the teas you buy in the store, so you have to treat them a little differently. Not to mention there are a few tricks to making the perfect cup."

The smile froze on Eleanor's face, and for a moment, I thought she was going to snatch the bags from my hands and order to me to sit down. But with some effort, she smoothed out her expression. "Of course. That makes perfect sense. Let me show you to the kitchen." She turned and started down the hallway. "You'll have to excuse the mess," she said over her shoulder. "We clean up after every meal, of course, but now we are prepping for supper."

"Of course," I said. "You should see my kitchen when I'm cooking. I'm a regular slob." I meant it to be a joke, but based on what I could see of Eleanor's profile, she wasn't amused.

The kitchen was as huge as the living room, although its vastness may have been due to the lack of appliances. There were two gas stoves, two refrigerators, and a wooden knife block, but that was it. A large farmhouse sink sat against one wall, and a row of frying pans hung overhead. Two women were standing by the counter peeling potatoes. One had blonde hair and was very thin and bony, all angles and sharpness; the other had dark hair, a pleasant face, and a soft roundness to her that was a nice contrast to the other. They both started when they saw Eleanor walk in.

"Why don't you two see if you can help Francine?" Eleanor asked. Her voice was amicable, but its effect on the two women was jarring. They both immediately put down the potatoes, even though one was almost done, and quickly left the room.

"Don't be too long," Eleanor called out. "Maybe 30 minutes or so."

I heard mummers of "yes ma'am," followed by the sound of the door opening and closing again with a gentle click.

"Well," Eleanor turned to me, her smile a little brittle. "Shall we begin?"

"I didn't mean to interfere with your meal preparation," I said.

Eleanor waved a hand. "Don't worry about it. They're two of my fastest workers and can probably make up the time. The worst thing that can happen is supper getting delayed a half-hour."

I couldn't figure out if she was trying to be reassuring or critical in a passive-aggressive way. I returned her smile, making an effort to have it appear a little more natural than hers. If she was upset, I wanted to diffuse it as much as possible. I still wanted a chance to look around myself. "Okay, I better get started. Is there a kettle anywhere?"

She opened a cupboard and pulled out a dented black kettle and handed it to me. I took it to the sink, filled it with cold water, and put it on the stove. She stood in the kitchen, her sharp eyes watching my every move, which made me feel self-conscious and clumsy … especially since I ended up fumbling for a few moments with the burner, trying to get it to light.

Once that was taken care of, Eleanor located a teapot as I measured the leaves in a tea ball I had brought with me.

"I've never heard of the Church of the Forgotten before," I said, breaking the silence as we waited for the water to boil.

"I'm not surprised," Eleanor replied. "We keep to ourselves."

"I can see that. May I ask what you're about? I mean, your beliefs and such." I felt like an idiot babbling away, so I forced myself to close my mouth.

"It's mostly about getting back to a simpler time," Eleanor said. "Society is moving at such a rapid pace, and it's just getting faster and more frantic by the day. Humans were never meant to live like that, separate and alone. Just look at the way most people eat nowadays. They're not even cooking their own food, much less growing and cultivating it. They live off of fast food or meals prepared by some big corporation that doesn't care about the people they're feeding. Humans are meant to live in a community, spending time together in person and on the land, tending the plants and animals that will nourish us. And that's what we've created here."

I hated to admit it, but she made more sense than I'd expected. Listening to her, it almost seemed like *I* was the crazy one. "I can see the draw in that. How long has the c - ... the church been around?" I caught myself before letting the word "cult" escape my lips. I didn't think Eleanor would appreciate that very much.

"Oh, years," Eleanor said. "I've lost count."

"Wow, years?" As soon as the words were out of my mouth, I could hear how shocked I sounded, and I tried to mitigate the damage. "Sorry. Like I said, I've just never heard of you before."

An amused smile touched her lips. "I understand. But yes, we are a very old church with a lot of history."

"Where did you all live before you moved here?"

"Oh, different places." Her voice was vague. "Nothing was a good fit, though. Not like here."

"I take it this is home, then?"

"Absolutely." Her eyes lit up, and her face noticeably brightened. For the first time, Eleanor looked truly happy. "We've been waiting and praying for this property for years and years now. It's perfect for us. We're so excited to be here and can't wait to fully renovate it and make it our true home."

"That's fantastic. I'm so glad it worked out so well. I'm sure having it tangled up in that trust all those years was difficult."

The light faded from her eyes. "It was definitely a challenge. But it all worked out in the end, so that's all that matters."

"I agree." The water had started to boil, so I moved to pour it into the teapot. "I'm curious ... how did you work it out with the trust? From my understanding, the chances of that happening were pretty small."

"That certainly seemed to be the case for a very long time. But sometimes, people have a change of heart. And that's what happened."

"That was pretty fortunate."

"It certainly was. But I have a feeling there was a little push from the other side," she said with a mischievous twinkle in her eye.

"Well, that's certainly helpful." I poured the tea carefully into two chipped, mismatched mugs. "See what you think."

Eleanor picked up a mug and blew on it before carefully taking a sip. "That's good," she said. "This is the Deep Sleep?"

"No, that one's the lavender-lemon." I tried mine, as well, wanting to make sure it tasted right.

"Well, this is wonderful," she said, taking a longer drink. "I would love to be able to offer this to our members. Shall we talk price?"

I gulped. Even though I knew this would likely come up at some point during our conversation, I hadn't exactly thought through how I would handle it other than figuring I'd somehow put her off. "Um, well, what are we talking about in regard to quantity?"

She flashed me another smile. "Well, that depends on you."

"Me? You want me to figure out how much you need?" Oh boy, things were getting even more complicated. How was I supposed to figure out how much tea the Church of the Forgotten would drink?

"In a way." She put the mug down. "You see, we don't use money unless it's absolutely necessary. We think it's part of the toxic culture we're trying to get away from."

"I see," I said slowly. "So, you're looking for me to donate it?"

"Oh, heaven's no. We're not a charity. No, what we would like to do is barter."

"Oh." I flashed back to the first time I had seen Eleanor standing in Aunt May's with her basket. Chrissy's absolute disdain for doing any business with them had been more than a little obvious. I had a feeling she wouldn't be any more thrilled about having their vegetables and eggs in our kitchen. "Um ..."

"Our vegetables are all organic," she said quickly. "Same with our eggs. You probably saw the chickens in the yard. Every day, they're let out of their coop to wander around the yard and enjoy the fresh air and sunshine. And happy chickens lay the best eggs."

"I'm sure your eggs and vegetables are wonderful," I said when I was able to get a word in. "I just have no idea how to barter something like that. I've never done any type of trading before."

"I completely understand. It might take a little time to get your head around it but, before you make your decision, let me show you around, so you can see for yourself what we're doing." She straightened up and stepped away from the counter.

"Oh, okay," I said, setting my mug down on the counter. Could it be so easy? Was I really going to get a look around after all?

"Great, just follow me, and I'll give you the grand tour." She started to walk briskly out of the kitchen.

I was about to follow her when I caught sight of the mound of unpeeled potatoes still on the counter. "Would you like me to put the mugs in the sink or anything?" I thought about how those two women were already behind on their supper preparation, and there I was, leaving more of a mess for them to clean up.

Eleanor glanced over her shoulder. "Oh. Don't worry about it. They can take care of it. You're a guest, after all." She threw me a smile as she strode out of the kitchen.

Her response wasn't all that surprising. I wouldn't let anyone clean up my kitchen, either. But there was something about it that didn't sit right with me. I also remembered how quickly the two women had jumped to obey Eleanor. Either she ran a very tight ship or there was something else going on.

"As you know, this property was completely rundown when we took over," Eleanor said as she opened the door and gestured for me to follow her out. "It had been years since anyone lived here. In fact, you should have seen this house. Even though it wasn't the original, it was still completely rundown. We had to do a lot of work to fix it up. Anyway, as you can imagine, we still have a ton more to do on the property as a whole."

"I bet," I said as I followed her out of the house and down the porch stairs. "So, where was the original house? Or was it torn down?"

"No, the original house was next to the gate. Apparently, the owner wanted more privacy, so he decided to build a second house further in and let his farm manager live in the original house."

Oh, that made more sense than having a little guard house there.

"Most of these buildings are from the previous owner then?"

"Not most, all. Except for those." She waved her hand toward the manufactured homes. "We had to bring those in, as we didn't have enough housing for everyone."

"Too bad you couldn't use the buildings that were already here," I said.

She sighed. "Yes, it certainly would have saved us a ton of money. But alas, they weren't in any shape to be used as homes. But they're on the list to be fixed up because we're going to need them all."

Eleanor continued on about the property and how difficult it was to get the fields plowed and the crops planted, but I was only half-listening. My eyes were focused on the huge, ancient barn in front of us. The wood was dark with age and exposure to the elements, and there were holes in the roof where some of the beams had fallen down. In fact, the more I looked at it, the less safe it appeared ... like it was a heartbeat away from collapsing into a pile of rubble.

Still. There was something about it that made me unable to look away.

Though I hoped Eleanor would give me a tour of the barn, or at least let me poke my head in for a quick look around, I was doomed to disappointment, as she was already veering to the side and heading toward the chicken coops.

"There's no comparison to fresh eggs," she was saying as we approached the coop. The chickens let out a few squawks as we entered their area, and several of them fluttered closer to us, as if expecting food. "Especially ours. Once you try them, you'll never be able to eat store-bought eggs again."

I wasn't sure how to respond, so I kept my eyes on the chickens, especially one particularly assertive bird. It kept staring at me with its beady eye, like it was trying to decide if it should attack me or not.

I took a step away from the fence.

"Becca." Next to me, Eleanor cleared her throat, putting an end to the strange and uncomfortable staring contest I'd found myself in with the chicken. "I have something to confess."

"What?" Now she had my full attention. I couldn't imagine what she was about to say. Was it possible she knew I had seen one of her girls in the woods after all? But how could she? I highly doubted Daniel would have said anything.

"I admit I wasn't … excited about you coming here. We value our privacy. The world can be a … well, a cold place when one doesn't agree with our views. So, we need to protect ourselves."

"Understandable." I wasn't quite sure where the conversation was going, but it seemed to be heading away from anything that would get me the scoop on whether or not any children had run away from their property.

"But having you here, talking to you … I'm realizing that your coming here was exactly what was supposed to happen. So, I want to apologize if I seemed … less than welcoming."

Oh, an apology. That was nice but … disappointing. I waved my hand. "Don't worry about it. There's no need to apologize. I completely understand. People can be cruel, especially about things they don't understand."

She took a step closer. Those blue eyes, so piercing, locked onto mine. She smelled like soap mixed with something else. Was it smoke? It seemed unlikely that Eleanor was a closet smoker, but people could be surprising. "I knew you were the right person to help us," she said, her voice low and almost hypnotic. "I feel so ... connected with you."

Did she say "connected"? I wondered. Every part of me automatically recoiled. But to my surprise, even though I wanted to back away, I found I couldn't move. My limbs were heavy and thick, almost like I was trapped in a dream, unable to run.

Her lips parted as if she were about to say something else when a loud voice yelling Eleanor's name cut in.

Immediately, the expression on her face turned sour, and she broke eye contact. "What is it?" she directed at a young man running toward us. While she didn't exactly snap, there was a definite undercurrent of annoyance in her tone.

The moment she stepped away, I found I could move again. The air whooshed into my lungs like I had been holding my breath, though I didn't think I was.

The man approaching was tall and scrawny, reminding me of a scarecrow. "There's a ..." he hesitated for a moment as he glanced at me. "There's a problem. Can you come?"

Eleanor turned toward me. "Do you mind? I should only be a moment."

"Of course not," I assured her, trying not to reveal how relieved I was to be away from her presence, even if only for a few minutes.

"Thank you. It should only be a moment." She turned back to the young man, and the two of them hurried across the field, heads bent together in conversation. The other members remained at their posts, but I noticed how they all lifted their heads and watched the two as they went by.

As soon as Eleanor was gone, the haziness in my head seemed to lift, and I could focus again. I took several deep breaths, filling my lungs with the sweet scent of growing plants mixed with the stench of the chickens, who were still clucking away next to me. One in particular was staring at me, and I absentmindedly wondered if it was the same one as before. I couldn't tell, since they all looked alike, but I took another few steps away just in case.

What did Eleanor mean about feeling so "connected" with me? Even thinking about it caused a cold shiver to run down my spine, despite the heat of the sun on my skin. Was she going to try to recruit me or something? Ugh, I didn't even want to think about it. There was no question I wanted nothing to do with the Church of the Forgotten, but my response to her—or lack thereof—continued to bother me. Why didn't I tell her I didn't feel the same, or move out of the way? Instead, I had just stood there, ensnared in her gaze, like hapless prey to a hypnotizing snake.

Eleanor and the young man disappeared from view, and the other members had turned their attention back to their gardening. The only being paying any attention to me was the chicken.

It occurred to me that I was wasting a perfect opportunity to do a little search of my own. Of course, my options were limited. If I headed toward the field, I would certainly get the attention of the other members, who might even try and stop me. I also didn't want to go far, as who knew how much time I had. Therefore, some of the other structures were likely out, too.

But the barn behind me …

I took a quick peek in that direction. No one was there. I also checked the fields again, but there was no sign of Eleanor, and all the members had their heads down.

This was my chance.

I backed up a couple of steps, moving to the shade of the barn where I hoped I would be less noticeable. Then, I hurried around to the front. As I got closer, I could see the boards were in even worse shape than I first thought. There were big cracks running through them, and I wondered again just how smart it was to be poking around. The thought of it collapsing while I was inside was almost enough to stop me, but then I thought about how irritated I would be with myself if I let an opportunity this perfect slip through my fingers.

I put my hand on the doorknob and attempted to open it. Initially, it resisted, and I couldn't figure out if it was stuck or locked. I jiggled it, then tried again. This time, it opened with a very loud groan. I quickly looked around, sure someone had heard, but all I saw behind me was the wind gently swaying through the long grass.

I poked my head in, but it was nearly impossible to see anything in the dimness, even with the holes in the roof letting in little pockets of sunlight. It certainly smelled like an old barn, though. My nostrils filled with the scents of dusty hay and faint horse manure. I dug my phone out of my bag, clicked on the torch app, and shined it around. It looked like a typical barn, with stalls on either side and a large loft with a rickety wooden ladder leaning against it.

I gingerly stepped inside. It appeared safe enough, at least for a few minutes while I took a quick look around.

I started with the stalls, pausing in front of each one to peer inside. They were all empty. Not even a mouse in sight.

Next, I checked the loft, standing up on my tiptoes and holding the phone above my head. Unfortunately, it was way too high to see anything. I wanted to climb up there, but there was no way I was going to use that ladder. The rickety, unstable barn looked as solid as granite next to it.

I swung the phone around, checking to see if I had missed anything and trying not to feel too disappointed. Again, it was probably a long shot to think I would find anything, especially since it wasn't even locked. If it was, I might have actually been onto something.

I was about to pick my way back out when my torch light illuminated what appeared to be a second door. It was tucked away in the corner, so it was easy to miss, especially if the light didn't shine on it exactly right. I walked toward it to take a closer look. It appeared to be in better shape than the rest of the barn, likely because it was mostly shielded from the elements. I reached to open it, but it wouldn't budge.

I tried jiggling it like I had the first door, thinking it might just be stuck, too, but it didn't work.

I let go of the doorknob and shined the light around the frame, trying to see if it was jammed or warped. Nothing popped out at me until I got closer to the doorknob. That was when I saw it.

The deadbolt.

This door was locked.

The lock was black, and the door was hidden in the shadows, which explained how I missed it at first. I reached out to touch it. It was cool and only slightly dusty.

It also looked brand new.

Why would anyone put a brand-new deadbolt on the inside door of a broken-down barn?

What were they trying to hide?

I leaned closer, pressing my ear against the wood to see if I could hear anything. I knew it was a long shot, but since I was there, I figured it was worth a try.

Of course, I heard nothing. The wood was smooth and cool beneath my ear. Definitely in much better shape than the rest of the barn.

I was about to pull away when it happened. It was soft—so soft, I thought I was imagining it.

The sound of a cough.

I gasped and jumped back. The door was locked because someone was in there!

"Becca?"

I let out a shriek as I spun around, dropping my phone with a clatter. The light bounced around the barn in a weird, psychedelic fashion.

Eleanor was standing there. Watching me.

I pressed a hand against my chest. "Oh, you scared me." A part of me wanted to demand that she open the door and show me who she was keeping in there. Was it the girl in the woods? Or Jill? But another part cautioned me not to show my hand. If she knew I suspected there was someone behind the door—if I asked her about it and told her I'd heard a cough—she might decide she couldn't let me leave the property. I was all alone, without a weapon or even quick access to my car. Even if I could get to whomever was locked inside without a key, the odds of getting both of us safely off the property were slim. A much smarter move would be to call Daniel and have him come riding in with the cavalry. Otherwise, I might end up trapped on this property along with whoever else was being held prisoner, in which case, I wouldn't be able to help anyone.

"What are you doing in here, Becca?"

I had to think fast. If I couldn't challenge her about the locked door, I needed to come up with a plausible excuse. "Oh, I was ... I was just looking around. I've always loved old barns. The play of light and dark, the weathered wood. As a kid, I used to spend days in front of one sketching it ..." I was babbling, and I knew it. With some effort, I shut my mouth.

Eleanor was still staring at me. I couldn't make out her expression, as her face was hidden in shadow, and I started to feel a trickle of real fear. Other than Daphne, no one else knew where I was. If Eleanor decided I needed to be locked in that room as well, I wasn't sure there was much I could do to stop her. Not only was she between me and the door to the outside, but she had an army of men out in the fields who could easily overpower me. Whatever I did, I couldn't allow that. Whoever was trapped in that room was depending on me.

"Old barns are certainly lovely," she finally said. "But it's not safe in here. Surely, you must have seen how deteriorated it is."

I hung my head. "I did. But I thought it would be okay if I took a quick look around. I apologize if I overstepped."

She didn't respond. The barn was hot; I hadn't realized how stuffy it was. I could feel the sweat drip down my back, soaking my shirt. Why didn't I bring some sort of weapon with me? Even a pocketknife would have offered me some protection, or my pepper spray. Instead, all I had was my bag, which was practically empty without the tea and my phone.

Boy, I was turning out to be one heck of an investigator.

I was wracking my brain trying to figure out something else to say to get me out of the mess I'd created for myself when Eleanor spoke again.

"No, there's no need to apologize. It's my fault. I should have been more clear about the barn being off-limits. We don't want the liability should anyone get hurt. You understand."

"Of course," I said, nearly holding my breath. Was this going to turn out okay after all?

"Why don't you grab your phone, and let's finish this outside?"

"Sounds great," I answered, bobbing my head up and down like a fool as I bent to retrieve my phone. It seemed I wasn't going to be locked in the room after all. I was so relieved, I felt the urge to thank her—so much so that I had to practically bite my tongue to keep from saying the words.

She waited for me to collect my phone before stepping aside so I would walk in front of her. I was a little nervous having my back to her, but knew I didn't have much choice if I wanted to get out of that barn. I focused on keeping a casual pace, like I was in no rush to leave.

I assumed Eleanor fell into step behind me, but she moved so quietly, I didn't hear her. Nonetheless, nothing else happened in the barn, and I began to relax again.

Until the moment I stepped outside. Edward was standing there, arms folded across his chest and a scowl on his face. I took a step backward, and without breaking eye contact, fumbled around in my bag for something—anything—I could use as a weapon. My fingers touched my keys, and I quickly grabbed them. I had no idea if they would do much damage if I needed to defend myself against Edward, but I had to try.

"Edward is here to take you back to your vehicle," Eleanor said behind me. "I'm afraid we're going to have to cut our tour short, as I have some pressing matters I need to deal with."

My legs suddenly went hollow as the relief flooded through me a second time, and it was all I could do to keep from collapsing. Of course, Edward was there to drive me back to my car. That made more sense than him kidnapping me.

"I understand," I said. "I need to get back, as well."

Eleanor nodded. Her face was expressionless, so it was impossible for me to get a sense of what she was feeling. Had she bought my silly excuse about sketching barns? I couldn't tell. I was sure the guilt was written all over my face.

"Call me when you've had a chance to think about what sort of arrangement you'd like to set up."

I blinked at her. Arrangement?

Upon noticing my expression, she clarified. "For tea. Think about what you might consider a fair barter, and let's go from there."

"Oh, of course." How could I have forgotten? "I'll do that and give you a call."

"Perfect." She smiled at me, but it seemed perfunctory.

Edward was watching us, his whole body practically vibrating with impatience. He turned, and I saw his old, battered truck in the same place it was before.

We were about halfway there when Eleanor called my name. My heart leaped into my throat. Was she going to tell me the gig was up? Order Edward to grab me? My hand tightened on my keys, and I could feel the metal dig into my flesh. I slowly turned toward her.

"Your tea," Eleanor said. "Should I run into the house and fetch it for you?"

I sucked in my breath. "Oh, no. That's fine. You can keep it."

Eleanor's brow furrowed. "Are you sure? There was a lot left."

I waved my hand. "I'm sure. Think of it as my gift to you for your hospitality."

"Well, then." She flashed me that toothy smile again. "Thank you."

I turned around on wobbly legs to see that Edward had almost reached the truck. I took another steadying breath and forced myself to start walking.

It will be fine, I told myself. *Just one step in front of the other. It will all be fine. Soon I'll be out, and I can call Daniel.*

All I had to do was keep walking.

Chapter 23

"You went to the Church of the Forgotten? *By yourself?* What were you thinking?" Daniel looked like he wanted to throttle me.

"You're missing the most important part of the story," I said. "I found the missing girls. They have to be locked in that barn. Or at least one of them."

Despite my worries about not being able to leave the property, the drive to my car had been uneventful. Edward didn't say a word to me, nor did I try to start a conversation like I had before. I was too afraid I might say the wrong thing, and he might decide I shouldn't be able to leave the property after all.

But nothing like that happened. He drove to the gate and parked to one side, just like before. I headed to my car, which was waiting in the same place as before, as Edward opened the gate. My car started just fine (much to my relief, as it not starting had become yet another fear), and I was able to leave without incident.

I wanted to pull over right then and call Daniel, but Edward would have seen me, as he was still fumbling around with the gate and lock. So, as soon as I was no longer within eyesight, I pulled over and grabbed my phone. I started to call Daniel, when I remembered that Daphne was likely staring at her phone waiting for me to text her, so I thought I'd better start with her. I texted Daphne that I was fine and would fill her in later. Then, I decided it might be better if I talked to Daniel in person and drove straight to the police station.

But now, taking in Daniel's murderous expression, I was starting to second-guess myself. Maybe it would have been better to call him after all.

"Becca, there are so many things wrong with what you just said, I don't even know where to start."

"Well, now's not the time anyway," I said. "There's a girl who needs saving. Save her first, and then you can tell me all the things I did wrong."

"But that's part of the problem," Daniel said, raking his hand through his hair. "I can't just search a private property without a warrant."

"Well, get a warrant then," I said. "You can tell them what I saw. Or I'll tell them what I saw."

"And what exactly was that? A locked door in a barn?"

"It wasn't just locked. It was deadbolted."

"Believe it or not, people are allowed to install deadbolts on doors they own. It's not a crime," Daniel said.

I shot him a look. "I get that. But this barn was falling apart, and the door looked new. So did the deadbolt. Why install a locked door in a dilapidated barn? It's simple—because they're hiding something."

Daniel sucked in his breath, like he was trying very hard to be patient. "First off, what makes you think the door and deadbolt were new?"

I stared at him. "Well, because they looked new."

"How did they look new?"

"For starters, neither were falling apart like the rest of the barn."

"As you said, the door was inside, so it wouldn't be exposed to the elements the way the rest of the barn was."

Ugh. I shouldn't have told him that. "But even so, it still looked a lot newer than the rest of the barn."

"Even if that were the case—that this door was new, or new-ish—you don't know if the Church of the Forgotten installed it."

"Well, of course they did. Who else would have? According to everyone in town, no one has lived there for years."

"Just because no one lived there doesn't mean the people who actually own that property didn't decide to install a locked door in their barn."

I threw up my hands. "But why would they do that? The barn is literally falling apart, Daniel. Again, the only reason to do that would be if you were hiding something."

"Who knows why people do the things they do," Daniel said. "Trust me, as a cop, you would be amazed at the choices people make. And even if you're right, and they *are* trying to hide something, it seems a stretch to think there's a person in there."

"But I heard a cough."

"You *think* you heard a cough," Daniel pointed out.

I put my hands on my hips. "You don't know what I heard. I'm telling you, I heard a cough."

"Maybe it was Eleanor. Or one of the workers outside."

I shook my head. "It wasn't Eleanor. When she came back, she was behind me. What I heard came from behind the door."

"Of an old barn," Daniel added. "IF you heard something, which is a big if, it was probably far more likely the creaking and groaning of the old structure than a person coughing."

"I know the difference between an object and a person," I said, frustrated. "But why are we arguing about this? Maybe you're right, and there's no one there. Shouldn't you at least check it out?"

"You're not getting it," he said. "I CAN'T go check it out, unless I have a warrant, and the questions I'm asking you are the same ones a judge would ask, if I went after one. And honestly, Becca, that judge would probably be less impressed by your answers than I am."

"Maybe a judge would be more open to saving someone's life than you appear to be," I threw back, stung by his words. "There's no harm in asking those people to open the door, especially when there might be two missing girls in this town."

He rubbed his face, suddenly looking old. "Judges don't work like that. Their job is to make sure people's rights aren't being trampled on. Maybe if there was an actual kidnapping, it would be a different story … but we don't even know if there truly *are* any missing girls."

"Okay, so maybe Jill is a stretch, but I saw a girl in the woods dressed like someone from the Church of the Forgotten," I reminded him.

"And they were asked about it. They said they don't have any girls as members."

"But they're lying," I said.

"You don't know that."

"They must be. Those outfits they wear are too distinct."

"It's still only circumstantial evidence," Daniel said. "We need proof. Actual proof."

I glared at him. I wanted to argue. Actually, I wanted to shake him. But I knew it wouldn't do any good. He was right. All his points made perfect sense. And I had nothing. A door with a deadbolt that may or may not have been installed by the Church of the Forgotten. The sound of something on the other side of the door, which could be nothing … or a person being held against her will.

Not only that, but it was true that just because the girl in the woods was dressed in the same clothes as the members of the Church of the Forgotten wore, it didn't mean she was a member. It could be some strange coincidence. And I didn't even know for sure where she currently was. She might not even be at the church. She could still be in the woods, or maybe in a completely different state.

The truth was, I had nothing that a reasonably competent defense attorney couldn't successfully poke a lot of holes in. No wonder Daniel didn't want to touch it.

Daniel was still staring at me, but his expression had softened. "Look, I know you've been under a lot of stress lately …"

My head jerked up. "What are you talking about? What stress?"

"I'm assuming the stress from these so-called 'cases,'" Daniel said. "But as you're not talking to me, I don't know for certain."

"I do talk to you," I snapped, a little more forcefully than I meant to. "I'm here, aren't I? And I've been trying to get your help with both of them."

"I know." He reached out to touch my hand, but I flinched. "And I'm glad you're doing that. But I also know there are other things going on with you, too."

I eyed him warily. I didn't like where this was going. "Like what?"

"Like the fact you think you're being watched. And that someone is messing with you."

I briefly closed my eyes. "Like I said, maybe I was letting my imagination run away from me ..."

"Maybe you were and maybe you weren't," he said. "Maybe there is someone trying to screw with your head."

"But?" I already knew where he was going.

He sighed. "Look, I know it's not your fault. You just seem to be more susceptible to ... mental hiccups."

"Is that a clinical term?"

"You know what I mean," he said. "You didn't remember what happened to Jessica for years and years. You had at least one nervous breakdown that landed you in the hospital. For a while, you were plagued by headaches all the time. There are certain over-the-counter medicines you have to avoid because it can cause mental problems. It's like you have a weakness in your brain that can easily get triggered. But it's nothing to be ashamed of. Lots of people have weaknesses. It's just like how people with asthma are susceptible to lung problems."

I picked up my bag where I had dropped it. "So, you think I'm crazy."

"No!" He shook his head. "I don't think you're crazy at all. But I do think your mind has a propensity for playing tricks on you."

I slung my bag over my shoulder. "I didn't imagine the garden tools. Or the dead mouse."

"I'm not saying you did. Nor is anyone else. But ..." he paused and sighed again. "It's just difficult to understand when Mia isn't having the same experiences as you. Maybe if you were able to talk to Chrissy ... or if you want, I can talk to her ..."

"No, it's fine. I can handle it." I turned on my heel and marched off. I heard Daniel call after me, but I was too upset to stay in the conversation.

I was angry that he didn't believe me or back me up, but if I was honest, it was more than that. I was also afraid. Deep down, I had been wondering if it was all in my head. Perhaps I hadn't felt anyone around the house. The dead mouse and the garden tools likely had logical explanations. In fact, the more I thought about it, the more it occurred to me that those WERE pretty flimsy reasons to think someone was watching me. Taking tools out of a shed? What would that even mean? Leaving a dead mouse for someone would send a message, but if that were the case, wouldn't the person want to include a note to make it more obvious it WAS a threat?

No, neither of those incidents were overly damning in and of themselves. So why did I immediately jump to the conclusion I was being watched? Sure, it had felt that way at the time, but could I really trust my feelings?

Once I reached the car, I unlocked the door and slid inside. I put the key in the ignition, but I didn't turn it on. Instead, I just sat there, forcing myself to think ... to face what I didn't want to face.

The thing that no one was saying.

Be careful. Now that you saw her, she sees you.

A tendril of pain slithered up my neck and clamped onto the back of my head with vice-like jaws before worming its way to my temples. I closed my eyes and started massaging my forehead, trying to push it away, even though I knew it would do no good.

All of this had started when I saw the girl in the woods. A girl no one else had seen, except for maybe Maude, who actually did have an untreated mental illness.

Not only had no one else seen her, but no one had even reported a missing girl.

Was it possible there was no girl at all?

Chapter 24

I stood in a darkened kitchen making a cup of tea. I would have preferred wine, but I didn't want to mix alcohol with pain medicine. Plus, I had finally found the tea recipe Aunt Charlie used to make me to help with my headaches as a child, so I thought it would be a good time to test it.

My head was still throbbing, but the ibuprofen I had swallowed the moment I walked in the door was starting to kick in and take the edge off. Food would probably help as well, as I realized I hadn't eaten lunch. Nonetheless, I wasn't all that hungry. I considered my options, since I didn't think I had to worry about feeding anyone else; Mia was working the night shift, and I was pretty sure Chrissy had said something earlier about going out with her friends. I contemplated heating up a can of soup to eat with some crackers.

Just then, I heard the door open and close and light footsteps coming toward the kitchen. "Don't turn the light on," I called out just as I heard the switch snap on. I squinted and held my hand over my eyes, trying to block the light.

"Oh, Becca, sorry," Chrissy said, turning it back off. "What are you doing in the dark?"

"I have a headache," I said.

Chrissy took a few steps toward me. "Oh, bummer. Is that why you're drinking tea?"

I grimaced. "You know me too well."

She flashed a grin. "Why don't you sit down? I can make you something. I'm guessing you haven't had dinner yet either."

"You guessed right," I said, picking up my cup and walking over to the table. "But you don't have to bother. I was just going to heat up some soup."

"Nonsense," Chrissy replied, going over to the sink to wash her hands. "I've got just enough time to whip you up a quick omelet. Doesn't that sound better than canned soup?"

"Actually, it does," I answered as my stomach rumbled. "I appreciate you doing this."

She flashed her bright smile as she opened the fridge. "Does mushroom and Swiss sound good? I could throw in a little spinach, as well."

"Sure," I said as she started pulling out the ingredients. "You're not working tonight, are you?"

"Naw, I'm seeing Brittany later. We're going out for pizza." She selected a knife from the block and started chopping. "It's been a while since you've had a headache. Or ..." she paused, knife mid-air, her brow furrowed. "Are you starting to get them a lot again?"

I shook my head. "No. This is my first in months. I think it's just stress."

She cocked her head as she resumed chopping. "What are you stressed about?"

"Just ... nothing." I flapped my hand, trying to make it seem like it wasn't a big deal. I didn't feel like talking about it, especially to Chrissy, who was still a teenager and didn't need adults dumping their problems on her.

Chrissy eyed me. "It's more than nothing if you're getting headaches again."

I sighed. Chrissy wasn't going to let me get off so easy. "Truly, it's nothing. With all of the stuff happening in Redemption—the gangs and the Church of the Forgotten and Penny dying—I've just let my imagination run away with me once or twice. That's all."

Chrissy glanced up to look at me again, an unreadable expression on her face, but then went back to cooking. I sipped my tea, which did seem to be working. The pain was starting to ebb to more tolerable levels. Although maybe it was the ibuprofen.

"You know," Chrissy said as she dropped a couple of pieces of bread in the toaster. "You've never struck me as someone who lets her 'imagination run away with her,' whatever that's supposed to mean. You've always seemed to have a pretty good sense of what's really going on, especially if it's hidden beneath the surface."

I stared at her. "What are you talking about? My brain has let me down all sorts of times over the years. You were even witness to it."

She shook her head as she slid the omelet onto a plate. "That's not what I remember. What I remember is people TELLING you what they wanted you to believe, but you always knew otherwise." She added the toast and brought it over to the table along with silverware and butter. "It seems to me what you really need to do is learn how to trust yourself." She stepped back and did a little flourish. "What do you think?"

I was so busy staring at her, I barely even glanced at the food. "When did you get so smart?"

She shrugged, but I could see a faint blush color her cheeks. "I've had a good teacher. Oh." She made a face as she dug her phone out of her pocket. "Brittany is texting me. I've got to go."

"Okay, thanks again."

She glanced at the kitchen. "You can leave the dishes. I'll take care of them when I get home."

"Don't be silly. I think I can manage to wash a few plates." I waved at her. "Go on. Have fun."

"Okay, but honestly, if you're still not feeling up to it, I don't mind cleaning up later." She tucked her phone back in her pocket and started to walk out.

I wasn't going to ask. I had pretty much decided while sitting in the car that it didn't matter if Chrissy had left the garden tools out or not. The tools weren't important. Nor the dead mouse. They were just symptoms of a larger problem, which was that something was going on with my brain. Whether it was just a glitch or something more serious was yet to be seen. That was what I needed to focus on … not on a couple of odd occurrences.

When I first had that thought, it seemed right. I was going to stop obsessing about things I couldn't control and start focusing on my mental health.

But despite all my good intentions, something compelled me to call out to Chrissy. "Hey, did you leave the garden tools out?"

She was already in the living room, so I couldn't see her. "Garden tools? What are you talking about?"

"A little hand trowel and cultivator, and some pruning shears. I keep them in the shed out back."

Chrissy had come back into the kitchen and was looking at me with a perplexed expression on her face. "Why would I have anything to do with your garden tools? You know I don't garden."

"I do know that, but I just thought you maybe used them for something else."

She was shaking her head. "Like what? I have no use for things like that."

"Well, maybe your friends used them?"

She shot me an "Are you kidding?" look.

I changed tactics. "What about Oscar? The other day, when Mia was here, did you let him out?"

"Again, no. Why would I? He's your cat."

"I've seen you feed him."

She rolled her eyes. "I give him treats occasionally. I only feed him when you ask me to."

"Okay. I was just curious. Thanks."

She shot me a funny look. "Becca, are you sure you're okay?"

"Yeah, I'm fine. Don't worry about me. Say hi to Brittany for me."

Chrissy looked like she wanted to say something else, but her phone buzzed again, so she gave me a little wave and headed out the door.

I took another sip of tea before picking up my fork. *It doesn't mean anything,* I told myself as I took a bite of the omelet. *It could still be kids. It probably was kids.*

It certainly didn't mean I really was being watched.

But if I *was* right about that ... was it possible I was right about everything else, too?

It seems to me what you really need to do is learn how to trust yourself.

I sat in the dark, eating my omelet and drinking my tea as my headache slowly drained away. I concentrated on thinking objectively about everything. What I needed was a way to prove I was right or wrong about one thing. If I could do that, then maybe I could start to untangle what was really going on in Redemption and within myself.

The phone rang as I was finishing eating, making me jump. At first, I wasn't going to answer. Chances were, it was either spam or something to do with the business, and I was in no shape to deal with that tonight. Either way, they could leave a message.

But despite my best intentions, I found myself standing up, walking over, and picking up the phone.

"This is all your fault, you know."

The voice on the other end was very deep, very angry, and very male. I didn't recognize it, although there was something familiar about it.

"Who is this?"

"If you weren't meddling with things that didn't concern you, none of this would have happened."

Something clicked in my head. "Zane? Is that you?"

"If she dies, her blood is on your hands."

My breath seemed to catch in my throat. "If who dies? What are you talking about?" An image of the girl in the woods flashed through my head, and I was suddenly terrified about what I had done. Was it possible that Eleanor decided to get rid of whoever was in the barn? That she was too much of a liability, now that I had seen that door?

"Who do you think? Wendy."

"Wendy?" It was so unexpected, it took a moment for my brain to catch up. "What's wrong with Wendy?"

"She's in the hospital, that's what. Thanks to you."

"What happened to her?"

"They almost killed her."

"What?" It felt like my whole body had been dunked in a bucket of ice water. "Who almost killed her?"

"This is a warning. You need to stop. Or you're going to kill us all." The line went dead.

I remained frozen in place, the receiver pressed to my ear as I listened to the dead air.

They almost killed her.

This is your fault.

Her blood is on your hands.

You're going to kill us all.

I squeezed my eyes shut, trying to block out the words. I needed to think objectively.

Was this the sign that I had wanted? Some sort of proof that I was right?

At the same time, everyone said Zane was crazy. He certainly sounded unhinged on that call. Not to mention that nothing he said could be construed as proof.

Yet if someone *had* tried to kill Wendy, wouldn't it be clear that something deeper was going on? Like she really did have a daughter named Jill who really was kidnapped?

Then again, Zane was the one who had forced her to lie. So why in the world would he tell me that Wendy was almost killed?

A loud beeping sounded through the phone, startling me so I nearly dropped the receiver. I hung up the phone and stared at it.

If Wendy was a victim of attempted murder, then the cops would investigate, which meant I wouldn't have to. And if it turned out Wendy really did have a daughter who was kidnapped, and her attempted murder was a part of that whole scheme, then the cops would be back on that case, as well. That would be the best-case scenario for everyone concerned. It was even possible Daniel would be able to convince a judge to search the Church of the Forgotten's barn.

Maybe this would all have a happy ending after all, and it could all happen without my getting any more involved. I could focus on my business and my mental health, which was surely a better use of my energy.

I moved to the table to pick up my plate and carry it to the sink, determined to let the cops deal with it. My job was done. Yes, it was unfortunate if my actions caused Wendy to almost be killed, but she was still alive, right? And maybe it would end up being the best thing that could happen, because Wendy would get her daughter back.

If she dies, her blood is on your hands.

I froze again, the dirty plates in my hands. Deep down, I knew what I had to do. No matter how ill-advised it might be.

Chapter 25

"She's stable," the nurse said, staring at the computer screen. She was plump, with straggly, limp, mud-brown hair and oversized, black-rimmed glasses. "Although she might be a little out of it from the meds. It looks like she just had her psych eval. I'll need to check if she can have visitors or not."

A psych evaluation for the victim of an attempted murder? It must have been really traumatic.

"What happened to her?"

"Slit her wrists." The nurse clucked her tongue as she shook her head. "It was bad, too. Good thing a neighbor stopped by and found her, or she would have bled out."

Slit her wrists? That didn't sound like attempted murder. "I thought someone tried to kill her."

"It was attempted suicide, not murder," the nurse corrected as she picked up a phone. "I'll go check to see if she can have any visitors. Your name?"

"Becca," I said.

"You family?"

"Cousin," I quickly answered. I wasn't sure if they'd let me see her if they knew I wasn't family, and it now felt even more urgent that I talk to her.

Why did Zane lie? Was it his paranoia telling him attempted suicide was actually murder?

Was it a euphemism? Blaming me for Wendy trying to take her own life?

Or was something else going on?

The nurse finished her conversation and was getting up from her chair. "If it's okay with her, you can see her. Let me go ask her if she wants any visitors."

Uh oh. I wasn't sure how Wendy would react to suddenly having a cousin named Becca. I guessed I was about to find out.

I watched as the nurse walked down the hallway and knocked on a door. She waited a moment, then opened it and stuck her head in. After a brief conversation, she turned to me and gestured for me to join her.

"Don't stay too long," she said, holding the door open for me. "She needs her rest."

"Of course," I agreed, stepping into the room as the nurse closed the door behind me.

Wendy was propped up in the bed, eyes closed. Both of her arms were heavily bandaged. An IV dripped fluid into the back of her hand as other machines quietly beeped. I could see two cameras pointed at her bed. The room smelled of disinfectant and old blood.

I took a tentative step forward. "Wendy?"

Her eyes opened, and she stared at me. Both were purple with bruising, and she was very pale. "Becca?" Her voice was hoarse. "How did you know I was here?"

I went to the side of her bed and took her hand. It was ice cold. "Zane called me."

She let out a deep sigh. "Poor Zane."

I didn't think that was how I would describe him, but it certainly wasn't the time or place to argue. I gently squeezed her hand. "How are you doing?"

"Tired. My arms hurt." Her lips quirked up in a small smile. "That's probably no surprise."

"No, not really." I paused, biting my lip as I tried to figure out how to ask what I wanted to without upsetting her. "I know we don't know each other very well, but you can always call me. Anytime."

Her expression was puzzled. "Why would I want to call you?"

"Well, if you were ..." I gestured to her hands. "Struggling."

She still looked perplexed.

Apparently, I was going to have to say it. "If you ever feel the urge to ... hurt yourself. Please call me. You're not alone."

She stared at me for a moment, and then her eyes went wide. "You think I tried to commit suicide?"

"Well, yeah ..." my voice trailed off as she was starting to get agitated.

"I would NEVER try to kill myself. That's not an option for me. I can't do that to ... I can't do that."

I wondered what she had been about to say before she corrected herself. Was she going to bring up Jill? If she was, did it mean Jill truly existed, and she had lied about making her up? Or did it mean that Wendy had some deep mental issues herself, and was now trapped in the delusion of having a child again? "But the hospital ..."

She shook her head violently, her greasy hair flying around her head. "Never mind the hospital. I thought you said Zane called you?"

"He did."

"Well, then you know the truth." She looked at me triumphantly.

"You were ... someone tried to kill you?"

She nodded, her eyes filling with tears.

"But ... how?"

She lowered her voice. "It was like before. They got into the house somehow and attacked me from behind. I blacked out. The next thing I know, I was in the hospital with my arms feeling like they were on fire and being told I tried to kill myself."

"So you don't know who did this to you?"

She shook her head.

"Did you see anything at all?"

"Nothing."

"How did they get into your house?"

She shrugged. "It's mom's house. Who knows who she gave a key to."

My mind was whirling. If Daniel thought Wendy had tried to kill herself, he wasn't going to open any investigations. Which meant, if this was truly an attempt on her life and "they" were serious about killing her, she would be left completely vulnerable.

"Have you talked to the cops?"

She made a face. "Like they would believe someone like me."

She had a point. Especially with her wrists all bandaged up. Would Daniel believe someone drugged her and cut her wrists, or would he be more likely to assume this was another of her delusions?

I had a feeling I knew the answer, and it left me with a sinking pit in my stomach.

"Wendy, if I'm going to help you, you have to tell me the truth. Do you have a daughter named Jill? And was she kidnapped?"

Wendy stared at me for a long moment, her expression slowly going flat. "Who said I'm asking for your help?"

"But ... I don't understand. You just said someone is trying to kill you, and the cops aren't helping ..."

"I don't want your help." She yanked her hand away.

"Wendy, I'm not trying to upset you. Don't you want someone in your corner?"

Her eyes narrowed. "If you were truly in my corner, you would leave it alone."

"But ..."

"No." She sat up suddenly, leaning so close to me, her lips were near my ear. "Listen to me." She spoke quickly, her voice low. "You can't help. No one can. It's all on me. I shouldn't have said anything to you. Because you said Zane called you, I thought … it doesn't matter. Do you understand? They're every-where, watching. I can't afford another mistake."

There was that "they" again—just like what Zane had said. "Who is watching?" I kept my voice equally low.

Wendy shook her head slightly. "I've said too much. About all of it. And I shouldn't have said anything at all to you. I'm not in my right mind. Sometimes, I make things up … like having a daughter. I'm still grieving for my mother, and I was just so de-pressed and weak. I shouldn't have tried to take my own life."

I stared at her, a little horrified by the words coming out of her mouth. "Wendy, you don't mean all of that."

She glared at me, her expression determined. "I do. And it's what I'll say if anyone … ANYONE … asks."

I couldn't believe what I was hearing. "Wendy, I know you're in trouble. I can help you. Daniel can help you. But you have to tell me the truth."

She turned her head away. "I'd like you to leave now."

I didn't want to. I wanted to try to convince her to be rea-sonable. Not only was she in terrible danger, but so was her daughter. She needed help.

But looking at her unyielding face, I knew there was no con-vincing her. At least not now.

As if to underscore the point, there was a knock at the door, and the nurse poked her head in. "Visiting time is over. Wendy needs her rest."

"Of course," I mumbled, gathering up my purse and getting to my feet. "I'll see you later."

Wendy didn't respond. She didn't even turn her head to watch me go.

The nurse, however, had a sympathetic expression on her face. "I know it's tough seeing her like that," she said to me after I was in the hallway and the door closed again. "Give her some time. She just came through a very traumatic event."

"I get it," I said.

She patted my arm. "It's good you're here. She's going to need all the support she can get, even if she pushes you away."

I nodded and thanked her. The good news was that Wendy's reaction to me wasn't raising alarms.

Now I just had to figure out if I could truly let it go, as everyone seemed to want me to.

Chapter 26

Help me.

I awoke with a jerk, sticky with sweat and my blankets twisted around me.

Again, I had dreamed of the girl in the woods. She was begging me for help, just as she had before. And just as before, I was trapped in the long, bony branches of trees that dug into my skin like sharpened bones, unable to move as the flames slowly crept closer and closer …

I shivered, despite the sweat, and started untangling myself from the sheets. Oscar lifted his head from where he lay on the pillow, watching me. The light shining through the window was a silvery gray.

Dawn was coming. Which was a good thing as I was sure I wasn't going to get any more sleep.

Oscar hopped off the bed with me and accompanied me downstairs, where I gave him an early breakfast and made a pot of coffee. I poured a cup and sat at the table, positioning myself so I could look out the window as I tried to ignore the uneasy feeling that still lingered from my dream.

Help me.

I gave myself a quick shake and sipped my coffee. I was now convinced that the girl in the woods wasn't Jill. She was someone else entirely, and likely connected to the Church of the Forgotten.

If she really existed.

I clutched my mug, trying to warm my fingers that had turned ice cold. The house was a comfortable temperature, not too warm or cool, but I was freezing. I considered grabbing an afghan from the couch to wrap myself in.

In my head, I knew there was nothing I could do. Wendy had made it clear she didn't want my help, and she would tell anyone, including Daniel, that she had tried to kill herself. So, who would believe me if I said she had told me otherwise? Especially if she followed it up by saying she often got confused and made stuff up. I would only be further damaging her already-ruined reputation.

As for the girl in the woods? I wasn't even sure she existed, let alone have any idea who or where she was. Yes, there was a deadbolted door in a barn on the church's property. So what? There was also a gate around the whole complex and no good way for me to get in.

So, really, there was nothing I could do, and I knew I needed to let it go. Not just for everyone else's sake, but for my own mental health. The smart thing to do would be to focus on my business and self-care.

Yet, no matter how much I told myself that, I wasn't convinced.

A flicker of movement caught my eye. There was something by the trees in the woods. I saw it again. A flash of light, as if a bit of glass caught the edge of the rising sun. Then, more movement as something disappeared into the brush. Something big.

I was on my feet immediately, my nose pressed against the window as I searched the trees for some sign. But there was nothing there.

I could hear Daniel's voice in my head: *It's probably an animal. Most likely a deer. It's that time of year, when they are most active.*

It made sense. But it didn't explain the flash of light.

I could almost see his expression. He wouldn't straight out say that I had imagined it. He would likely blame it on my being stressed and upset about my dream. I probably did see a deer, and the flash of light could have simply been the sun sparkling on the dewdrops dripping from the leaves.

Maybe.

What you really need to do is learn how to trust yourself.

The words flashed through my mind clear as day, and all of a sudden, something snapped inside me. I was sick of it. Sick of no one believing me, sick of not even being sure if I believed myself.

Both Zane and Wendy had told me that Wendy hadn't tried to kill herself. Both claimed she had almost been murdered.

I was not imagining it.

And it was time to prove it.

* * *

It wasn't quite 9:00 a.m. when I began pounding on Zane's door.

I wanted answers. Even if there was nothing more that I could do. Even if there was nothing concrete I could go to Daniel with, I had to know. For my own peace of mind, I needed to understand what was going on.

Zane didn't answer, so I kept pounding. When he still didn't respond, I started shouting. "Open up, Zane. I know you're in there. I'm not going away, so you might as well open the door and talk to me."

"Stop shouting," came the muffled voice from the other side of the door. I heard the locks being disengaged, and then, the door flew open.

Zane stood there, wearing a baggy pair of gray sweats and an old gray tee shirt. "Are you trying to let everyone in the neighborhood know my business?"

I spread my hands out. "What 'everyone'? You're in the middle of nowhere."

He glared at me and crossed his arms. "What do you want?"

I glowered right back at him. "Who is trying to kill Wendy?"

"That's not your concern." He started to slam the door shut, but I was faster, wedging myself in the doorway. He sighed and rolled his eyes. "Are we going to play this game again?"

"It's not a game," I said. "And I'm not going away until I get answers. So unless you're prepared to have me show up here every single day for a repeat performance, you might as well talk to me."

"I'll call the cops," he threatened. "I'll get a restraining order."

"Fine. Do it. I'll be happy to tell Daniel about Wendy lying about attempting suicide when it was actually an attempted murder."

He snarled at me. "No one is going to believe you, especially when Wendy denies it."

"Maybe," I said. "Want to put that theory to the test? Even if it means going against whoever is doing this and bringing attention to their handiwork?"

Zane's face worked. I could see how much he wanted to call my bluff and get the police involved. But his distrust of the police and the law ran deep, and he finally seemed to decide talking to me was the lesser of two evils. "Fine. What do you want to know?"

I leaned forward. "Who is trying to kill Wendy?"

"The same people who are trying to kill all of us 1888ers."

"And they are ..."

"Our mortal enemy."

I rolled my eyes. "That's not helping."

His eyes narrowed. "It's best not to name them. You have no idea the kind of power they have."

The back of my neck prickled, my nerves acutely alert and on the lookout for danger. I pushed the thought aside. Spending time with paranoid people was definitely bad for my mental health. I needed to focus on what I could control, not conspiracy theories. "That doesn't help me know who they are."

Zane almost smiled. "Ah, but you do know who they are."

I pushed my surprise aside. "Who?"

He cocked his head. "Redemption is changing a lot. A lot of new people suddenly moving in. Have you thought about why that's happening?"

"People are always moving to Redemption. So what?"

He made a face. "You and I both know Redemption decides who comes and goes. Why would it suddenly allow a whole bunch of new people to make it their home?"

I stared at him. "Are you saying that Redemption—the town itself—is trying to kill you?"

His expression shifted, and for the first time, I saw real fear in his eyes. "I don't know," he said, his voice low. "For so long, I didn't think so. I thought Redemption was protecting us, at least as best it could. But now ... I can't explain it."

"Explain what?"

"Why Redemption let them in."

The sky darkened as a cloud passed over the sun. A cold wind breezed across my skin, leaving a trail of goosebumps. Somewhere close by, a crow called out.

"Who did Redemption let in?" My voice was barely above a whisper.

Zane's face was pale, and his eyes were focused on something beyond me. "The new people."

A part of me wanted to reach out and throttle him. Could he be any more obtuse? How was I supposed to figure out which new person of all the people who had moved to Redemption he was referring to?

And then it hit me. He didn't say "person." He said "people."

"You mean The Church of the ..."

"I told you, don't say their name," he snapped.

"Sorry," I quickly apologized, not wanting to upset him and risk him clamming up. "Are they the ones who took Jill?"

There was a long pause. His eyes were still fixed on something beyond me, and he seemed practically hypnotized. I wanted to turn around and see what he was looking at, but I was too afraid to make any movement, in case it would put an abrupt end to our conversation. Instead, I stayed as still as I could, hardly daring to breathe. Again, the crow cawed.

Finally, his eyes shifted, and he focused on me. "Yes."

I tried to keep my expression neutral but could feel my eyes widening on their own accord. "So Jill *does* exist."

He blinked, and just like that, the moment was broken. Anger seeped back into his expression, and he glared at me. "Haven't you done enough damage? Go away and leave us be. We don't need your help."

"But ..." I started to say, but he was already shoving me out the door. I lost my balance and fell on my butt. Again. Good thing I had some cushion back there, or I might have ended up hurting myself.

Zane glowered at me from the doorway. "Don't come back here again," he barked before promptly slamming the door.

I sat there for a moment, trying to collect myself. The crow cawed a third time. I turned and saw it standing on the overgrown, weedy lawn, watching me.

Prickles of unease ran across both of my arms. There was something about the way it was looking at me that was bothering me. It felt almost human.

I gave myself a quick shake. What did I think was going on? That I had somehow fallen into a real-life version of Hitchcock's *The Birds*? I got to my feet, brushed myself off, and headed to my car.

The crow never moved. It stood in the same place, watching me get into the car. Only when I slammed the door did it finally take off, flying away with its big, black wings.

I ran a hand through my hair. I definitely needed to limit my time around paranoid people.

Starting immediately.

I pulled my phone out of my front pocket. It was still recording. I hit "end" and then pressed "play."

After a few moments, I heard a tinny version of Zane's voice ask me if I wanted to let everyone in the neighborhood know his business.

I stopped the recording and smiled. I finally had my proof.

Chapter 27

Daniel's face was troubled as he clicked on the stop button. "Can you send me the recording?"

"Of course," I said, picking up my phone. "It's enough, right? For you to get a warrant for the barn?"

Daniel scrubbed at his face. "I'm not sure. Neither of you actually said the words, 'The Church of the Forgotten.'"

"That's because he interrupted me."

Daniel gave me a look. "I know ... I heard."

"That's the only thing that makes sense," I said as I clicked on the buttons to email Daniel the recording. I knew I was babbling, but I couldn't stop myself. Finally, I had proof. Finally, people would have to believe me.

And the best part was that finally, Jill would be saved.

"And we even know where she is. In the barn, behind that locked door. It must have been Jill I heard after all ..."

Daniel held a hand up. "I get it, I get it. So, send me the recording ..."

"I did. It's sent." I held up the phone.

Daniel reached for his mouse to click through to his email. "Great. As soon as it comes through, then I can do something."

"Starting with that barn ..."

He held up his hand again. "Becca, let me do my job. I see the recording, so thank you. I'll call you later."

I chewed on my bottom lip, feeling oddly unsettled. I wanted to keep talking to him ... to hear him to tell me that yes, he was going to get a warrant and go out to the Church of the Forgotten and save that poor girl.

But I also understood that he knew the system better than I did, and it was not my place to tell him what to do. Not to mention the longer I stood there talking to him, the longer it was going to take for him to get to Jill.

"Let me know as soon as you can," I said.

His eyes flicked up at me. "Don't worry, I will."

I was going to have to be satisfied with that.

I went home and immediately headed to my garden. Mia was still in the kitchen, and as much as I wanted to tell her *I was right*, I also knew it was now an active investigation, and I should probably wait until Daniel arrested the perpetrators. In fact, having Daniel tell Mia that because of me, the cops were able to solve the case, might be even more satisfying.

I had my phone with me, and I kept an eye on it as I worked, not wanting to miss a call or a text, even though I had to keep telling myself it might be a while. Who knew what they were going to find when they finally got that door open? It might be something so big that they would end up working all night.

The sun had just started its downward slant when I decided it was time to call it quits. I was tired, but it was a good tired. It had been far too long since I had a decent physical workout, and gardening all day was exactly what I needed.

I had just stood up, my arms full with my gardening tools, when I realized I wasn't alone. Daniel was standing near the side of the house.

"Oh," I called out. "I didn't see you there."

He didn't answer, just stood there watching me. I wondered if he heard me, so I started walking toward him.

"I didn't get a text," I said as I got closer.

"That's because I didn't send a text," he said.

His face was in the shadow of the house, so I couldn't see it well, but there was something about the way he was standing that was giving me a bad feeling. Sweat had dripped down the back of my shirt, soaking through the fabric, and it left me suddenly cold.

I stopped dead in my tracks as the sudden realization of what Daniel must have found exploded inside me, practically shattering my internal organs with its force. The tools slid from my numb arms and landed in the soft grass. I felt like I could barely breathe. "She's dead, isn't she?" I finally whispered.

I was too late. I should have confronted Zane earlier. I should have trusted myself. Chrissy was right.

Daniel folded his arms across his chest. "Who's dead?"

"Jill, of course. Although …" a more horrifying thought occurred to me then, and I pressed my hands against my mouth. "Oh, don't tell me they're both dead."

"Both?"

"Jill and the girl in the woods." Something was definitely wrong. Was it even worse than I was imagining?

Daniel still hadn't moved. "No," he finally said. "They're not dead."

"Oh, what a relief!" I dropped my arms to my sides, but the uneasy feeling instantly returned and was slithering around inside me. Why was Daniel acting so strangely? "Are they hurt badly?"

He came toward me slowly, his steps carefully measured. "No. They aren't hurt."

"Then what is it?" He didn't respond, just kept moving closer in that same, ponderous way. "What's going on? Daniel, you're scaring me."

His eyes never left mine, but he finally stopped just a couple of feet away from me. "They aren't dead, and they aren't hurt … *because they don't exist*."

My jaw dropped. "What?"

Daniel released his arms to his sides, which is when I finally, belatedly, recognized the emotion he was struggling to contain.

Anger.

"Do you have any *idea* what you've done?" His voice was low, but it vibrated with fury. "If I don't get fired, it will be a miracle."

I cupped my elbows with my hands, holding my arms against my body as if to shield myself. "I don't … I don't understand."

"Oh, you don't understand? Let me spell it out for you. *There was nothing there.*"

My mouth was so dry, I wasn't sure I could push any words out. "Wha … What do you mean?" I stuttered. "You didn't find the door?"

"Oh. Oh, no. That WAS exactly where you said it would be. Probably the only thing in this mess that you had right."

"Then I don't understand. What was in that room?"

He leaned toward me. "Files."

I blinked stupidly at him. "Files?"

"Yes. Files. Taxes. Financials. Things like that."

"But why would files be locked up in a broken-down barn?"

He threw up his hands. "Becca, don't you get it? It doesn't matter why! What matters is that there was no sign of anyone in that room, child or otherwise."

"Then they must have moved her. Don't you see? I told you to check it out immediately …"

Daniel was shaking his head violently. "Enough. This ends now."

"But …"

He glared at me. "I talked to Zane. And Wendy. I even played Zane your little recording." He took another step toward me. "Want to know what he said?"

I swallowed hard. "What?" My voice was small.

"He said you have been harassing both him and Wendy. That you refused to leave either of them alone. Is that true?"

"Wendy? What does this have to do with Wendy? Besides, Zane said Jill existed. You heard him on the recording."

Daniel stared up at the sky. "Becca, you're still not getting it." He lowered his head and looked at me. "He claims he only said that so you would stop coming around and bothering him. He said he made up the whole thing to get you to leave him alone. And if you didn't, he was going to get a restraining order. Wendy too."

I gasped. "But I'm trying to help ..."

"No, you're not. Because there's nothing to help them with. There is no case here. Wendy is a troubled woman who tried to commit suicide, in part because you won't drop it ..."

"She said that?" I couldn't believe what I was hearing.

"Becca, what do you think I've been telling you? No one wants you interfering, and if you kept insisting, you would likely have found yourself facing some sort of lawsuit." He paused and lifted his hand to wipe the sweat off his forehead. "And now I've let you drag me into it, as well."

I bit my lip as the realization that Daniel might also be affected started to sink in. "But what I don't understand is why you're taking Zane's word that he lied on the recording. Why not assume he was telling the truth on the recording, and lying now?"

Daniel lifted his head and looked directly at me. The anger had completely drained away, leaving his face looking hollow and exhausted. "I called around, asking if anyone had seen a little girl with Wendy. No one has. I even talked to the Historical Society volunteers, since they were the last to leave the reception. No one saw a little girl, nor had Wendy told any of them that she had a daughter. I can't find one single person to corroborate any of this."

I opened my mouth, then shut it. My legs were wobbling, and it suddenly felt like I was trying to stand under a thousand-pound weight.

"Let it go," Daniel said, his voice ragged. "Please. I'm begging you. For the sake of all of us, just. Let. It. Go."

I stared at the ground. My tools were still lying where I'd dropped them. I had completely forgotten about them. I studied the cultivator, noticing the dirt on the edge of it. I hadn't cleaned it. I should have cleaned it.

"Becca?"

I couldn't even lift my head. All my strength seemed to have drained into the ground. Finally, I nodded.

There was a long silence. Then Daniel turned and walked away, leaving me standing there.

Alone, with my tools.

* * *

"You know," Daphne said, picking up her glass of wine but not drinking. "I don't think you're crazy."

I let out a laugh that sounded like a yelp. "You're pretty much the only one."

It had been three days since Daniel told me there was nothing in the locked room in the barn. Three days of enduring Mia's pitying gaze and Daniel's "checking in" texts. Both of them were strongly suggesting I make an appointment to see a therapist.

I hadn't yet, although a part of me felt like it would be the right thing to do.

But it also felt as if I would be admitting to everyone I had been wrong if I did.

And I wasn't wrong. I knew the truth.

No one else heard what Wendy had said to me in the hospital. And no one else had seen the look in Zane's eyes when he admitted that Jill existed.

I knew the truth, even if I still didn't know why they were lying. The problem was, I had no way to prove it.

I reached for the bottle to top off my glass before offering it to Daphne, who shook her head. We were alone in the kitchen; both Mia and Chrissy were working. Normally, I would have wished one or both of them were home. But, since that terrible afternoon, I lived for these times.

"Well, it helps that I was there the first time you saw Zane," Daphne said, playing with her glass. She hadn't touched the wine yet, which wasn't a big surprise, as it was the middle of the day. Normally, when Daphne visited at that time of day, I would offer her tea.

It's amazing how much can change in three days.

"It also helps when you discover certain things that don't add up," she continued.

I was about to take another drink but paused, my hand still in the air. "What do you mean?"

She threw me a sideways glance, a hint of a smile on her lips. "Well, you know what they always say, right? Follow the money."

I put my glass down, without drinking it. "Yeah?"

"But the Church of the Forgotten claims they don't use money. They wanted to barter with you to get tea."

"Yes." I couldn't figure out where Daphne was going. Was this a distraction to keep me from drinking?

She looked directly at me. "Then how did they get the Hoffman land?"

"What do you mean?"

She waved a hand in the air. "Think about it. This was a piece of property that had been tied up for years because of some legal red tape. How on Earth did some group of people with no money cut through all that tape and end up on that land? They did something that developers with their deep pockets weren't able to do. Live on that land."

I sat up straighter, a flicker of excitement starting to stir in me. "You're right. I hadn't thought about it like that. But how could we find out?"

She flashed me a sly smile. "A friend who knows how to hack computers is an excellent place to start."

My eyes widened. "You didn't."

She waved her hand. "Never mind the technicalities. Want to hear what I found out?"

"Of course."

She paused, as if trying to milk the moment for as long as she could. "So, it does appear like the Church of the Forgotten is renting the property. But they're not renting it from the trust."

I frowned. "They're not? The trust doesn't own it anymore?"

"Apparently not."

"Then who does?"

"An LLC."

I stared at her. "What?"

"Weird, isn't it?"

"What LLC?"

She frowned. "It's got a strange name. The Jolly Roger."

"The Jolly Roger?" I was sure I heard her wrong. "Like a pirate ship?"

"Not so much a pirate ship, but the pirate flag," Daphne said. "The black flag with a skull and crossbones on it is called 'The Jolly Roger.' It's also the name of Captain Hook's ship."

"Captain Hook?" I was having getting my head around what she was telling me. Maybe I shouldn't have started with the booze so early. "Like from *Peter Pan*?"

"The one and the same."

"Why would an LLC choose the name of Captain Hook's pirate ship?"

"I haven't a clue."

This was getting stranger and stranger. "Do you know who owns it?"

"That I can't find out."

"Of course not. That would make things too easy," I said, drumming my fingers on the table. "Do you know why they would rent the property to the Church of the Forgotten?"

"Not a clue. However ..." she leaned forward, her eyes dancing. "That's not the only interesting tidbit I discovered. Ready for more?"

"Of course?"

"The Hoffman property isn't the only property the Jolly Roger owns. Apparently, Penny willed her house to it."

My mouth fell open. "Penny? As in Wendy's mother?"

"The one and same."

"But ..." I was having trouble wrapping my head around these new developments. "Why would she do that?"

Daphne shrugged. "You'd have to ask Penny."

"What about Wendy?"

"Penny may have willed the rest of the estate to her, but not the house."

I sat there, stunned at the news. "Do you think Wendy knew?"

"No idea." She cocked her head and looked at me. "But it's kind of odd that an LLC I've never heard of suddenly owns two properties in Redemption, don't you think?"

"Yeah," I said, my mind whirling. "Very odd."

Chapter 28

"Becca. I'm so glad I caught you."

Eleanor was standing on my porch, smiling her signature smile that didn't quite reach her eyes.

"Eleanor." I was suddenly very aware that I was alone and would likely be for a few more hours. "What can I do for you?"

"I was hoping we could talk. Just for a minute." Her smile stretched a little further. "I promise it won't take long."

I wanted to say no. Whatever she wanted, I was sure it wasn't good. After all, I had told the police about the locked door in the barn.

No, my instinct was to send her away.

But I was also curious. Why would she come all the way out to my house to see me? She appeared to be alone, as well. I didn't even see the old, beat-up pickup truck she must have driven into town.

Plus, I still had the tea business facade to keep up.

"It will just take a minute," she said again.

"Okay," I agreed, stepping out onto the porch with her and shutting the door firmly behind me. I gestured to the porch swing. "It's such a nice day. I thought we could sit out here. Plus, we'll have a little privacy."

One eyebrow rose. "You have company?"

"Roommates," I said, moving to sit on the swing while making a show of sliding over to give her room. "One of them is taking online classes, and it's probably best we don't bother her."

"Of course," Eleanor murmured as she sat down next to me.

We rocked back and forth in silence for a moment. I was about to ask her what she wanted when she started to talk.

"I thought it best to clear the air, so to speak," she said.

"Oh?"

"Yes. About the barn."

I sucked in my breath with a hiss, but didn't say anything.

"It's true that the barn is old and falling apart, but not all of it. There's a section that is new—a new roof, new walls, new door." She eyed me. "New lock."

There was no sense in trying to pretend otherwise. "I saw."

Her nod was barely perceptible. "I'm not sure who built it. It was there when we arrived, but it was clear it was meant to be ... well, a hiding place, if you will. When we moved in, there was a desk, some shelves, and some metal filing cabinets in there. Empty, of course. When we asked about it, well ..." she gave a delicate shrug. "Whoever had been using it had found ... other accommodations. So, since it was already set up as an office, we moved our files in. It was perfect, actually. As a community, we don't believe in locking doors as a general rule. But there are some things, mainly financial records, that the rest of the members don't need to see."

"Of course," I said, but still, I wondered. Was it truly as simple as that? A place to store files away from prying eyes?

It seemed a little too pat.

"I can see how it would seem ... questionable to you," she said. "And why you would call the cops." Her smile was flat.

"I'm sorry about that," I said quickly, but she waved me off.

"That's not why I'm here," she said. "Truly, I understand."

I thought about the two women peeling potatoes, and how quick they were to obey her, immediately dropping half peeled potatoes the moment she asked them to leave. Despite her warm words, Eleanor didn't strike me as someone who liked having her authority challenged.

And me telling the cops about the locked door, would definitely qualify as challenging her authority.

She must have seen something in my face, because she continued talking. "I understand, because ..." she leaned closer to me, and I caught that strange smoke-like scent again. "You saw her, didn't you?"

What? She couldn't mean what I thought she meant. My mind flashed to Maude. *You saw her. In the woods. You know who.*

She nodded again when she saw my face. "It's okay. You see, at one point, we did have a mother and a child staying with us. A little girl. She was about ten. But a few weeks ago, she left."

"She ... left?"

Eleanor nodded. "Yes. The mother had some family issues she had to deal with, so she packed up her daughter and left. For a while, she said. She'll be back once she's straightened things out."

I blinked, feeling a like I had lost my bearings. "But ... you said a few weeks ago, right? Whoever I saw, I saw more recently."

"I know she has family scattered all over, even in different states, but she does have a few family members living here in Redemption. I would imagine she was staying with them when you saw little Mabel."

Again, like the explanation for the room in the barn, there was something a little too ... perfect about her story.

I didn't trust it.

"But I can imagine how shocking it would be to have seen Mabel in the woods dressed the way we dress, and then the locked door in the barn, so I'm not at all surprised that you would draw the conclusions you did. That's why I wanted to clear it up."

"I appreciate it."

She smiled again and stood up. "Now that we got that out of the way, I hope you'll consider being our tea supplier. We're still interested."

"Let me give it some more thought," I said, getting to my feet as well. "I still need to work out the barter thing."

"I understand." She smiled again and turned to leave.

Something was niggling at me ... something that didn't fit.

I watched Eleanor walk down the steps and move toward the driveway before it hit me. I called after her.

She half-turned, fixing those piercing blue eyes on me again. "Yes?" Her tone sounded normal, like what anyone would say in this same situation, but the expression in those eyes was almost ... predatory.

I found myself taking a step backwards and reaching behind me to put my hand on the doorknob. Even though she was far enough away, I was sure I could get into the house before she could reach me, it made me feel better to have it in my grasp. "How did you know I saw Mabel in the woods?"

Her face broke into a real smile, and she clapped her hands together. "I knew I was right about you."

I looked at her in confusion. "Right about me? What are you talking about?"

She lowered her hands and stared at me, her eyes narrowing ever so slightly. And just like before, when I was by the chicken coop, I once again found myself unable to move, unable to breathe. All I could do was stand there, helpless, as she pinned me with her gaze. "You'll understand soon enough."

With that, Eleanor turned and headed down the driveway, leaving me alone on the porch, gasping for breath.

***

I wiped the sweat off my hands one last time before I mounted the stairs to the porch and rang the doorbell. A part of me was sure this was a terrible idea.

Another part of me didn't care.

The door opened, and Wendy stood on the other side of it. Her face was flat. "What do you want?"

"I wanted to check on you. Make sure you're okay ... after your suicide attempt." I deliberately dropped my eyes to the white bandages on her wrist. She folded her arms against her chest, as if to hide them from me.

"I told you to leave us alone." Today, she looked like she had at least showered. She was wearing a pair of jean shorts and an old tee shirt. There was a streak of dust across the shirt, and behind her, I could see boxes.

"Are you moving out?"

She shifted uncomfortably. "It's not safe here."

"Nor do you own it."

She blanched. "How do you know?" The moment the words left her mouth, she mashed her lips closed and dropped her gaze to the ground.

I took a step closer to her. "I know a lot of things. Like you really do have a daughter named Jill who was kidnapped."

Her head shot up. "I told you. None of that is true."

I didn't respond, just stared at her.

Finally, she relented. Her eyes shifted to my pockets. "I suppose you're recording me, too." Her voice was bitter.

I pulled my cell phone out of my purse and showed it to her, then held my arms straight out. "I'm not recording you. You can check me if you want. Not that it would matter if I was, since no one would believe a word of it anyhow." I scowled at her. "You and Zane managed to completely destroy my reputation."

Her eyes went wide. "Oh, that's our fault? We kept telling you to leave it alone, and you wouldn't. What did you expect us to do?"

"I was trying to help you."

"We didn't need your help. Or want it. And we made that pretty clear." Her voice was flat.

I closed my eyes briefly and forced myself to take a breath. I didn't come here to fight, even though I was still angry. I came here because I had no choice. And antagonizing Wendy wasn't going to do a bit of good. "I know. I get it now. I shouldn't have interfered. I'm sorry."

She looked at me in surprise, but there was a wariness there, as well.

"I mean it. You did keep telling me that, and I didn't listen. I just ... look, I know what it's like to move somewhere new, especially a place like Redemption. Half the people in this town don't like me either, because of my aunt. It's tough. And with your history and mother ... I thought you might be feeling as alone as I did, and I wanted to help. But I should have listened to you instead of continually pushing it."

She chewed on her lip as she mulled over what I said. "You weren't ... wrong." Her voice was halting. "I did feel alone. And I ... I did appreciate you reaching out to me. But ... Becca, there are things going on that you don't understand. Dangerous things. It's safer for you if you don't know."

"But what about you?"

Her shoulders sagged. "I was born into this. I don't have a choice. But you do."

I thought about Eleanor and the way she looked at me. Almost as if she ... knew more about me than she should. "I don't know if that's true."

She gave me a sharp look. "Of course it is."

"The Chur ... the new people," I corrected myself, thinking about how upset Zane got when I started to say the name. "They've been pursuing me, too."

The blood seemed to drain from her face. For a moment, I was afraid she might faint. "What?"

"Yeah, they want me to make teas for them."

I could still see the horror in her eyes, but there was puzzlement there, as well. "Teas?"

"I have a business making teas. It was my Aunt Charlie's, but I took it over. I'm not sure if you'd remember her or not."

"Wait," she held up a hand. "You're Charlie Kingsley's niece?"

"Oh, you knew her?"

"Does that mean you're living in Helen Blackstone's house?"

"Yes."

The puzzlement was gone, but the horror was back. "Becca, you must be careful. Promise me. You're not safe either."

"Why?"

"I can't tell you. You just ... you need to be very careful. And stay away from the new people. Promise me."

Wendy looked legitimately frightened. I wondered why she would be so terrified of the Church of the Forgotten.

Unless they truly did have her daughter.

"I promise," I said. "On one condition."

The wary look was back. "What?"

"Tell me the truth. Do they have Jill?"

Her mouth opened. I could practically see the "no" start to form.

"Please," I said, my voice breaking. "I really need to know the truth. I'm not going to do anything about it. I just need to know."

Wendy paused. I could see her wrestling with herself.

Finally, she took a step forward and leaned in very close to me. "Jill is safe," she whispered. "She's with family. But please, you must drop this. You can't keep digging. You're putting us in danger."

I had been so focused on the words "Jill is safe," I barely heard the rest of what she said. But the meaning behind her words started to penetrate. "Wait, was that what happened to your arms?" I gestured toward the bandages.

Her breath hissed in her throat. "I've said too much. Please. Drop this. For all of our sakes."

"But I have so many questions. Like, why are you lying?"

She was already shaking her head. "I can't tell you. Just ... please. Stay away from the new people. And drop it. Okay?" She started backing into the house.

"Wait. Can you at least tell me where you'll be staying?"

She had started closing the door, but she paused. "I'll be with Zane."

"Zane?" Although it probably shouldn't surprise me, it did.

"At least initially, until we figure out somewhere safer. But ..." a ghost of a smile touched her lips. "You really don't want to visit me there. Zane is not your biggest fan."

"I know."

Our eyes met, and something passed between us. It felt like an understanding. "Be careful, Becca," she said, and she shut the door with a quiet click.

For a moment, I didn't move. Everything she had told me crowded together in my head. But the most important part was that Jill was alive.

I was right.

In that moment, it didn't even matter that I couldn't tell anyone. All that mattered was that I knew.

A crow cawed to my left. I turned and saw the big black bird on the grass in the yard, staring at me.

An uneasy feeling began to prickle at my spine. It looked just like the one that seemed to be watching me at Zane's house.

I was suddenly very aware of how much I still didn't know.

And how many secrets Redemption was still holding onto.

A note from Michele

I know, I know. It's only part 1. But part 2 is coming in September, 2023: *The Room at the Top of the Stairs.*

Becca has always known something is off about that room. The one at the top of the stairs. She'd always dismissed what she had heard as rumors, but now, something has changed. And she can't ignore what's going on anymore …

Preorder your copy right here:

https://www.amazon.com/dp/B0BTMLPGHG.

★ ★ ★ ★

You can also check out exclusive bonus content for *The Girl Who Wasn't There*, including a short story called *The Missing*, which takes place in 1888, right after the adults disappeared. Here's the link:

https://MPWNovels.com/r/girlwhowasnt-bonus

The bonus content reveals hints, clues, and sneak peeks you won't get just by reading the books, so you'll definitely want to take a look. You're going to discover a side of Redemption that is only available here.

★ ★ ★

If you enjoyed *The Girl Who Wasn't There*, it would be wonderful if you would take a few minutes to leave a review and rating on Amazon:

www.amazon.com/dp/B0BG621VNZ/#customerReviews

Goodreads:
goodreads.com/book/show/62710406-the-girl-who-wasn-t-there
or Bookbub:
bookbub.com/books/the-girl-who-wasn-t-there-a-psychological-sus-
pense-novel-secrets-of-redemption-book-6-by-michele-pariza-wacek
(Feel free to follow me on any of those platforms as well.) I
thank you and other readers will thank you (as your reviews
will help other readers find my books.)

All of my series are interrelated and interconnected. Along
with my psychological thrillers, I also have a cozy mystery series
that takes place in the 1990s and stars Aunt Charlie. (It's called
the Charlie Kingsley Mysteries series.)

You can learn more about Redemption and my other series
at MPWNovels.com. You'll also discover a lot of other fun stuff
such as giveaways, puzzles, recipes and more.

More Secrets of Redemption *series:*
It Began With a Lie (Book 1)
This Happened to Jessica (Book 2)
The Evil That Was Done (Book 3)
The Summoning (Book 4)
The Reckoning (Book 5)
The Girl Who Wasn't There (Book 6)
The Room at the Top of the Stairs (Book 7 coming soon)
The Secret Diary of Helen Blackstone (free novella)

Charlie Kingsley Mysteries:
A Grave Error (a free prequel novella)
Ice Cold Murder (Book 2)
Murder Next Door (Book 3)
Murder Among Friends (Book 4)
The Murder of Sleepy Hollow (Book 5)
Red Hot Murder (Book 6)
A Wedding to Murder For (novella)
Loch Ness Murder (novella)

Standalone books:
Today I'll See Her (free novella or purchase with bonus content)
The Taking
The Third Nanny
Mirror Image
The Stolen Twin

Access your free exclusive bonus scenes from *The Girl Who Wasn't There* right here:
https://MPWNovels.com/r/girlwhowasnt-bonus

Acknowledgements

It's a team effort to birth a book, and I'd like to take a moment to thank everyone who helped, especially my wonderful editor, Megan Yakovich, who is always so patient with me, Rea Carr for her expert proofing support, and my husband Paul, for his love and support during this sometimes-painful birthing process.

Any mistakes are mine and mine alone.

About Michele

A USA Today Bestselling, award-winning author, Michele taught herself to read at 3 years old because she wanted to write stories so badly. It took some time (and some detours) but she does spend much of her time writing stories now. Mystery stories, to be exact. They're clean and twisty, and range from psychological thrillers to cozies, with a dash of romance and supernatural thrown into the mix. If that wasn't enough, she posts lots of fun things on her blog, including short stories, puzzles, recipes and more, at MPWNovels.com.

Michele grew up in Wisconsin, (hence why all her books take place there), and still visits regularly, but she herself escaped the cold and now lives in the mountains of Prescott, Arizona with her husband and southern squirrel hunter Cassie.

When she's not writing, she's usually reading, hanging out with her dog, or watching the Food Network and imagining she's an awesome cook. (Spoiler alert, she's not. Luckily for the whole family, Mr. PW is in charge of the cooking.)

Made in the USA
Monee, IL
05 May 2023

33131466R00157